a.D. W

THEY CAME TO CASA GRANDE

Cooper Dundee—Thrown in jail, framed for the murder of his passengers, his life was never in greater danger, but Cooper would come raging back to defend himself.

Regan Dundee—With her baby due any moment, her husband at the mercy of a vengeance-seeking town, she must summon all her courage to fight back against the cruel stranger who is causing her family's suffering.

Jonathan Dundee—Cooper's half brother, who will risk everything to regain the family business.

Adam Becker—Fueled by bitterness, his sick fires of revenge threaten to destroy Cooper, Regan, and Dundee Transport.

D0801985

The Stagecoach Series
Ask your bookseller for the books you have missed

STATION 1: DODGE CITY
STATION 2: LAREDO
STATION 3: CHEYENNE
STATION 4: TOMBSTONE
STATION 5: VIRGINIA CITY
STATION 6: SANTA FE
STATION 7: SEATTLE
STATION 8: FORT YUMA
STATION 9: SONORA
STATION 10: ABILENE
STATION 11: DEADWOOD
STATION 12: TUCSON
STATION 13: CARSON CITY
STATION 14: CIMARRON
STATION 15: WICHITA
STATION 16: MOJAVE
STATION 17: DURANGO
STATION 18: CASA GRANDE

STAGECOACH STATION 18:

CASA GRANDE

Hank Mitchum

Created by the producers of
Wagons West, White Indian,
and Saga of the Southwest.

Chairman of the Board: Lyle Kenyon Engel

BANTAM BOOKS
TORONTO • NEW YORK • LONDON • SYDNEY • AUCKLAND

STAGECOACH STATION 18: CASA GRANDE

*A Bantam Book / published by arrangement with
Book Creations, Inc.*

Bantam edition/June 1985

*Produced by Book Creations, Inc.
Chairman of the Board: Lyle Kenyon Engel*

ISBN 0-553-24949-5

Published simultaneously in the United States and Canada

PRINTED IN THE UNITED STATES OF AMERICA

H   0 9 8 7 6 5 4 3 2 1

STAGECOACH STATION 18:

CASA GRANDE

ARIZONA TERRITORY 1881

CALIFORNIA

PRESCOTT

DUNDEE TRANSPORT ....

Colorado River

Gila River

Salt River

PHOENIX

CASA GRANDE
DUNDEE RANCH

YUMA

PICACHO PASS

FORT LOWELL

0   55   100
      MILES

TUCSON

Santa Cruz River

San Pedro River

+ DUNDEE TRANSPORT CO. +

©1984 BECK CREATIONS INC.

RON TOELKE '84

Chapter One

Cooper Dundee stood at the window of the Phoenix office of Dundee Transport, his eyes on the red brick office building directly across the street. He was feeling more than usual curiosity; his interests ran deeper and were of a more personal nature. So personal that the tight knot at the pit of his belly had worsened with each passing day.

A new sign had just been fastened into place on the brick facade of the structure, and Cooper felt a stifling surge of anger sweep through him as he spied the bold "D" that dominated the placard. The sun flashed against the gold lettering as Cooper read the name beneath the large, block "D" and swore. *"Jonathan Dundee, Attorney at Law."* "Damn!" he cursed, repeating the word a second time. "Damn!"

Regan Dundee entered the room from the back door. Her eyes swept the lean figure at the window and she smiled. "You knew he was coming back, Coop," she said softly to her husband.

Without turning around, he put his arm out and made a place for her at his side. "Yeah, I knew," he breathed. He nodded across the street to where the new sign now hung. It angered him, the blatant way Jonathan chose to announce his return to Phoenix—by opening a law office directly across the street from Cooper's transport company, when there were many other suitable locations in Phoenix's bustling business district.

Regan shook her head, scolding her husband's window reflection with her eyes. "It's been more than a year, Coop. He's your brother. . . ."

"Half brother," Cooper corrected. He wondered where it was written that a man had to like his brother or, for that matter, respect him.

1

Cooper's thoughts drifted back to the time growing up when he and Jonathan, separated by much more than the five years' difference in their ages, fought and battled their way from one scrape to another. It seemed natural enough at the time, two brothers competing for the love and companionship of their much absent father, but then it changed.

The childhood fights became genuine contests of temperament, with the elder brother, Jonathan, using the advantage of age and size to impose his will on Cooper. And when Cooper was finally able to match him in physical combat, Jonathan used words. After their father, Malachai, had died, Jonathan skillfully used those words to bind Cooper and his mother, Teresa, to agreements and financial reports, contracts and complex litigations. His methods had succeeded until a final confrontation almost two years earlier in 1879, when Cooper had foiled Jonathan's plan to sell the family business and had instead won from Jonathan in a card game his one-third share of the Dundee stagecoach line and the family ranch at Casa Grande.

All Jonathan had left was his wife Angela's one-third share, Cooper reminded himself, still bitter. He had never been able to reconcile himself to the marriage between Jonathan and the young woman their father had adopted and who had been raised as their sister.

Regan's gentle touch roused Cooper from his dark musings. She reached up, taking his hand and rubbing the tightness from the long tendons in his clenched fist. "It's time to forgive and forget, Coop." Her fingers worked their magic, and she felt him relaxing. "Time to bury . . ." Immediately, she regretted her choice of words.

"Like we buried Teresa?" Cooper interrupted sharply. His hand made a fist again, and he pulled away from his wife. The memory of his mother's death still haunted him—how she had been murdered by the henchmen of Logan Montgomery, the man to whom Jonathan had been preparing to sell the line, when Montgomery grew tired of waiting for Teresa to agree to the sale.

Regan's whole body tensed and then went slack as she sighed. She felt a brief twinge of anger at her husband's stubborn reluctance to let go of the past. "I want to see Angela, Coop. I want to be able to invite Angela into our home."

Cooper's jaw tightened. He understood what Regan was saying, just as he understood the thing she had so carefully avoided saying. Angela would not feel welcome in their home if Jonathan was not welcome, too.

Cooper reached out, taking Regan in his arms and holding her close, wanting to do what she was asking and not sure that he could. On the new law office across the street, the sign with its gold logo—the bold Dundee "D"—mocked him. "I can't change what I feel about Jonathan, Regan." She stirred against his chest, and he held her even tighter, willing her to remain silent until he finished. If he ever hoped to purge the hatred, the words had to be said. "There are times," he began, "when I'm sorry I didn't kill him that night in the office at Tucson, after I'd killed Montgomery. I wanted Jonathan dead, too." It was true. For one terrible, black moment he had wanted his brother dead—even though he knew Jonathan was only indirectly involved in his mother's death. He wanted to be the one who killed him.

There was a subtle movement against Cooper's chest as Regan shook her head. "You were hurt, Coop. And you were angry." She remembered his rage—the terrifying bloodlust she had seen in his eyes. "You *love* Jonathan, Coop. You've always loved him." She said the words with the simple, strong conviction of a woman who knew her husband's capacity for loving.

"But I don't *like* him!" he protested. In spite of himself, Cooper laughed, his mood changing. His hands were on her upper arms now, and he gently pushed her away from his chest. "I'll try," he promised. "For your sake . . ." The smile grew as one hand drifted down her arm to rest on her prominent belly. ". . . and for his."

It was Regan's turn to laugh. In the first weeks of her pregnancy, she had been annoyed at Cooper and his need to touch her stomach. And then, as time passed and she realized how much their child meant to him—how he longed even now to touch it—she almost encouraged his caresses. She caught Cooper's hand in her own and pressed it even tighter against the child growing in her womb. "Hers," she corrected, knowing that it didn't matter to either one of them what sex the baby was, as long as it was healthy. *As long as it survived.*

Cooper sensed the sudden desperation in his wife. He pulled her close in a tight hug. He had been so concerned with his own feelings that he had forgotten what Regan had been through in the year and a half since their marriage. There was her business in the East, the consulting company she had started years before and longed to continue. There was her twelve-year-old son, Michael, who had been raised by Regan's brother and now thought of Regan as his aunt. Now that her brother was dead and she was raising Michael, she desperately longed to tell him the truth but did not know how, afraid that the truth would drive them apart. There was their first baby, which she had miscarried when she was alone at the ranch at Casa Grande. And now this pregnancy was taking its toll in sleepless nights and bouts of early morning nausea.

"Maybe it will be twins," he whispered, teasing her. "Think of it. Twin boys. Just like Michael." Then he had a truly inspired thought. "Just like me and Jonathan!"

Regan was laughing. "Oh, God," she groaned. "Anything," she pleaded, "anything but that!" The laughter was genuine, and it ended with a long kiss that aroused something much more than paternal feelings within Cooper.

They parted reluctantly, knowing that this was neither the time nor the place. Cooper's fingers lingered at his wife's cheek. "Early supper?" he asked, hoping that she would say yes.

Regan hesitated before answering. "We're eating out," she began. There was no point in not saying the rest. "Angela has invited us to have dinner at the hotel. I told her we would be delighted."

Cooper was shaking his head, but he was smiling. "You had this planned all along," he accused. "You and Angela."

Regan nodded her head. "Ever since they first got here," she said truthfully. "*Before* they got here."

"And Jonathan agreed?"

Regan stifled a laugh with both hands. "If he hasn't, he soon will!" She imagined Angela being in Jonathan's office at the same moment, doing just what she was doing: pacifying, cajoling, using all the feminine tricks and wiles Regan had always detested. "Are you angry?" she asked, facing Cooper directly.

He loved her too much to ever stay angry with her and wondered if she was aware of that love. "Would it make a difference?"

Her mood changed, and she was suddenly serious. "If it really mattered, Coop. Or if I didn't really think it was for the best."

"I'm not mad," he answered. And in truth, he wasn't. As angry as he was with Jonathan, as deep as the old animosities ran, he still wanted to see Angela. *And their baby,* he thought. He did want to see Angela's little boy.

"Six-thirty," Regan reminded him.

Cooper touched her face again. "You owe me one, woman," he grinned. "And I intend to collect."

"Tonight," she promised. "If you're a very good boy and you mind your manners . . ." There was a provocative cant to her head when she said the words.

Cooper smacked her playfully on the rear end when she walked away. *God, I love her,* he thought. *I will always love her.*

Michael Patrick O'Rourke sat on the back step of the porch of the house he shared with his aunt and her husband, Cooper Dundee. He had been inside the company office earlier, after he had come home from school, and had seen the tender exchange between Regan and Cooper. He left before they saw him, feeling the intruder.

It was, he decided, that damned baby. That's all Regan and Cooper ever talked about anymore. He failed to see what there was about a baby that made supposedly sane, adult people go soft and silly. *Babies,* he fumed. *All they are good for is getting wet at one end and throwing up at the other.*

Almost absently, the boy began unwrapping the tissue casing on the cigar he had pilfered from the container on Cooper's rolltop desk in the front parlor. The thick stogie suddenly became the total focus of the boy's attention. He performed the ceremony he had watched so many times before, wetting the length of the cigar with his tongue and then biting off the end. He did all these things without really knowing why, pleased that he did them so well. It was important to him that he succeed in this task.

Michael was tired of the teasing he took from the older boys at school who taunted him about his overprotective aunt and his store-tailored clothes, and about the fact that he was never allowed to play in the alleys and vacant lots on "that" side of town.

He was going to learn how to smoke. And then one day, after school—or maybe even during recess—he would simply light up a smoke and puff away in front of everyone. That would rock them back on their heels, he thought smugly. He paused, striking a wooden match on the rough-hewn stairway as he closed his eyes and visualized the smoke rings he would learn to make, blue and heavy on the air, one inside the other.

"Michael!" The voice penetrated the young boy's day-dreams, vague and not quite real. And then it increased in volume and intensity. "Michael Patrick O'Rourke!"

The boy scrambled to his feet, dropping the still-lit match. The smell of sulfur-tipped matches lingered, and in-stinctively his hand—and the cigar—disappeared behind his back. "Regan!"

The woman was on the porch stoop, the screen door still held open. She looked like the wrath of God, her face show-ing a mixture of anger and consternation. Her right foot tapped impatiently on the threshold. When she was finally able to speak, her voice was quiet, firm. "What have you got behind your back, Michael?"

The boy recognized the woman's tone and knew he was in big trouble. He debated the wisdom of telling the truth and decided that a lie would serve him better. "Nothing," he mumbled.

"Show me," Regan ordered.

Michael's face colored, and for an instant he actually hated the woman and the way she constantly nagged him. Reluctantly, he put out his right hand, opening the fingers to display his barren palm.

Regan's right eyebrow arched, and she nodded slowly. "And now the other one," she urged. When it was clear the boy intended to withdraw one hand before he produced the other, she stopped him, her fingers closing around his thin wrist. "The other one, Michael," she ordered again.

Grimly, the boy brought out his left hand. The cigar was still firmly clenched between his forefinger and middle finger.

Cooper Dundee appeared at his wife's back, a heavy towel in his hands. He had just finished washing up and was still shirtless. It took him only one quick glance to see what was happening between Regan and the boy. More, what was going to happen to the boy if he didn't intervene. "I can't find my clean shirts, Regan," he said softly.

It was plain from the look on his wife's face that she didn't exactly welcome her husband's interference, and yet, not knowing what else to do, she yielded. "I don't want him getting away with this, Cooper. Not this time."

He smiled at her. "I'll take care of it," he promised. When she started to object, he raised his hand, crossing his heart. *You spoil him*, she signaled with her eyes. *You let him get away with too much.* He read her silent message and flashed one of his own: *Not this time.*

Michael was still holding the cigar. He watched the silent exchange between Cooper and Regan, relieved when she finally went inside.

Cooper sat down on the top porch step and draped the towel around his neck. "I want you to go in the house, Michael," he said finally. "I want you to get another cigar and bring it back out here."

Puzzled, the youngster hesitated. And then he bolted up the steps. He was gone but a minute, and when he returned, the second cigar was clenched firmly in his fist.

Cooper took the fresh smoke from Michael's hand. Methodically, just as the boy had done earlier, he unwrapped the thin paper wrapper and moistened the stogie end to end. He bit off the nub and spit it into the dirt between Michael's feet, and then he lit up. He took his time, filling his mouth with the potent smoke and then slowly exhaling. His match still flickered between his fingers.

He did a surprising thing then. Reaching out, he took the cigar the boy was still holding and placed it in his own mouth just long enough to get it started. It was a thing of awe for Michael, watching the man puff on two cigars at the same time, even if it was just for a moment.

Michael was even more dumbfounded when Cooper handed him back the lit smoke and gestured for him to sit down.

"You know, Michael, a cigar is truly a fine thing." Cooper was staring straight ahead, the hint of a smile creasing the skin at the corner of his eyes. "It finishes off a good meal"—he pulled his own smoke out of his mouth and studied it for a time—"and tops off a glass of fine wine." Two blue smoke rings appeared above his head when he exhaled. "Even helps a man celebrate. His wedding. A successful business deal. The birth of his child."

He paused, taking another puff. The cigar was firmly clenched between his teeth at the side of his mouth. "Smoke it, Michael," he said finally, pointing to the boy's cigar. "All of it." The congenial tone of only moments before was gone.

Michael stared across at Cooper and then at the still-smoldering cigar he held in his own hand. Warily, he lifted it to his lips.

Cooper watched as the boy inhaled. He kept watching, no sympathy in him as he continued his false instructions. "Suck up, boy," he ordered, watching as the youngster's cheeks filled with air and smoke. Michael swallowed, his face turning gray, then white, and then a sickly ash-blue.

Eyes watering, Michael dropped the cigar. He was dismayed to see Cooper pick it up. The man pushed it back into his hand. "All of it, Michael," he intoned.

The boy choked back a sob. His stomach was convulsing, waves of nausea sweeping up his gullet and burning at the back of his throat. "I can't," he whined.

Cooper was unrelenting. "Sure you can," he urged. "Big man like you. Someone who can steal his smokes right out of the front room." He stuffed his fingers into the boy's shirt pocket and extracted a handful of wooden matches. "Steal matches out of his mama's—" he caught himself, grateful that the boy was too sick to comprehend "—out of the kitchen." He forced the cigar back into the boy's mouth. "Sure you can," he repeated.

Michael felt himself getting sick, sicker than he'd ever been in his entire life. "Please, Coop," he begged. "Please?" And then he was sick.

Cooper pulled the towel from around his neck and crammed it beneath the boy's chin. He held him, his arm around Michael's shoulders as the youngster lost what was left of his noontime meal. The pain of retching after his stomach was empty was even worse, and the boy began to cry.

Cooper's mood changed, and he was almost sorry. "I catch you with another cigar, Michael, and we'll do this again. I want you to understand that."

Michael nodded his head. Even that small effort hurt him.

From beyond the screen door, Regan watched the interplay between Cooper and her son. *Her son.* She wondered if she would ever have the courage to tell him.

The Imperial Hotel was on the main street of Phoenix. It was a long adobe-brick building that had been given a veneer of white stucco to smooth the rough, uneven facing. In spite of the fact that there was no second floor, it was the largest building in the city. It was also the most elegant and most expensive.

Cooper held the door open, waiting for Regan and a still-pale Michael to pass. He dreaded this dinner and the anticipated meeting with Jonathan—so much so, that his stomach was already rebelling. His hand on Michael's shoulder, he followed his wife into the lobby, wishing that he and the boy were somewhere else.

Regan summoned the room clerk with a single ping of the brass bell. He came out of the back office, staring at them over the top of a pair of wire-rimmed glasses, clearly annoyed that his own supper had been interrupted. "Yes?"

"Mr. and Mrs. Jonathan Dundee," Regan answered, her tone matching the man's. "We're meeting them here for dinner."

At the mention of Jonathan's name, the man's manner changed. Jonathan Dundee had rented an entire suite of rooms and had paid in advance. The clerk wiped his mouth with the napkin that had been stuffed in his collar and reached for his coat. "Back there," he said, pointing the way. "If you'll follow me . . ."

Regan led the way. She reached back, taking Michael's hand when it appeared that the boy was falling behind. "A united front, if you please," she whispered, groping for Cooper's arm.

The dining room was full. This was not the usual transient crowd that gathered for a night's lodging, or the ordinary collection of drummers and tradesmen. These were the winter visitors, the moneyed cream of an Eastern society fleeing the snows of the Midwest and the bitter winds of the Atlantic coast.

There were foreigners, as well. Gregarious European adventurers who had come seeking excitement in the wild West. It seemed to Michael that all eyes turned toward them when they entered.

Jonathan had chosen a long table at the rear of the room—purposely, Cooper knew, so that he and Regan would be properly impressed with the surroundings. Appearances had always been important to Jonathan: appearances and what other people thought.

Their greetings were restrained and properly polite. There was something almost fearful in Jonathan's eyes when he extended his hand, and Cooper was tempted for a moment to ignore the gesture. His moment of hesitancy was immediately sensed, and when their hands did meet, the handshake became a contest of strength. "Jonathan," Cooper smiled. His face remained calm, impassive, and he yielded not one mote to his elder brother's continued pressure.

The women were less concerned with the formalities or the polite gestures, and there was no sense of competition between them. Angela's face shone with pleasure, and she embraced Regan, openly unabashed in her joy. Her happiness extended to Michael, and she planted a warm kiss on his forehead. "I'm so glad you came."

There was an awkward pause as the young woman waited for some response from Cooper. She toyed nervously with the curl of blond hair at her ear, afraid to make the first move. And then he was in front of her, and she was swallowed up in his arms. Relieved, she buried her head against his chest, unable to stop the tears. "Oh, Coop . . ."

He held her for a time, no longer angry at her. Her marriage to Jonathan seemed insignificant now that he had her in his arms. "I've missed you, brat," he murmured. Sensing her relief, he let go. "Welcome home, Angela."

Cooper's words seemed to break the fragile cloak of icy tension that hovered over them. Jonathan exhaled loudly, as if he had been really holding his breath in anticipation of some nameless trouble, and signaled for them to sit down. "Wine," he said expansively. "I've brought a bottle of imported wine."

Regan's hand found Cooper's. She held out her own glass, smiling as Jonathan poured. "I'm going to be drinking Coop's share," she smiled. There was both pride and humor in her voice as she continued, her words light and conversational. "Marriage has reformed him." She laughed, nodding at his upturned goblet.

Cooper joined the game, realizing how important it was to Regan that his refusal of the wine not become an issue. He toasted Jonathan with his water glass. "I've seen the light, big brother! No wine, no women, and—" his gaze fell on Michael, the smile growing "—only occasionally, a good cigar!"

Jonathan's initial discomfort eased, and he filled his own glass with considerable pleasure. *As if Cooper's acknowledged inability to drink was somehow an endorsement of his own great self-control.* He lifted his glass in a salute of his own. "I can only hope you've learned moderation in other things, as well." He smiled.

Cooper endured the meal with the grace and determination of a man caught in a social dilemma over which he had very little control. Jonathan dominated the conversation, making pronouncements and asking only an occasional question. And when those rare queries occurred, they were phrased in such a way that Cooper soon found that they were sparring with their words.

At last the meal was over. Jonathan poured himself a glass of brandy, warming the glass between his palms as he watched Cooper drink yet another cup of strong coffee. "How's business?" he asked finally.

Cooper smiled into his cup and took a long drink before answering. "Which business?" He had long ago learned the wisdom of answering Jonathan's questions with a question of his own.

Jonathan frowned. "Dundee Transport," he breathed. "I was asking about Dundee Transport." *As you damn well know*, he fumed silently.

"Why?" Cooper set his cup down on the table, both hands wrapped around the fragile china vessel. His gaze crawled across the damask cloth and up Jonathan's arm to meet the man's eyes.

The tense silence that had preceded the meal returned, and the invisible walls that separated the men began to grow. Both women sensed the change, and both of them spoke, hoping to avoid what they instinctively knew was about to happen. "The baby," Regan said, hoping to distract the men.

'I'm still waiting to see your baby. . . ." Hopefully, she pushed her chair away from the table.

"He's growing, Regan! It amazes me, how fast a baby can grow." Angela's words were directed as much at her husband as they were at her sister-in-law.

The women's ruse failed miserably. Neither man responded. They sat facing each other, as if they were the only two at the table.

Jonathan's face betrayed the anger that was mounting within him. He stared across the rim of his glass at his younger half brother, his eyes tracing Cooper's features as he tried to read something—*anything*—in the man's impassive expression. "I have a right to know, Coop," he began. When there was no response, he continued. "You may own two-thirds of Dundee Transport, now, but I still have a one-third interest in the line, Coop; in the line and everything else."

Cooper shook his head. "*Angela* still has a one-third interest, Jonathan. Not you."

The elder Dundee was having a great deal of difficulty holding his temper. Without taking his eyes off his brother's face, he addressed his wife, his tone so harsh that the woman was visibly startled. "Angela!" There was an irritating air of false condescension in his manner when he spoke to the woman. "I want you to ask Cooper how the business is going. How things stand financially. Now, Angela."

Cooper's jaws tightened. He resented the way Jonathan had drawn Angela into their quarrel. His hold on the coffee cup increased, the fragile, translucent china suddenly shattering between his fingers. The great self-control he was exercising made him impervious to the scalding heat, and he continued speaking as if nothing had happened. "Angela gets a yearly report, Jonathan, and a financial statement from the bank at the end of each quarter. What she does with those reports is none of my business." He forced a smile, his voice lowering. "Just as it's none of *your* business." Still smiling, he reached out and wiped his coffee-wet fingers on Jonathan's clean napkin.

"I read those reports, Coop!" Jonathan retorted. He was suddenly smug. "Angela asked me to read them. You're in trouble. You're up to your neck in debt, and you've had to turn down contracts because you don't have the equipment or the men to handle an increase. And you can't get any financing!"

Cooper was fully aware of the heads that had turned in their direction, but he refused to indulge Jonathan's flair for the dramatic or the man's need for an audience. "You're right about the debts, big brother," he breathed. "What you've forgotten is just where they came from and who was responsible for them." He was silent for a brief moment, wishing, for the first time in more than a year, for a drink. He settled for a hand-rolled cigarette.

Jonathan snorted. "Company debts, Coop. All I left you with was company debts."

"Bullshit!" Cooper's single-word reply came with a thick cloud of acrid blue smoke. "You lived high for a long time, Jonathan—at the company's expense. Your business dinners . . ." An old wound was reopening, a gaping wound that had never properly healed. "The investments and the proposed expansions . . ." Cooper's chest tightened, and he tugged absently at his tie. "Montgomery and his damned railroad."

The mere mention of Logan Montgomery's name brought a strained, ominous hush to the small gathering, each of them locked in his own dark memories of that time.

Jonathan was the first to speak. "That's all past, Coop." The guilt that he had felt following Teresa Dundee's death had been short lived, and he no longer blamed himself for it. All that remained now was a feeling of regret for the emotions that had prompted him to let Cooper take control of the stage line on the turn of a card. "Far in the past."

Cooper shook his head. "Maybe for you," he whispered. "But not for me, Jonathan. And not for Teresa."

"Teresa's dead," Jonathan replied, his voice flat. "And none of it was my doing."

"It was *all* your doing," Cooper retorted. Simultaneously, both men shoved back their chairs and rose to their feet. Their quarrel was no longer a private affair. Without realizing it, their voices had risen, too, and now the entire room was aware of the disagreement.

The two women were painfully aware of the strain between their husbands and the very real potential for a violent confrontation. Regan rose up from her chair. "You'll have to excuse us, Angela. All of us." Resolute, she placed her hand on Cooper's shoulder.

Michael watched with interest as Cooper and Jonathan held their ground, neither man yielding. He felt a familiar flush of pride at Cooper's total lack of fear and the way he refused to let Jonathan's size and bulk intimidate him. More than ever, he wished that Cooper was his father, his real father.

Her fault, he pouted, his gaze shifting to Regan. *It is her fault that Coop hasn't adopted me.* Just like it was her fault that he and Cooper were here in a place they didn't want to be.

He slid off his chair and marched around the table, reaching out to take Cooper's hand. "I want to go home, Coop. Please take me home."

Chapter Two

Regan sat at the desk in Cooper's inner office, absently toying with the long black curl that had escaped the ribbon securing her hair at the nape of her neck. Silently she reflected on the things that had happened the night before. How could it be possible, she wondered, for so much to go wrong in so short a time? Jonathan and Cooper had almost come to blows before she and Angela succeeded in restoring some semblance of peace, and even now she found herself wondering what would have happened if Cooper hadn't been concerned about Michael.

A shadow appeared across the open pages of the ledger spread before her and roused her from her melancholy. Startled, she looked up, the surprise filling her with a fleeting moment of panic. She had heard nothing, not the opening of the door nor the sound of footsteps. Recovering her composure, she spoke. "May I help . . . ?" There was a pause, and then a smile as she recognized the man who stood before her. "Estevan!"

Estevan Folley returned Regan's smile, his brown eyes filled with the woman's image. He took her hand, bowed at the waist, and kissed her fingertips. "Mrs. Dundee," he greeted.

Regan's laughter was genuine. So was the confusion she was unable to conceal. She withdrew her hand and rose up from her chair to make a proper, if somewhat awkward, curtsy. "Señor Folley."

Her eyes swept Estevan from head to toe, and she was amazed at the change. Even his clothing was different. Instead of the usual well-tailored suit, he was clad in the

15

traditional garb of a working cowhand. A vaquero, she thought, correcting herself.

Like Cooper Dundee, who was one-fourth Apache, Estevan Folley was the product of two distant cultures. A subtle blending of his Anglo and Mexican heritages had given him a complexion neither white nor brown, and his skin contrasted sharply with his dark hair and ebony eyes. There was a fineness to his features, something deceivingly delicate, yet there was no softness in him.

Regan allowed her curiosity to get the better of her. "We weren't expecting you, Estevan. At least, not yet." It was, she knew, too early for his yearly trip north to the capital at Prescott, where he served as a territorial legislator.

He seemed to know what she was thinking, and he answered the question before she asked it. "I've resigned, Regan. I was in Prescott just long enough to give Governor Frémont a letter explaining the—" he paused, smiling "—*official* reason for my resignation. . . ." The words were left hanging, and he was quiet for a long time. "Where's Coop?" he asked finally.

Regan was toying with the papers on the desk. The color had returned to her cheeks, and she had the look of a child who had been caught writing dirty words in the margin of her McGuffey's reader. "I hope he's still busy trying to find out what's wrong with our stagecoach driver—he didn't show up today." Guilt prompted her to explain further, though not fully. "He's worried about the baby, Estevan. And about me. He doesn't want me working." She indicated the pile of papers and the ledgers still open on the desk. "Not even this."

Estevan's eyes danced. "Pregnant, cooking, and cleaning," he laughed, tidying up the original phrase for the woman's benefit. "He always said that when he took a wife, that's how he'd keep her!"

Regan canted her head, her right eyebrow raising. It was a look that Estevan recognized. She patted her stomach with one hand, using the other to shake a finger at her tormentor. "He may have me pregnant, but it will be a cold day in—" Michael came through the door "—Phoenix," she intoned, "before he chains *this* wife to a stove and a mop!"

Estevan laughed and turned to greet the boy. "*Qué tal, niño!*"

"Estevan!" Michael's pleasure was as great as Regan's. He allowed the man to give him a quick hug, ducking away with a squeal when Estevan pretended to want a kiss. And then, remembering the reason for his mission, Michael turned to Regan. "Coop told me to find you." Michael seemed to enjoy the next. "He knows you're working."

"Damn!" Regan rarely used profanity, and the word came with a great deal of intensity. She cast an accusing eye at the boy. "Did you tell him I was here, Michael? Before he asked?"

Estevan saw the boy's pout and felt the tension between the woman and the child. He watched, waiting for the youth to answer, troubled by the obvious animosity.

"No!" Michael's reply was curt and sullen, his usually pleasant face marred by a jaw-jutting belligerence. *"No!"*

"I beg your pardon," Regan said quietly.

Michael stared at the floor for a time before he answered. "No, ma'am," he said finally. And then, without asking to be excused, he ran out of the room.

"Regan?" Estevan suddenly felt his problems were very small compared to the woman's.

"He's upset with me." She stared after the boy, watching through the door as he raced down the street. "If Coop can't find another driver, he's going to have to make the Prescott run himself. And if he does, Michael wants to go with him. I said no." She exchanged a long look with the man. "There are times, Estevan, when I think that he hates me."

"Growing pains," Estevan volunteered, wanting to reassure her. "He's too old to be babied and too young to turn loose." He smiled and touched Regan's arm, his hand sliding down her sleeve to hold her hand. "It's like that with little boys. Sometimes it's like that with the bigger ones, too."

Cooper Dundee arrived and, concealing his surprise at seeing Estevan, eased through the front door. He grinned and cleared his throat. "If I had a suspicious mind, *compadre,* I'd think you were trying to seduce my wife and steal my unborn child!" He made a loud *tsk-tsk* with his tongue, shaking his head. "I've seen men get killed for less."

It was always the same when the two friends met—the playful banter, the good-natured teasing, which was their way of expressing their love without having to say the words.

Estevan shrugged. "And just when she was about to say

yes." He sighed. Unable to help himself, he began to laugh. Just as quickly, he sobered. "I need to talk, Coop."

Regan was relieved that Estevan had provided a means of escape for her. She excused herself, her fingers leaving a warm place on Cooper's arm as she went away.

Cooper leaned over the litter on the desk, stretching to open the bottom drawer. "She thinks I'm going to forget about this." He grimaced, nodding at the ledgers. Straightening, he produced a bottle of amber-colored rye. "I probably will."

Estevan took the bottle. He worked the cork free and took a long drink. "I quit, Coop. I told Beitermann and the other legislators to stick the whole shebang up their self-righteous rear ends, and then I resigned." Only then—and forgetting that Cooper no longer drank—did he offer his friend the bottle.

Cooper shook his head. "I learned the hard way that it doesn't do much more than dull the pain for just a little while," he said quietly. "You looked like you could use a temporary pain killer."

Estevan laughed, but the sound was totally devoid of humor. "Nine years, Coop. I've served in the legislature for nine years and have yet to see one bill I've introduced make it out of committee." His brow wrinkled, and he started to take another drink, then changed his mind. "I'm going back to the law, Coop. Try and make things work for my people from this end." *To make things work for my mother's people*, he promised silently.

Cooper inhaled. He chose his next words very carefully. "Here, Estevan? You plan on opening an office in Phoenix?"

Estevan turned to face his friend, surprised that he would ask the question. "You sound like you think it would be a bad idea, Coop." There was a whiskey edge to his voice, to his words.

He doesn't know, Cooper thought silently. Aloud he said, "You might find it a little crowded, *compadre*." He beckoned and led him to the window.

Estevan's lips grew thin, his mouth a tight line beneath the dark mustache. He could see the law-office sign with the bold Dundee "D" and Jonathan's name underneath. "I thought he was still back east in Washington," he said finally. He forced his eyes away from the sign, staring hard at his feet.

His shoulders lifted and then fell. "I don't know why I'm surprised. Frémont hasn't appointed an attorney general yet, and Jonathan's got as good a chance as any of the other bootlickers." He was silent for a moment, his gaze still fixed on the toes of his boots. "Coop, how is Angela?" he asked softly.

Cooper would have given his soul to be able to say Angela was unhappy and that she regretted having married Jonathan, but he could not. "She—*they*—have a baby, Estevan, a little boy."

There was a long silence as Estevan pondered Cooper's words. He had loved Angela for a long time. *He still loved her.* Forcing a smile, he lifted the whiskey bottle and saluted the building across the street and the unseen people behind its doors. "I love Angela too much to wish her any grief, Coop." The empty smile became a sheepish grin. "But that doesn't stop me from wishing Jonathan would fall down a flight of stairs and break his neck!"

Cooper's laughter was spontaneous. He clapped Estevan on the back. "Are you in any big hurry to open that law office, *hermano*? Or do you think you could spare a couple days off for a trip back to Prescott?"

"With *you* driving?" his friend replied, laughing.

"And why the hell not?" Cooper's tone became conspiratorial, and he draped an arm around his friend's shoulders. "It'll be like the old days, *compadre*. Just you and me on a pleasant, uneventful jaunt across the plains. . . ." He was talking like a brochure for a stage line interested in luring a gullible greenhorn into a trek across Death Valley. "Consider it," he said, still holding Estevan tightly under his arm. "The two of us, out in the fresh, clean air, heading into the mountains on a comfortable coach drawn by fleet and surefooted steeds. . . . Think of it as an adventure."

Estevan snorted. "It's easier to think of it as a royal pain in the ass," he said knowingly. Already, he could feel the dull ache deep in his bones, remembering the grinding pain of hip joints and a tailbone that always seemed to take forever to heal. Still, it would be a chance to consider his plans for the future. "Why not," he said finally. His eyes were on the red brick building across the street. "Why the hell not?"

*　　*　　*

Jonathan's private office had the smell of new furniture and freshly tanned leather. He had spared himself nothing, from the luxurious oriental carpet to the complementing black velvet draperies that hung at the floor-to-ceiling multipaned windows. A six-foot-long mahogany desk with ivory and gold inlays dominated the room, the polished top uncluttered and free of litter. Nothing in this inner sanctum was out of place: not one chair, not one ashtray. Even the books that lined the identically spaced shelves on all four walls sat upright, carefully catalogued and indexed according to author and title.

The room was a startling contrast to the almost spartan simplicity of the small outer office that was occupied by Jonathan's secretary. This room faced the street, a desk on one side of the wide front door, a long, unpadded deacon's bench on the other.

Regan's first thought, as she entered the small anteroom, was to turn on her heel and leave. She attributed her feeling of panic to the austerity of her surroundings and the guilt she felt in having come here without telling Cooper. Worse, for having waited until Cooper and Estevan had left for Prescott.

The middle-aged man at the desk did little to ease her discomfort. He sat, his index finger skimming the sparse entries in the appointment book, and then pompously addressed her. "You do have an appointment, madam?" he asked, staring up at her over a pair of wire-rimmed spectacles. Like the cook and the nurse Jonathan employed, this man was also from the East, and there was a blatant attitude of superiority in him. *As if*, Regan thought, *he had found himself, a sinless Gentile, cast among a tribe of ignorant heathens.*

There was more. She discerned a sneer that touched the corners of his mouth as he appraised her, head to toe. It was obvious that he felt she had breached some strict code of etiquette, appearing in public when she was so obviously with child. Regan refused to be intimidated by the man's attitude.

"Mr. Dundee is my husband's brother," she said quietly. "And Mrs. Dundee—Angela—is a very close friend."

The small man's demeanor immediately changed. He rose up from his chair, apologizing profusely for his error as he headed for Jonathan's door. He disappeared into the inner office and, just as quickly, reappeared. "Mr. Dundee will see you in just a moment," he bubbled. Politely, he nodded at the uncomfortable bench.

Regan remained on her feet. She stood at the window, her eyes on the street. And then, catching his reflection in the window, she saw Jonathan. He stood in the doorway of his office, visibly drawing himself taller before he called out to her.

She turned, facing him, before her name died on his lips. "Jonathan," she greeted.

He nodded in greeting but did not speak to her. Instead, his words were directed at his secretary. "We're not to be disturbed, Peters." And then, almost cautiously, he invited the woman to join him.

The difference between the outer waiting room and Jonathan's inner office was overwhelming. Regan knew that her response was anticipated, just as everything about Jonathan was carefully planned and orchestrated. He knew how to impress, even more than he knew how to manipulate. She gave the devil his due. "It's very nice, Jonathan." Her appraisal of the room continued, and she wondered how much of this was Angela's doing.

It was, she decided, a man's domain, meant to impress other men with money.

Jonathan was standing behind one of the chairs that stood in front of his desk. He kept his place, lingering at her back for a moment, until Regan finally sat down. Even carrying his brother's child, she was still an incredibly beautiful woman.

She felt him at her back and knew instinctively what he was thinking. It was strange how things had worked out. Before coming to Phoenix, Regan had owned and operated O'Rourke & Associates, a Chicago consulting firm of which she still held the controlling interest. She had founded the business-management company herself, at a time when women in business—any business—were as much a curiosity as they were a rarity. Not that she had not had her share of important backers. Robert Lincoln and George Pullman had not only given her the financial backing she had needed—she had worked for them both—but endorsements that brought her only the best clientele. And as she earned the respect of her peers, the business had flourished.

When Regan's brother and sister-in-law had died, she

had decided to come to Arizona to assume guardianship of her son, Michael, and so she had accepted Jonathan Dundee's offer to hire her to assess and appraise the stage line. For a time she had been attracted to him, just as he had been attracted to her—before she and Cooper had fallen in love.

Regan cleared her throat, relieved when Jonathan took his place in the chair behind his desk. "I want to discuss the line, Jonathan."

He smiled. "I was willing to talk the other evening, Regan," he said. "When we were having dinner. It didn't work. Coop wouldn't let it work."

It took all the calm Regan could muster to keep from losing her temper. She had wanted to keep the discussion on a business level, knowing that there was no hope for any kind of an amicable agreement if they continued to allow their personal differences to cloud their thinking. "You weren't without fault, Jonathan." She raised her hand when he started to speak. "None of us were without fault." Her eyes lifted and met the man's, and she continued. "Angela and I were wrong to attempt a forced reconciliation between the two of you. Cooper was wrong to imply that you had no interest in the line. And *you* were wrong to make the kind of demands that you were making." Already, Regan could feel herself losing control of the situation.

Jonathan was unrelenting. "You can't deny that Coop— that the line—is in serious financial trouble," he declared. "He's going to lose it all, Regan." Jonathan didn't even try to hide his satisfaction. "If Coop doesn't listen to me, if he doesn't let me help, he's going to lose it all."

Regan couldn't help but admire the man's steadfast belief in his own self-worth. There was absolutely no humility or doubt in him. "What do you want, Jonathan?" she asked finally.

"A partnership," he announced. "An equal partnership in return for my financial backing."

"Like before?" Regan asked, already knowing the answer.

"*Exactly* like it was before," Jonathan answered.

Regan was already shaking her head. "No," she murmured. And then, more strongly, "No."

Jonathan's face colored. "You won't like the alternative, Regan," he breathed. "I'll sell . . ." He saw the look on the woman's face and corrected himself, silently cursing her for making him feel it was necessary. "I'll convince Angela to sell her share." He grew smug. "She'll do it, Regan, if I ask. You know that she'll do it."

It was true. Regan didn't doubt for a moment that Jonathan could convince the young woman to sell. Worse, that Jonathan would convince her to let him handle the sale.

She knew the kind of buyer Jonathan would seek out: a dummy company set up by the railroad, which would purposely expose the line to ruin, with little regard for the small businessmen who would suffer also.

Jonathan's voice cut into her thoughts, rudely jarring her to her senses. "You tell Cooper I want my share of the line back, Regan," he ordered quietly. "You tell him I want things to be just like they were before. Or . . ." There was something ominous in the way he left the sentence hanging, and something even more sinister in his smile when he continued, "Or he can sell the ranch, Regan." His voice lowered. "He can sell *me* the ranch at Casa Grande."

Regan rose up from her chair. It would hurt Cooper to lose the line, but it would destroy him if he were to lose the home place at Casa Grande. Especially to Jonathan.

Regan realized now just how much he intended taking. When she spoke, her voice was as firm as Jonathan's, and her eyes burned with the same stubborn intensity. "I won't let you do this to him."

Jonathan's patience had reached its limit, his old resentment of the woman—of the fact that she had spurned him and chosen to marry his half brother instead—fueling the anger. "Before long, you won't have any choice," he whispered. "He has ten days to make up his mind. He agrees to the partnership, or I find a buyer for *my*"—he purposely emphasized the word—"share of Dundee Transport."

Regan spun around and left, sorry that she had come. Jonathan hadn't changed. After everything that had happened in the past, after all the pain he had caused, he hadn't changed.

Thirty miles north of Phoenix, at the way station at New River, Cooper and Estevan stopped for a change of horses and their midmorning meal. They sat at a long table in the summer kitchen, competing with newly hatched botflies for a lunch of chili and warm tortillas spread with freshly churned butter.

They were no longer alone. Two others, a young man and a young woman who earlier had arrived at the way station from one of the small nearby towns, were seated at the opposite end of the table. Covertly, Cooper watched the pair. Finally, he placed the young man and turned to Estevan to confirm his speculations. "That's Aaron Beitermann's kid, isn't it?"

Estevan answered without speaking, nodding his head as he chewed on a mouthful of beans. "Tad," he said, swallowing. Estevan found it hard to believe that this young man could be the same snot-nosed brat that Beitermann used to drag to legislative meetings at the capitol. All of a sudden he felt old, even more so as he recognized the young woman. "The girl is Leona Simpson," he finished. He studied the pair briefly, smiling when he saw the way they had locked out the rest of the world. It dawned on him then where he had seen that kind of pleasant isolation before. It was when his cousin had married, and she and her husband were about to embark on their first trip as man and wife.

Cooper recognized the look, too, just as he was aware of the young man's furtive glances in his direction. Wiping his mouth, he rose up from his seat, shaking his head when Estevan started to join him. "I'll be right back." He grinned.

The coach was in front of the way station. It sat motionless, the empty traces waiting for the animals that would bring life back to the wood and the iron-bound wheels.

Intent on his mission, Cooper hoisted himself up into the driver's box. His carry bag, the canvas sack he used to carry a change of clothes and his toiletries, lay beneath the seat. He dug into the sack, grinning when his fingers closed around a short love note from Regan and a want list from Michael, digging even deeper as he searched for the bottle.

The magnum of imported brandy had been with him for a long time. He had bought it more than a year before from a liquor salesman on his way through the territory to greener pastures in San Francisco. That was the same day he had taken his last drink. *The same day he had promised Regan he would never drink again.* Now he carried it as a reminder.

Tad Beitermann was talking to Estevan when Cooper returned to the table. The flush of embarrassment was still on the young man's cheeks, and there was a hesitancy in him as he extended his hand. He was painfully aware of the animosity that had long existed between Cooper Dundee and his father, who hated Indians with a vehemence that extended to the prominent, part-Apache stage-line owner. "Mr. Dundee," he began, still unsure

Cooper shook the youth's hand heartily. "Tad," he greeted. Gingerly, he lifted his other hand and displayed the jug. "A toast for the newlyweds." He smiled.

The young man laughed, relief flooding him. And then his face turned red again, and he glanced at his wife. "I didn't think anyone could tell." He smiled. Suddenly, he felt a kinship with Cooper, a kinship that came with the knowledge that he, too, had done something that his father would not approve. "We're taking your stage north to tell our folks," he said. "They had a big wedding planned for June." He paused and chewed on his bottom lip for a moment, and then, feeling a need for a man-to-man confession, continued, "We couldn't wait." He knew at once that Cooper understood.

Estevan had gone into the back room for glasses, returning with the stationmaster and his wife in tow. "It's a big bottle, Coop," he grinned.

Cooper nodded. "What about the others?" he asked. He could see the hostler at the coach, busy greasing the right rear wheel, and the young stockman in the corrals just beyond.

The stationmaster eyed the bottle, counting heads before he made his decision. "I don't abide the help drinking, Mr. Dundee. Not on the job."

Cooper almost choked. Titus Bragg had been with Dundee Transport for as long as he could remember and had always been able to hoist a glass with the best of them. He also ran a thriving bootleg business on the side. Cooper looped a friendly arm around the man's shoulder. "It's a special occasion, Bragg." He lowered his voice, gesturing toward the young couple. "They just got married."

The old man's face split in a wide grin. Weddings, like new babies, brought out the best in all men. "Why the hell didn't you say so in the first place?" he groused. His voice rose, and he summoned the help. "Yo!" he bellowed, waving them in with his outstretched arm. "Babcock! Spencer!" Puzzled, the hostler and the stockman joined them. "A wedding," Bragg announced, as if the whole thing had been his idea. "We're celebrating us a wedding!"

Cooper was concentrating his attentions on the bottle. Carefully, he peeled off the sealing wax and, just as carefully, loosened the cork. One by one, he filled the glasses. "To new beginnings," he grinned, touching the edge of his own glass to Estevan's before he touched it to the others. "To new beginnings," they echoed. Only Estevan was aware that Cooper's glass was empty.

Babcock finished his drink, refusing another with a polite nod when Estevan made the offer. "Still got that rear wheel to grease." He smiled amicably and rubbed his beard. He was still grinning when he departed.

The man's smile dissolved as soon as he turned his back. His dark eyes were warmed by a fire more intense than any inner heat caused by the glass of potent brandy, and his fists were knotted at his sides. He needed something in his hands, something that would hide the eagerness and anticipation that had begun to fill him. Back at the coach, he dropped down on one knee and resumed his chores, plunging his hand into the bucket of thick, yellow grease.

His real name was Adam Becker. Two years before he had run the Dundee Transport way station midway between Phoenix and Casa Grande. Malachai Dundee—Cooper's deceased father—had hired him more years ago than he cared to remember, and he had grown fat and comfortable in a job that had required little more of him than the ordering about of another man to do the actual work.

And Cooper Dundee had fired him from that job—had beaten him almost senseless and stripped him of his manhood and his livelihood—just because Cooper didn't like the way he beat and kicked some damned mongrel dog.

And later, much later, when he had tried to kill Cooper Dundee in revenge, Cooper had sent him to prison.

The black memory of Yuma Prison swallowed him up, and he instinctively gulped a lungful of cool air as the remembrance brought back the old fears and the even older hate. He remembered the long hours in the stifling cells that had been carved out of the very bowels of hell, just as he remembered the endless days he had spent on the country road crews.

It was those long, grueling hours of hard labor that had

melted the flesh from him. At first, his soft hands had bled, and the white flesh on his back had burned and blistered. And then, as the days stretched into weeks and the weeks into months, his entire body hardened. After the first year, he could stare at his own reflection and wonder about the face that stared back at him.

He had changed so much, including adding a beard, that even Cooper Dundee did not recognize him. He laughed. Only moments before, he had shared a drink with the man whose testimony had sent him to prison—and shared a drink with the man's attorney, Estevan Folley—and neither one had known him!

Finished with his chores, he stood up, smearing yet another glob of thick grease on the large wheel hub. It was an effective cover for a lug nut he had loosened. It was going to work, he thought smugly. This time, after all the waiting, all the careful planning, it was going to work.

And before the day was over, Cooper Dundee would be dead.

Chapter Three

Estevan sat beside Cooper, staring straight ahead at terrain that, like the big canyon north of Flagstaff, never seemed to be the same. It wasn't only the subtle differences brought on by the change of the seasons or the corresponding positions of the sun in the heavens, it was the wildness of the place. The native scrub poked up from the rock-strewn earth with the kind of stubborn tenacity that mortal man could only admire and rarely attain. It was as if nature were trying to take back what man had stolen from her.

Sprouting shoots of juniper root forced their way out of the yellow sandstone at the side of the hand-hewn roadway, obscuring the marks of the pickaxes and shovels that had torn at the earth when the road was built. The gnarled tendrils ate away at the soil, eroding the man-made embankments of piled stone, pushing aside the smaller rocks until the larger boulders gave way. And then the spring rains would come, and whole sections of the roadway would give out and be swept away.

Estevan pondered these things, as wary of the fickle changes in the terrain and the weather as he was of the sad condition of Cooper's rolling stock. He had noticed the patched and reworked harness and the mended wheels when they were still in Phoenix, but back there—with Cooper explaining his need to economize—it didn't seem so bad. Here and now, however, on top of the coach, behind the six-horse hitch that plunged forward in response to Cooper's whip, his viewpoint was radically changed, and he began to worry.

His concern, he rationalized, was foolish and unnecessary. Cooper would never do anything that would put the line and its passengers—young Tad Beitermann and his new wife—in any real jeopardy. Still silent, Estevan mentally apologized to his friend for doubting him. He told himself that Cooper was too well acquainted with tragedy to be careless, and too familiar with death to do anything that would expose man or beast to needless risk.

As if sensing Estevan's concern, Cooper slowed the team a little as he came into the grade that rose before them. The natural upward rise of the roadway would take away the remaining momentum. The horses would be barely moving when they reached the crest of the hill.

The road narrowed, funneling upward along the edge of the mountain, and the coach almost scraped against the hewed-out embankment. On the opposite side, it seemed to hang over the steep drop as they made the first switchback, and Estevan closed his eyes in a quick need for prayer.

The stage lurched a bit to the right just as Cooper was straightening out on the final curve. It seemed natural enough, the big rear wheels sliding across the loose gravel. And then, terrifyingly, it was as though the right rear wheel dropped over the edge and away. The seat on that side of the driver's box dropped suddenly at a sharp angle, and both men scrambled to keep their places on the box.

Still moving forward, the inside of the stage rose higher and higher. Cooper could hear the splintering of the back axle and braced himself for the inevitable jolt that came when the rear axle frame was torn away from the body of the coach. There was a sudden shift as the rear of the big Concord collapsed into the roadbed, the sharp whine of wood and iron against rock piercing the air.

Desperately, Cooper called out to the team, urging the horses on in an attempt to offset the drag of the crippled coach. It was useless, the animals' shod hooves sparking against the rock-hard roadway as they tried, and failed, to gain ground. The old Concord dragged them back, the pull of a dead weight in excess of a ton too much for the horses as the back end of the coach dropped over the side of the cliff.

Estevan felt rather than heard Cooper's urgent command, *"Jump!"* and then felt himself propelled from the seat. Single-handed, in a burst of superhuman effort, Cooper lifted him up and over the side.

Cooper's own effort failed. He was half erect in the seat, and the coach was increasing in its momentum as it tumbled

backward down the face of the cliff. The rising seat slammed
into him, knocking him off balance, his own cries mingling
with the terrified screams of the panicked horses. And then,
suddenly, he was flung out into space.

He spun through space, nothing more than a child's toy
floating on the still air, instinctively compacting himself into a
tight ball just before he hit the ground. He rolled and tumbled down the side of the mountain, following the wide path
cut by the careening coach, until they both disappeared and
were swallowed up by a great cloud of thick yellow dust and
debris.

The Concord seemed to explode on impact. The wood
door panels heaved outward and then collapsed into the
silent interior, and then it was still.

An unnatural quiet descended on the canyon. Nothing
moved. Nothing, it seemed, lived.

Michael was prowling the back streets of Phoenix, still
nursing a bruised ego. Not only had Regan had the effrontery
to tell him he was too little—*little*, he fumed—to go with
Cooper and Estevan, she had added insult to injury and
ordered him to his room to take a nap when he continued to
argue.

He went to his room, all right. And as soon as the door
was closed behind him, he promptly escaped out the window.
"Naps," he muttered, talking to himself as he played a solitary game of kick the can. "Babies take naps!" He gave the
battered tin another swift kick with the toe of his boot. "I
sure ain't takin' no damn nap!" The tin can bore the brunt of
yet another attack, this time lifting into the air and disappearing into an alleyway between two buildings.

The boy pursued the can, a sudden flush of excitement
in him as he realized where his forbidden wanderings had
taken him. He was filled with the titillation of a secret
trespasser. The pathway that spread before him led, he knew,
straight to the back doors of hell.

Inadvertently, Michael had wandered into the garbage-
littered alleyways behind the red-light district of Phoenix. A
long row of saloons and bordellos spread out before him,
their rear entrances not unlike the back doors of the more
respectable buildings that lined the main street. Not sure

what he expected, the youngster tiptoed down the yawning passageway, his heart thumping loudly in his chest.

This was a different kind of fear. It wasn't the same thing he felt when he had done something wrong and knew he was about to be caught. It was more the kind of terror he remembered from the night when he and two of his friends had snuck into the back room of the undertaker's. They had wandered about, poking and sniffing at all his strange paraphernalia, until they stumbled on the room where he did his embalming.

The mortician's teenaged son had somehow known they were coming. And he waited for them, spread out silent and holding his breath beneath a sheet on the gray marble slab. It was scary-funny now, remembering what he felt when the sheet-covered body rose up off the table. But then, in the cold darkness of that smelly room, it was the same as what he felt now. . . .

A brief flash of motion caught the boy's eye, causing him to visibly panic. He caught his breath, drawing himself up small against the side of the building at his back as he forced himself to explore the black shadows with his eyes. *It's a cat,* he told himself, hoping it was true. *Just some damned old cat* . . . But the fear didn't go away.

He heard the laughter then, a soft, teasing sound that came to him out of the darkness. And then there was another spurt of movement, of cloth and flesh, and the sound of bare feet padding down the alleyway.

Curious, he followed. The wraithlike presence seemed to be everywhere at once, ahead of him for a time, then in the darkness at his side. And then, inexplicably, behind him.

"Stand still, dammit!" he called.

The soft laughter answered him. "Make me," a voice taunted.

Michael spun around. The voice seemed to come from behind him again, from behind and above. Cautiously, he retraced his steps, his right hand brushing lightly across the sides and tops of the empty crates and boxes that lined the pathway.

A handful of packing excelsior dribbled down from above his head, and then another. And again, the sound of childish giggles.

Michael waded into the crates, clambering up and over

the wooden boxes. He caught sight of a slim ankle and reached out, his fingers closing around a fistful of air. The near miss made him even more determined.

They played a game of hide-and-seek the full length of the alley. Michael's anger at his unseen quarry faded and gave way to good-natured laughter, only to return again when the spirit-child refused his invitation to come out and laughed at him again.

Discouraged, he plopped down on an empty packing crate to think, and then, cleverly, he pretended to give up. Hands thrust in his pockets, whistling nonchalantly, he marched out of the alley.

Stifling a laugh, he ducked behind a pile of trash and waited. He held his breath and strained for some sound that would tell him what he wanted, and then he flattened belly-down on the ground. One bare foot appeared before him only inches from his head, followed by the second foot, poised on tiptoe and ready to run. He waited until the second foot relaxed, and then he moved.

He grabbed both ankles, just below the frayed bottom of the other youngster's ragged trousers. "Gotcha!" he exclaimed.

Suddenly, he was like a dog who had captured a badger. His quarry turned on him, becoming the aggressor, and he felt the frustration of wanting to let go and not knowing how. Clenched fists pounded at his back and head, and he tried to defend himself. Together, they wallowed in the dirt, clinging to each other and too stubborn to let go as they rolled over and over.

Thoroughly winded, they stopped their struggles, neither one yielding, and in the end it was a joint truce. Warily, still facing each other, they rose up from the ground. They stood, nose to nose, appraising each other for a long, long time.

Michael studied the youngster who stood before him. The face was somehow familiar, yet vague. It was, he knew, no one that he recognized or knew from school. And still the image of the face—the remembered image—reached out to him from some small corner of his mind.

And then he knew. He had seen the child before, hovering in the background at the schoolyard and at the vacant lot where the town youngsters played ball. It was the same face he had seen last summer and all through the winter, and yet, somehow, it was different.

Softer, he thought, like the rest of the body that lay buried beneath the threadbare jeans and shirt. He explored that body with his eyes, his gaze finally lifting to the chest. The subtle beginnings of a pair of small breasts mounded beneath the thin shirt. "A girl," he announced, disgusted. "You're a girl!"

She tossed her head, both hands knotting into fists and going to her hips. "So?" she demanded.

"So I don't play with girls," he answered. He was rubbing his palms on his pant legs, as if he had touched something unclean and needed to wipe off the smell. "Even girls with short hair and long pants!"

The scornful reference to her clothes and her appearance hurt and angered the girl. She mustered all the spunk and pride of a twelve-year-old and silently dared him to say it all again. "Afraid?" she challenged. The blue eyes sparked, and she poked his chest with her index finger. "Scaredy-cat?"

Michael sniffed and wiped his nose with the back of his hand. "I ain't scared," he scoffed, sounding tough. There was an awkward pause between them. "You got a name?" he asked, making conversation.

She eyed him, suspicious. "Sure, I've got a name!"

They began circling again, squaring off. "Well, what is it?" the boy demanded.

She hesitated before answering. "Niña," she breathed, pronouncing it the way she had learned to say it. *Nee-nya*.

Michael snorted and then laughed. He repeated the girl's name over and over, exaggerating it more each time. "That isn't a name," he said arrogantly. He jabbed at her arm. "That's how they say *little girl* in Mexican."

"Is not!" she retorted.

Michael persisted, dancing around her as he repeated the word and its translation again and again. "Little girl," he teased. "Little Miss Got-No-Name!"

She hit him. It was a solid blow, brought up from the ground to connect with his pug nose. Michael never even saw it coming.

There was a sudden flood of bright red across the girl's fist, a dark flash of crimson that surprised her as much as it surprised the boy.

"What'd you do that for!" he yelped.

"I don't like to be teased!" The anger was leaving her, draining away with each splash of red that dripped from Michael's nose through his clenched fingers. "I'm sorry," she said, afraid that he might leave.

"It didn't hurt," the boy lied. He lifted his fingers away from the wound, allowing her a closer look and relishing her sympathy.

"It's pretty bad," she said demurely. Maternally, she tore off a corner of her shirt and dabbed at the place beneath Michael's nose. There was only a thin trickle of bright red now, from just one side, the blood already clotting.

They sat down side by side on an upended barrel. Seeing the girl's concern—her remorse—Michael felt duty-bound to say he was sorry, too. His apology was eloquent and brief. "Sorry," he said softly. A strange compassion moved him to say more. "About your name," he finished.

She nodded, saying nothing for a time, until she was satisfied the boy's nose had really stopped bleeding. "You got one?" she said finally. Her bare heels thumped rhythmically against the hollow keg. "A name?"

"Sure," he answered. "It's Michael. Michael Patrick . . ." There was a brief moment of hesitation. "Michael Patrick Dundee." It was more wishful thinking than outright deceit.

"Cooper Dundee," the girl-child volunteered, thinking aloud. "Cooper Dundee is your pa?"

Michael stared across at his companion, wondering what it was that made her so damned smart. It was beginning to bother him, the way one small fib led to another, but not enough to stop. "Yeah," he lied.

She answered his next question before he could ask it. "He used to come here to visit Dotty," she said matter-of-factly, nodding her head in the vague direction of the entire street. "And that Jonathan, too, before he went away."

Visit? Michael thought, ignoring the bit about Jonathan. Confusing pictures raced through his mind. There was no doubt about where this Dotty worked, just as there was no doubt about what she did. "Where's your ma?" he asked finally.

"Gone," the girl answered. Her mother, Dotty, like the other whores at the bordello, drifted in and out of her life as their moods and their profession decreed. Their absences, like their chosen profession, didn't seem to worry her, nor did she seem to feel any real shame. Someday, her mother would be back, just like some other day she would be gone again. "My ma's a whore," the child explained. She shrugged. "Sometimes, she just goes away. . . ."

This wealth of information only served to confuse Michael even more than he had been in the beginning. If there was something terrible about being a whore—a fallen woman, he thought, remembering Sunday morning meetings—Niña didn't seem to know it. Or if she did, she didn't seem to care. "When Coop . . ." his brow knotted and he corrected himself, not sure how to ask the question, "when my pa used to come here . . ."

"They'd go upstairs," she answered. "You know," she explained, "to be . . . alone."

"Alone," Michael echoed. It was still puzzling to him. What could possibly be so wrong—so dangerous—about a man coming to a place like this to be alone with some woman? Sure didn't seem like enough to burn in hell for eternity. "And?" he prompted.

Niña's mood was euphoric. This was the first time within her limited memory when she had spent so much time with someone so close to her own age. "They'd kiss!" she announced. "Like this . . ." She threw her arms around the boy's neck in an exaggerated parody of adult, two-dollar passion.

Michael's reaction was all boy. Flustered and embarrassed at her sudden attack, he struggled against the girl's embrace and, making a face, shoved her away. And then, afraid she would think him a coward and a baby, he returned the kiss. Hard, right on the lips, just the way he had seen Cooper kiss Regan.

He liked it! And the sudden realization that he *could* like it filled him with a strange sense of panic. Testing himself, he kissed the girl a second time and discovered that, instead of going away, the sensation intensified. She was so soft. Everything about her was so soft.

His nose began to hurt, and he had to reconsider. Her fist certainly hadn't been soft. But the rest of her . . . Timidly, he kissed her again, and just as timidly, she let him.

*   *   *

Estevan hovered between unconsciousness and a dream-like awareness of everything around him. He was crawling, climbing, working his way inch by inch up the side of the steep cliff, dragging something heavy and dead behind him.

The dead thing was his broken leg. It hung lifeless and useless from his right hip joint, impeding the torturous journey through the thick scrub. Time after time, his pant leg became entangled in the low-lying brush, and he would have to reach back with both hands to tear himself free before he could go on.

Mercifully, there was no pain. The shock of what had happened—what he had witnessed—had dulled the physical manifestations of his injuries, and head to toe, he was numb.

He had no concept of time. The sun was a blazing white orb that seemed to hang motionless above him, but it failed to give him any warmth, just as it failed to provide him with any gauge for the passage of time. He did know that he had to keep moving. From somewhere within, the primitive need to survive told him he must keep moving.

At last, just when he thought he could go on no longer, he pulled himself up and over the edge of the scarred roadway. He collapsed face down into the dirt, turning his head to stare down the mountainside.

He began to laugh, urgently, the sound of his own voice strange and distant. Then, as he marked his pathway up the side of the mountain, the laughter turned to tears, and he surrendered to the need for relief. Fifty feet, he reckoned silently, measuring the narrow furrow that had been left in his body's wake. And it had seemed like fifty miles.

A shadow appeared over him, blotting out the sun, and he felt himself shudder. "Help me," he gasped, spitting out the gravel that filled his mouth and scraped against his teeth. "For God's sake, help me . . ."

Adam Babcock dismounted. He took his time, staring first into the depth of the yellow canyon, watching hawklike for signs of any other life. There were none. The only indication that there was a survivor was the narrow dirt trench carved by Estevan Folley in his long climb up the hill. *Too much sign to hide*, he reasoned. Estevan, it seemed, was destined to live.

He made the man as comfortable as he could, using his bedroll for a pillow and his slicker for a blanket. There was a perverse satisfaction within him when Estevan tried to thank him, and he shushed Estevan as if embarrassed.

"The others," Estevan whispered. His fingers closed around Babcock's arm, and he tried to focus. "You've got to help the others. . . ."

Babcock nodded. "Sure," he grinned. "Right away."

Carefully, he picked his way down the side of the mountain, following the wide path cut by the wrecked Concord. It was less difficult than he had anticipated, and he was surprised at how fast he was able to reach the bottom.

The sour stink of death filled the air. All six of the coach horses were at the bottom of the canyon, already stiff and beginning to bloat from massive internal bleeding, and the stench of their urine was overwhelming.

Babcock picked his way through the carnage, feeling nothing for the horses that lay torn and broken among the rocks. But they held a macabre fascination for him, their stilted postures reminiscent of the things he had seen during the war, and for a moment it was as if he had stepped back in time.

He heard a sound then, a shallow whimpering from somewhere beyond the collapsed stagecoach. Instinctively, he drew his weapon. It didn't seem possible that anyone could have survived the long plunge down the cliff, and yet . . .

Cautiously, he skirted the remains of the Concord. A man's arm poked out from beneath the painted wood, the pale fingers of the left hand closed tightly around a handful of rock. Babcock saw the wedding ring and knew that it was the younger man and not Cooper Dundee who rested beneath the wreckage. He knew, also, from the great pool of dark blood that surrounded the arm, that the sound he had heard had not come from this particular place.

He canted his head, listening, and heard the same noise a second time. Fainter now and higher pitched than before, but still the same.

A subtle movement in the brush alerted Babcock, and he paused midstep. It was wrong, all wrong. The noise had come from somewhere ahead of him, not to the side. Cursing, he moved closer to the place where he had seen the feeble raising of a hand.

A man's hand, long-fingered and well tanned. *Cooper Dundee's hand!*

Babcock's first instinct was to kill the man. He strode through the brush, pistol in hand, sure that this was what he wanted. And then, coldly, his mind began to function more rationally. He couldn't shoot Dundee. It wouldn't make any sense, a bullet in a man who was supposed to have died in a stagecoach accident.

He found Cooper, the man's arms and legs akimbo as he lay torn and bleeding in a shallow pit in the shadow of a large boulder. Babcock hunkered down, measuring the extent of Cooper's injuries and taking delight in his suffering.

Cooper's clothes were torn to shreds, the majority of his body exposed and bleeding. Long, deep cuts lay in finger-size ruts on his legs and arms, and his face . . .

Babcock laughed, unable to suppress the glee he felt. Cooper's face was horribly bruised, a mass of contusions that already were turning black and blue, marring his handsome features. And his right eye—impaled in his right eye was a three-inch dagger of splintered white oak.

It would have been so easy to simply drive the long piece of wood through Dundee's eye and into his brain. But, Babcock realized, that would be too easy, too quick. There had to be a better way, he told himself. A way to make Cooper Dundee suffer for a long, long time.

He needed to think. Slowly, Babcock righted himself and made a slow circle around Cooper's still form. His mind cleared, and he remembered the sound that he had heard before, the quiet whimpering.

The girl, he thought. Tad Beitermann's young wife! *Aaron Beitermann's daughter-in-law*, he reminded himself.

The young woman lay in the dirt, a good ten feet away from the coach. She was as torn and as bruised as Cooper Dundee, but, surprisingly, more aware. *Too damned aware*, he thought, feeling the woman's eyes on him.

He needed a drink and took one from the full flask in his hip pocket. It didn't matter to him one way or the other if the woman lived or if she died, and he shrugged. Cooper, however, was another matter.

What Babcock had wanted in the beginning was revenge. Some form of . . . he searched for the phrase, laughing when he finally remembered it: poetic justice.

Yuma, Babcock thought. What he really wanted now was for Cooper Dundee to rot inside the hell that was Yuma.

A glint of sunlight off the amber slivers of broken glass gave Babcock the answer he had been seeking. He recognized the remains of the half-gallon bottle of brandy Cooper had opened at the way station and had given to the newlyweds, and he felt it was a sign from the gods.

The woman was going to die. He was going to kill her. And then, he would tend to Cooper Dundee.

Dispassionately, Babcock picked up a flat, saucer-shaped rock. He hefted it in both hands, testing its weight, and then, without a second thought, raised it high above his head. There was a brief moment of hesitation as the young woman's eyes focused on his face. She stared up at him, her mouth moving noiselessly as she tried to speak, her blue eyes reflecting the shock and the confusion that had robbed her of understanding. And then, suddenly realizing but not comprehending Babcock's intention, the cerulean orbs widened and she tried to scream.

The young woman's feeble cries tore into the unnatural quiet, as fragile and as full of confusion as the first squalling mews of a newborn infant. And like a newborn, the cries intensified and became stronger.

Leona Beitermann's life ended as abruptly as it had begun. Babcock brought the rock down on her head, hard—once, twice—until the crying stopped.

He pulled the stone away from her face, gagging at the impact of what he saw. Her eyes were still open, and she was staring up at him. *Accusing him* . . . In his panic, Babcock raised and lowered the dish-shaped rock a final time. He turned loose of the thing, feeling the warmth of the woman's blood on his fingers, careful to leave the rock covering the woman's face. *Her eyes.*

Coldly, Babcock composed himself. It was easier now, without the woman's eyes to torment him. She had become a thing again, and he could dismiss her from his thoughts as easily as he had dismissed the horses.

And now for you, Mr. Dundee, he mused silently. He sprinted across the rocky terrain to the place where Cooper lay and, pausing only to wet his lips, took the remainder of his pint of whiskey and emptied it across the man's chest and arm.

Carefully, he rolled Dundee over on his side, ignoring the cries of pain as he stuffed the empty flask into the man's back pants pocket. The damning charade was finished.

Satisfied, he turned loose of Dundee and began his long climb back up the side of the canyon. *Drunk*, he would tell them when he rode back to find help. *Even a fool could see that Cooper Dundee had been drunk.*

It wouldn't matter what Estevan Folley said. Not anymore. He was Cooper Dundee's friend and would be expected to lie for him.

And the others, all the others that could tell the truth, were dead. Babcock smiled. They were all dead.

Chapter Four

Regan stared at the stack of papers that lay before her on Cooper's desk, feeling that she had been shackled to her chair for an eternity. She had hoped, when she first started the audit, that she would find that the stage line was not as far in debt as it first appeared. But now, with her worst suspicions confirmed, she had no choice but to face the facts.

It was more than the day-to-day expenses. The young man Cooper had hired as a clerk during the first months of her pregnancy when she was so ill had been grossly inept. Payments on the bank notes and the bank deposits had been entered incorrectly, if they were entered at all, and the monthly billings for freight charges for the local merchants had been completely ignored. As it stood now, she had no way of knowing which bills their customers had paid and which bills were still outstanding. Even the simple entries for the passenger fares were incomplete. So incomplete that for the last month, there was absolutely no record of anyone having purchased a ticket.

Regan rose up from her chair. She stretched, using her fist to rub away the dull ache in the small of her back. She was tired, but it was not an ordinary fatigue caused by her pregnancy. The weariness came from knowing that somehow, by simply not being in the office to take care of the books, she had let Cooper down.

Regan was determined to help him. The stage line was in trouble, serious trouble, but the problems were not so bad that with some additional time and a comparatively small amount of money, they could not be overcome.

Jonathan could have helped, she thought bitterly. Instead, he had stubbornly insisted from the beginning that Angela's share of the earnings be paid in cash on a quarterly basis and not reinvested in the business. Those payments, once a mere inconvenience, had already become a hardship.

A wry smile touched her lips. She had no doubt that Jonathan had known all along that the time would come when Cooper would be faced with the problem of either expanding Dundee Transport or standing back and seeing the line put out of business by a larger company. So he had simply waited, biding his time, making sure that he had control of Angela and her share of the company before making his move.

A dark thought touched her then, and she wondered if Jonathan saw his marriage to Angela as little more than a marriage of convenience.

It was one thing for Jonathan to assert his will on Angela. It was another thing, she told herself, for him to attempt to assert his will on Cooper. He had done that once before, with tragic results, and she steadfastly refused to let it happen again.

Regan crossed the room to the tall filing cabinet behind the desk and pulled open the top drawer. She kept her own records here, the correspondence and papers relating to her business in Chicago. The feeling of pride was still there when she pulled out the first folder, the good feeling that came when she saw the embossed letterhead: *O'Rourke & Associates*. The company name was boldly and elegantly engraved in script above the LaSalle Street address.

She found it ironic that it was her husband's company that was in trouble now, and that she had been unable to help him. *Until now,* she reminded herself.

Jonathan was wrong when he assumed that Cooper had only two alternatives open to him for salvaging the stage line. His choices were not limited to accepting Jonathan's demands for a partnership or, in desperation, selling the ranch at Casa Grande. There was a third option.

Regan opened the file folder she had pulled from the drawer and spread its contents before her. O'Rourke & Associates was important to her. For ten years it had been her sole consuming passion, a passion that had driven her to succeed in a field totally dominated by men. She felt a small twinge of regret as she read through the papers, an inner voice scolding her for even thinking of selling her company in order to raise enough funds to help her husband. It was, she thought, like surrendering ten years of her life, ten years during which she had worked at a job that she loved.

Still loved, Regan reminded herself. She had hoped that after the baby was born, she would be able to go back to work again and open a branch office here in Phoenix. There was so much potential, so many places where she . . .

"No," she said aloud. Cooper needed money, and he needed it now. And she could raise that money by simply saying yes to the offer that had been made by the three men who were her associates.

A generous offer, she reminded herself. A large cash down payment, with the balance to be paid off within the next ten years, plus a two-percent share of the company's future earnings in exchange for allowing them to use her name, contingent upon her agreement not to open a business of her own for the next five years.

She sighed, wishing that life was less complicated. Whatever she did, Cooper would be angry with her—angry that she would even consider giving up her successful business in order to salvage his own deteriorating company. *Damned if I do, damned if I don't*, she mused.

But anything—even Cooper's anger—was better than yielding to Jonathan.

The sun had already begun to set when Regan stepped out onto the boardwalk and turned to walk home.

"Ma'am?" A voice called out. "Mrs. Dundee?"

Responding, Regan spun around, recognizing the young deputy marshal, Bucky Conners. He stood before her, grinning, a grubby-faced Michael in tow in one hand and an equally grimy little girl in the other. Seeing the unmistakable look of guilt on her son's face, Regan closed her eyes and counted slowly to ten.

Adam Babcock stood in the narrow doorway of the way station's back room. It was a good place to be, half in and half out of the small bedroom, in a position where he could watch as the army doctor worked on Cooper Dundee and Estevan Folley while still being able to answer the questions of the men who crowded the building's main room.

"He smelt like a damned gin mill when we found him!"

he declared, and heard a dozen voices agree with him. His voice lowered, and his tone became even more solemn. 'Damned shame," he breathed. "Killin' that boy and his wife like that. They was newlyweds, you know. Goin' home to tell their folks the good news. . . ." He shook his head, as if it really mattered to him that Tad Beitermann and his new bride were dead.

"Goddamned shame," the stationmaster echoed. His loyalty to Cooper Dundee was diminishing in direct proportion to the amount of anger and condemnation voiced by the others who were with him. He faced the roomful of men, eager to share Babcock's audience. "He was always a wild one," he announced, indicating the room at his back with a single nod of his head. There wasn't a man standing before him who didn't know he was talking about Cooper. "It's like that with the breeds. Can't hold their liquor any better than the reservation bucks, and twice as crazy when they go on a tear."

Babcock hid a smile with his hand, pretending to wipe his nose and scratch his beard. He'd been working on the crowd right from the first, when they'd responded to his plea for help and followed him back to the wreckage. And now, with their bellies full of Titus's bootleg whiskey, they were in the palm of his hand. "I keep thinkin' of that poor little girl," he breathed, pausing just long enough to let them remember. "Layin' there, broken like some china doll . . ."

One of the men spoke up, his tone the same as Babcock's. "I got a girl about her age. I kept thinking about her, how I'd feel if . . ." His voice faded off into a grim, reflective silence.

"Murder," someone in the back of the room said. "Ain't no different than if he put a gun to her head."

A second man added, "Any way you look at it, it's Dundee's fault. Man's got no business drinking on the job."

Another voice lifted over the grumbling speculations of the crowd. "I seen the tracks," he volunteered, and then held his glass out for a refill. "Looked like he ran the damn coach right off the edge. . . ." A dozen men spoke out in agreement, each offering his own opinion of what had happened and why the two young people had died. And the word *murder* was whispered again.

Babcock heard the quiet condemnations and rejoiced. Before it was over, he would have them all believing that

Cooper Dundee really was drunk, and that the accident was his fault. *That he was guilty of a heinous crime.*

In the small room at Babcock's back, Cooper woke to find himself on a narrow cot. He had no memory of how he had come to be in this place, just as he had no real memory of the reason for his pain.

He was aware of the voices—the voices and the light. The faint glow of the small lantern seemed to diffuse and filter through the heavy bandage that covered his right eye, bringing with it a terrible flood of excruciating pain. It was as if his eye had been torn from the socket and someone was holding the naked orb in a clenched fist and squeezing, constantly squeezing, so hard that the pain made him sick. He was convulsed with the involuntary need to empty his stomach. The continuing waves of nausea brought even more pain—sharp, stabbing pains that clawed at his ribs and radiated toward his spine.

He moaned, and a pair of strong hands held him down as someone forced the neck of a bottle between his clenched lips. He heard a faraway voice telling him to drink and knew from the taste that he was being given laudanum. Greedily, he swallowed a mouthful of the opiate, seeking release and finding it.

There was a sensation of lightness, his body numbing as the powerful drug possessed him, and he hovered for a time between this world and another in a pleasant fog that separated him from the pain. Words—snatches of words—echoed and reechoed in his head, the same angry words that had first roused him. They increased in intensity, growing louder, until they were buzzing inside his head like a swarm of angry bees.

His other senses responded to the drug. Blue-white lights exploded before his eyes, still brilliant when he shut them and tried to blot them out. And all around him was the stench of whiskey and the cold wetness of alcohol against his skin. Lightly, his fingers skimmed across his chest, and he touched the wetness, and when he drew his numb fingers away, the smell of rotgut was even stronger. A terrible fear gripped him then, the horrors of the old days when he could not control his drinking coming back to torment him. For a long, terrifying moment he questioned his sanity, and then the laudanum overcame him, and he slipped into a welcome void beyond the light and the babble of angry voices.

Regan stood in the middle of the street, firmly holding on to Michael's hand and listening intently as the young deputy catalogued the boy's many sins. "Bad enough, ma'am," he said solicitously, "that the boy was takin' himself a stroll on that side of town, but he had to get himself mixed up with this kind of trash. . . ." With that, he gave the little girl's arm a vicious jerk and then boxed her ears when she tried to pull away.

The child retaliated in kind. She bit the lawman, hard, choosing a tender spot on the back of his arm and sinking her teeth well in. And when that failed to win her release, she kicked him. He turned her loose then, hopping up and down on one foot as he massaged his shin, his pompous manner and his temper gone. "Why, you little bitch," he roared. He made a grab for her, only to find his way blocked by an equally angry and belligerent Michael. His frustration increased twofold when both youngsters disappeared behind Regan's skirt.

She held them in place behind her. As angry as she was with Michael, she couldn't help but be amused by the spunk and spirit both he and the young girl had shown. *And the loyalty,* she thought, remembering. Once, long ago, she and her brother had been like that.

There was more. She couldn't stand seeing the girl abused by the deputy, any more than she could stand by and listen to him call the child foul names. "I've heard all I want to hear, Mr. Conners." She held her hand up when the man started to protest. "I'm taking my nephew home."

Conners felt a need to assert his authority. "I caught them stealin' apples out of the barrel in front of Putnam's Mercantile," he said, not caring if anyone else heard. "And that one," he continued, pointing at the boy, "put a rock through the window when old man Putnam grabbed the girl."

Regan cast a fleeting look at Michael and knew from the look on his face that the deputy was telling the truth. She had the feeling that there was more. "And?" she said quietly.

Conners was grinning. "Preacher Davis," he answered. "He caught them—" The smile grew. "Well, let's just say he caught them." The man lifted his shoulders, his finger stabbing the air in the general direction of the little girl. "Like I told you, she's dirt, just like her mama. You let the boy run with her, and that dirt's goin' to rub off."

Regan shook her head. She could feel the girl's head pressed against her skirt. "She's a child, Mr. Conners. Just a child."

The lawman snorted. "She was born old, Mrs. Dundee. Another year—maybe sooner—she'll be earnin' her keep at Clancy's, just like her mama." He grinned. There was something obscene in the grimace.

Just like her mama. The words tore at Regan. Old memories, long buried, escaped the dark recesses of her mind, and she could see herself as a small child. The haunted look she had seen in the little girl's face was the same look she remembered from her own childhood. She had seen that same expression on her own face every time she looked into a mirror during the long years after her father had abandoned her mother.

The lawman's gruff tone jolted the woman from her reverie. Conners reached out, grabbing the little girl's arm in an attempt to pull her away from Regan's skirt. "You're comin' with me, missy," he growled. His fingers bit into the child's pale skin, the indentations mottling as he increased his hold. *"Now!"*

Regan yielded to her temper. Her voice dropped, the words coming with a chilling quiet that startled the man. He backed up a full pace, pulling the child with him. Regan followed him. "Take your hands off her, Mr. Conners," she breathed. When he failed to respond, she reached out and pried the child from beneath his fingers.

The girl became a link between the man and the woman. She was the object of a game of tug-of-war that the lawman seemed intent on winning. Putting his arm around her waist, he swept the child up off the ground. "I'm taking her to jail, Mrs. Dundee!" he declared, his voice raising as the child began to whimper. "And I'm keepin' her there until her mama—or that pimp of Clancy's—comes after her!"

Regan blocked the man's way. She stood, wedged between the lawman and an irate Michael, mindful of the eyes that peered at them from behind the closed windows and doors. There was a sickening awareness growing within her, gnawing at her subconscious: She could not let the man take the child.

"The broken window, Mr. Conners," she said quietly, fighting to keep her words civil, "and the apples. How much?"

Conners stared across the child's head, his mouth open as he struggled with his thoughts. "It don't work like that," he stammered. "There's got to be a hearin', and the judge . . ." He was stalling, and the woman knew it.

Regan dug into the side pocket of her smock. When she withdrew her hand, it was clenched tightly around a small wad of bills. She stuffed the money into the man's vest pocket, making no effort to hide what she was doing—hoping, in fact, that those who were watching would see. "I don't know what you intended on doing with that child," she murmured. "But if you take her, I'm going to convince every woman in this town that you took her with the intention of using her!" She whispered the threat, her words as effective as if she had shouted them. "I mean it, Mr. Conners."

It was a mixture of fear and guilt that prompted the lawman to release his hold on the child. He let go of her, as if her flesh blistered his fingers. "You'll regret this, Mrs. Dundee. You mark my words!" Conners made the threat in a futile attempt to reassert his authority. "Trash," he said again. "She's nothin' but trash!"

Regan turned her back on the man, both children firmly tucked under her arms. When the deputy's rantings continued, she gently covered the little girl's exposed ear and then cradled her head against her hip. "It's all right," she crooned, pulling the child closer. Behind her, the man's words continued.

". . . whore get! Just like her ma!"

Cooper was aware of motion. He lay, arms and legs held fast by sheeting, on a canvas stretcher inside an army ambulance. The side-to-side sway of the wagon had unleashed a score of hooved demons inside his head, jolting him into a tormented consciousness, and he heard himself cry out.

Something more terrifying than the pain tore at him. The muslin sheets that covered him had been folded and secured as effectively as steel restraints. He was a prisoner, bound to the narrow cot, a horrified victim of an animal fear that threatened to suffocate him.

A dark shadow loomed over Cooper's head, blocking out the light coming from the lantern that was suspended above the stretcher. "Dundee?" When there was no response, the man repeated the word louder. *"Dundee?"*

Cooper struggled against his restraints, the man's voice vaguely familiar, yet distant. *Dake,* he thought, remembering. *What the hell is a U.S. marshal doing here?*

Desperate to remember the thing that had happened, he shook his head in an effort to clear his mind. The pain was immediate and intense. The entire right side of his face seemed to explode. In all his life, he had never experienced such grave physical torment. Unable to stop himself, he screamed.

Ethan Dake threw himself across Cooper Dundee's prone form, amazed at the sudden surge of animal strength that raised the other man—in spite of his restraints—straight up from the narrow cot. "Doc," Ethan bellowed. *"Doc!"*

The physician scrambled to tend his patient, cursing at the narrow confines of the wagon as he and the lawman struggled to force Cooper back onto the stretcher. "It's the eye," he grunted through clenched teeth. "The pain . . ." The doctor stopped at midsentence, cradling Cooper's head in one arm as he forced the narrow top of the amber medicine bottle between his patient's tight lips.

Dake snorted, watching as the physician sedated Cooper. "The pain is the least of his worries, Doc," he breathed. "You should have let him die," he said quietly. "You'd have done him a favor, if you'd let him die."

The army doctor sat back on his heels, a hostility in him that belied his usual benign demeanor. "Just what the hell do you mean?" he demanded.

Dake rose up as far as the canvas-topped wagon would permit. The stooped posture and his sore back did little to enhance his already foul mood. "He's going to hang," he intoned, his voice flat, devoid of any emotion. When he saw the angry flash of disbelief in the physician's eyes, he continued, "You saw the Beitermann boy. And you saw what was left of that girl."

The doctor was shaking his head, not in a denial of the

man's words, but in utter disgust over his presumptions. "It's been my impression," he said, his tone matching the other's, "that a man—*any man*—is presumed innocent until proven guilty."

There was a brief silence that was followed by the lawman's quiet, mocking laughter. "He's got Indian blood," he began, shaking his finger and then pointing it at the still figure on the small bed. "And a breed, especially a *drunk* breed, ain't considered a man. Not in this place, and not in this time. If he's lucky, he'll hang. If not . . ." He was quiet, considering Cooper's options. "If not," he continued, "he'll rot in Yuma. You should have let him die," he said again.

Stubbornly, the doctor shook his head. "You're a piss-poor excuse for a lawman, Dake," he observed disgustedly.

The marshal laughed. "I'm a realist, Doc. It's your business to take care of people. It's mine to know them. All of them," he added, squinting into the growing darkness behind the slow-moving wagon. Two troopers were riding rear escort, and behind them, a ragged line of civilians formed an unofficial rear guard. He heard the strangely disquieting sound of shattering glass and knew that one of the riders had discarded yet another empty liquor bottle.

There is going to be some real hell raised before this is over, he thought grimly. Already he could feel the hostile mood of the growing crowd as more and more riders appeared out of nowhere to join them. If Cooper Dundee lived to stand trial, it would be with these men as jurors, and they had already convicted him. All that remained was the carrying out of the sentence.

Dake was not a cowardly man. He had faced more than one lynch mob in his long career, and each experience had left him with an emptiness and a coldness that time was never able to erase. He knew these men, could call some of them by their first name. It was bad enough shotgunning a man you didn't know. But to look a man in the eye, having eaten and drunk at his table, only to have to shoot him in the street in front of some cracker-box jail over a man who was in all probability as guilty as sin . . .

It stinks, he thought sourly. *The whole damned world stinks*. He would shoot them, the doctor would patch them up, and it would begin all over again.

Dake poked his head out of the canvas flap, angry when

he saw that one of the troopers was on the verge of dozing off in the saddle. Maliciously, the lawman pulled at the loose-hanging tarp above his head, snapping the fabric taut. The sound was not unlike the report of a small-bore pistol. Startled, the soldier snapped awake and fumbled for his revolver.

Still mad, Dake jabbed a finger at the man. "You watch our tail, sonny," he ordered. "I got a man in here I intend to take all the way to Phoenix, and you'd best know that." He grinned nastily at the young man. "They start anything," he said, nodding at the crowd at the soldier's back, "and you'll be the first to fall—likely from a bullet in the back." For effect, the lawman tapped the holster that hung at his belt. "You'd best remember that, sonny."

Dumbfounded, the trooper nodded. "Yes, sir," he answered. "Yes, sir!" Fully alert, he turned his horse and faced the crowd that followed behind. His sudden move startled the men, and they pulled to a quick halt.

The blue-suited cavalryman stood his ground. "You keep your distance," he shouted. His embarrassment at being chastized by the civilian lawman made him bold. "You bastards make damn sure you keep your distance!"

Chuckling, Dake withdrew into the interior of the ambulance. The smug laughter continued as he addressed the physician. "He'll get his trial," he grinned, nodding at Cooper.

He knew that now, just as he knew that the cluster of riders that had pursued them from the way station no longer presented any immediate cause for alarm. They had been stopped dead by a single trooper, and that, he knew, meant that they had no plan, just as they had no single leader.

Dake exhaled slowly. He rolled a cigarette and took considerable satisfaction in the sedative effect of the badly needed smoke. They were safe, he reasoned. For now, they were all safe.

Chapter Five

The private coach entered Phoenix from the south, the team of matched grays slowing to a brisk walk as the vehicle approached the outskirts of town.

Jefferson Kincaid sat closeted behind the ornate louvered windows. Already he was cursing the heat, the inside of the brougham a virtual sweatbox. Still he did not open the windows fully, choosing to sit back and survey the growing frontier city from behind the slatted shades.

The unplanned urban sprawl offended Kincaid's sense of neatness and order. He felt nothing but contempt for the stark mixture of Mexican and Anglo architecture and the haphazard way one building competed with the other. Red brick and white clapboard stood out against the rough-hewn and deteriorating adobe structures. Concrete walkways were interrupted by warped and sagging boardwalks that had sunk almost level with the unpaved street.

Jefferson Kincaid was a man used to wealth and comfort. He had been born in San Francisco forty-five years before into a family whose fortunes had been built and perpetuated on the backs of Chinese coolies who had died working in the Kincaid mines. Nothing had been denied him, and he bulled his way through life taking whatever he fancied, whenever he fancied. *The same way he had taken Regan O'Rourke.*

He thought of the woman, of the way she had been when she was little more than a girl. Even under all the filth, he had recognized a remarkable beauty and an even more remarkable intelligence. *Intelligence and innocence.* If he had been limited to only two words to describe Regan as a young woman, these were the words he would have chosen.

He had enhanced her intelligence. Just as he had robbed

her of her innocence. In the end, she bore him a child. It was this child that had brought him to Phoenix.

Kincaid thought about the past five years. So much had happened. In spite of the Eastern doctors, in spite of the pious donations to the church, an angry God had taken his wife and his sons. They had died within days of each other, their bodies ravaged by a fever that had touched no one else in the household. Even Kincaid had been spared, condemned instead to watch his fragile wife die without a whimper. His teenaged sons followed her two days later, refusing to fight their illness and begging for release.

Begging for death, Kincaid thought bitterly. In the end, he hated them all: his weak-willed wife for her complacent acceptance of her own death as preordained, and his sons for their weak refusal to fight the illness that consumed them.

God had taken his sons. The devil had reminded him that he had planted his seed in another place.

Kincaid remembered the joy he had felt when the Pinkerton agents he'd hired had traced the child to Fort Whipple. It had taken the detectives considerable time to discover that Regan had given her child to her brother, and even more time to locate the man. And then, when it was finally accomplished, it had all seemed so simple. He had planned to take the youngster, by force if necessary, and then battle the man and his wife in the courts. The corners of Kincaid's mouth twitched as he thought of the confrontation he had planned. He would have fought them all the way to the Supreme Court—because the power of his money extended all the way to the Supreme Court.

But when the time had come to act, Kincaid had discovered that Regan's brother and his family had died and that Regan had taken her child back. Now he would have to deal with her directly. He considered that for a long moment and then decided it didn't matter. Regan was evil. She had given away her child when it was born: She didn't deserve to have it now.

The carriage suddenly slowed. There was a sharp wrenching as the driver turned quickly to avoid a collision with another vehicle, and then the brougham rolled to a complete stop. Kincaid's fingers raked down the wooden louvers that covered the window at his shoulder, opening the thin slats,

and he watched as a slow-moving caravan made its way down
the center of the street.

Two uniformed troopers led the way, a military ambulance coming next, and behind the canvas-topped wagon
were two more troopers. More riders, these obviously civilian,
followed warily in their wake. There was something funereal
in the mood and movement of the mounted men, as if they
were accompanying a hearse, and for a fleeting moment
Kincaid wondered about the vehicle's passengers.

Once the grim cortege had passed, he lifted his silver-
headed walking stick and pounded on the small door at the
top of the carriage. His instructions were curt and precise.
"Dundee's office," he ordered, and knew from the immediate
forward movement that his orders had been understood.

Jonathan Dundee stood at the window of his office,
watching as the southbound army ambulance disappeared
down the street. His attention was only perfunctory, an auto-
matic response to something out of the ordinary. It would
help him pass time as he awaited the arrival of a new client.

Jefferson Kincaid, he mused. He had met the man just
briefly when they were both in Washington. Governor Frémont had arranged the introduction, enthusiastic because
Kincaid had expressed an interest in the governor's proposal
to create an inland sea and canal in the vast Arizona desert.
After speaking with Kincaid, Jonathan was convinced the man
was too good a businessman to be genuinely interested in
Frémont's farfetched fantasies. They had, in fact, privately
shared a bottle of brandy and a hearty laugh afterward.

And now Kincaid had sent word that he wanted to see
Jonathan at seven-thirty that night. More, that he wanted to
discuss a possible joint business venture.

As the clock in the outer office gently tolled eight o'clock,
Jonathan counted the final strokes as he checked his pocket
watch. More than a bit angry at being kept waiting, he
snapped shut the gold case and gripped the watch in the
palm of his hand as he debated his next move.

Kincaid would be a valuable addition to his meager list of
select clients. The man's reputation made him an important
prospect. Still Jonathan was rankled by the servile feeling of
having to wait for him, which gave Kincaid the advantage. He

had just made up his mind to leave when the door to the other office opened and his clerk made the awaited announcement. "Mr. Kincaid, sir. With apologies for his tardiness."

Jonathan nodded, taking the engraved business card that the clerk was holding. "Tell him that I'll be with him in just a few minutes," he said. It was Kincaid's turn to wait.

Regan was in the kitchen of the house she and Cooper had purchased in Phoenix shortly after they were married. It was not as grand or as spacious as the big house at the rancheria south of Casa Grande, but it was well kept, cozy, and with the help of a live-in girl, reasonably easy to maintain.

There were eight rooms in the house: a front parlor that was used only on Sundays and special occasions, three bedrooms, a dining room, the small parlor, a servant's room, and the kitchen. The kitchen had become the center of the home. It was a big room, dominated by a wood-burning cooking stove. Now, in the cool, late spring twilight, the warmth was even more inviting.

Regan had seen that both children bathed before their meal. Now Michael and Niña sat at the table eating a late supper, one on either side of her, and both of them considerably cleaner and more tranquil than they had been before.

Wisely, Michael was on his best behavior. Everything was "please" and "thank you," with a healthy dose of "yes, ma'am" and "no, ma'am" thrown in for good measure. The boy was, Regan mused, almost angelic, all scrubbed and combed and pleasantly polite.

Almost angelic, she reminded herself. The way he was behaving now did not make up for the way he had been behaving earlier. Running off after he had been sent to his room was bad enough, but the incident at the general store— the broken window—was an entirely different matter.

Determined not to lose her temper, Regan said, "We have to talk, Michael."

The boy, unfortunately, did not share her desire to keep the conversation civil. He stabbed his fork into the piece of meat so hard that the tines penetrated the beef and struck the plate. "You're going to yell at me," he accused.

Regan sighed, her eyes quickly going to the little girl, then returning to Michael. "No, I'm not going to yell."

"Sure you are," he pouted. "You always yell at me!" He looked across at Niña and found a sympathetic audience, and her pure admiration gave him courage. "I don't want to talk to you," he declared. "I don't *have* to talk to you!"

It took everything Regan could muster to keep her voice and her temper under control. She thought of all the other women up and down this very street, who stood out on their front porches keeping their children in line with less effort than it took to shake a finger, and she envied them.

And then it dawned on her, the thing she was doing that the other women were not. She had kept her problems with Michael a private thing, strangely fearful of sharing them with Cooper, and that had been a mistake. *Just wait until your father gets home, young man!* That was the simple magic the other women used. It was all so simple.

Smiling, Regan got up from her chair, fully aware that both Niña and the boy were carefully watching her. Still smiling, she moved to the boy's side and hugged him. "All right, Michael," she agreed. "You don't have to talk to me." She was almost ashamed of the vindictive pleasure she felt as she chose her next words. "I think we'll just wait until Coop comes home." With that, she planted a wet kiss on the top of the boy's head.

Michael's mouth opened and then just as quickly shut. "Regan," he began. His intended entreaty was interrupted by a sudden, harsh rapping on the door.

"Not now, Michael," Regan said absently.

She responded to the loud tapping, opening the door and finding herself face to face with Marshal Ethan Dake. At first, she assumed the lawman's visit had something to do with the incident involving the two children. But then she read the look in his eyes and knew that she was wrong. Mindful of the two youngsters who stood at her back—and grateful that the lawman was also sensitive to their presence— she shut the door and stepped out onto the porch.

"Marshal Dake," she greeted.

Immediately, the man removed his hat. "There's been an accident, Mrs. Dundee. Your husband . . ." He found, looking at the woman's face, that he couldn't continue.

She nodded her head, saying nothing for a time, and for a moment the lawman was afraid she was going to faint. Instead, she reopened the door, said a few words to the two children, and then took the marshal's extended arm. Instinctively, she headed for the doctor's office.

Dake realized her mistake immediately and felt the fool. He pulled her up short. "He's not at the doctor's office, Mrs. Dundee." There was an awkward silence as he tried to find a way to soften the blow. "The jail," he said finally, knowing that there was no tactful way to tell her. "I had him taken to the jail."

Regan's body tensed, and she withdrew her arm from around the man's elbow. "We're wasting time, Marshal Dake," she said evenly.

They continued their walk in cold silence, aware as they approached the jailhouse of the growing crowd of people outside the adobe building. Snatches of words drifted on the night air, inaudible mutterings that increased in intensity as the woman and the lawman approached.

Dake elbowed his way through the crowd, making a pathway for the woman. He was sorry that there was no way he could protect her from the flurry of speculative whispers that were purposely exaggerated for her benefit: "Murderer." "Drunken breed."

Regan moved through the crowd, painfully aware of the whiskey-primed hostility around her. She ignored the words, concentrating instead on individual faces that suddenly appeared and then just as quickly disappeared. Head held high, she met their scrutiny directly, refusing to look away or down until the crowd, of their own reluctant accord, separated and let her pass. Their new silence was ominous and as hostile as their once-loud rantings.

The interior of the jailhouse was dismal and oppressive. A wet, dank odor permeated the air, the only source of ventilation the narrow barred windows that were cut into the thick adobe only inches from the high, beamed ceiling.

Major Stockwell, the army doctor, was still with Cooper. He stood in the locked cell at the front of the corridor, hovering over Cooper Dundee's quiet form, his grim-faced countenance telling Regan more than she cared to know. He felt the woman's eyes before he actually saw her, and he shook his head to the question so obvious in her expression. When he spoke, he directed his words at the lawman. "Ethan," he began, the fatigue beginning to eat at him, "I want you to tell this presumptuous ass," he nodded at Deputy Bucky

Conners, "to unlock this cage. Dundee isn't going anywhere. You have my professional word on that."

Dake swore as he yanked the key ring from the hook on the wall and unlocked the door himself. "Mrs. Dundee," he said apologetically, beckoning the woman forward.

As gently as possible, Stockwell delivered his diagnosis. "His ribs are broken," he said quietly, his fingers in the air above Cooper's chest. "His left shoulder was dislocated, and there are contusions over his entire body." The dreaded hesitation came then as the doctor paused for breath, and when he resumed speaking, his voice had lowered to a hoarse whisper. "There's been extensive damage to his right eye, Mrs. Dundee, and his lungs . . ." For the first time, his gaze swept the woman fully, and he cursed himself for not realizing sooner that she was pregnant.

Numbly, Regan nodded her head. Her right hand rested lightly on Cooper's bandaged cheek. "How is Estevan?" she asked softly. "Estevan Folley."

Dake answered for the physician, amazed at the woman's composure, that she would be aware enough to be concerned about someone else. "He was thrown clear. He has a broken leg, some bumps and bruises. Doc felt he would be better off at the way station. At least for now." Somehow, he couldn't bring himself to tell the woman just how badly broken Estevan Folley's leg was. He had seen the yellow-white gleam of bone through the Mexican's torn flesh.

Again Regan's head moved up and down. When the two men began to speak simultaneously, she shushed them, listening instead to the wet rattle of Cooper's labored breathing. "I want the truth, Doctor," she began. "Is he going to live?"

Stockwell refused this time to mince his words. He gazed at the interior of the barren cell, sniffing the moldy air and choking on the musty scent. Already the strange dampness of the place was working its insidious evil on the tender joints in his hands and fingers, just as it was working on Cooper Dundee's damaged lungs. "Not if he stays here," he announced.

Regan lifted her head, her blue eyes boring into Ethan Dake's deep brown orbs. "Why is he here?"

Dake was taken aback by the directness of the woman's gaze as much as he was affected by her bluntness. The lawman was no hypocrite. He knew that there was nothing to be gained by some empty gesture on his part, so he told her the truth as he knew it.

"It appears that this wasn't just an accident," he began. He reached across in front of Regan, his thumb and forefinger rubbing at Cooper's tattered shirtfront. As if to reaffirm his suspicions, he held the two fingers beneath his own nose, and then hers. The bitter smell of the rotgut was muted by the odor of blood and laudanum, but it was still there.

"He was drunk," he continued. Regan was shaking her head in disbelief, and in spite of her silent denial, he went on, his voice lowering. "There were two passengers inside the coach, Mrs. Dundee. They're dead." He knew from the look on her face that he didn't need to say any more.

It was as if she hadn't heard him. She lifted her head, her eyes settling first on Bucky Conners's grinning countenance. The intensity of her stare wiped the smug expression off the man's face as effectively as if she had struck him. "I'm taking him home, Marshal Dake," she said finally, her gaze now locked firmly on the elder lawman's face. "Come hell or high water, I'm taking him home."

Resolute, Regan left the two men, moving out into the clean evening air. She was physically and emotionally drained, and she paused for a long moment to rest with her back against the jailhouse wall.

Jonathan, she thought silently. She had no time for second thoughts, any more than she had any time right now for foolish pride. Cooper needed an attorney immediately, and Estevan was unavailable. Taking a deep breath, she pushed away from the wall, well aware of the irony in what was about to happen. Jonathan would help Cooper. No matter what he felt, he would still help. His need to protect the Dundee name gave him no other choice.

Jefferson Kincaid sat in the chair directly in front of Jonathan's desk. "I'm not going to waste your time, Dundee, any more than I'm going to waste words. You hired a woman, a little better than a year ago. Regan O'Rourke. I want to know where she is, *exactly where she is*, and just what she's been doing since she left your employ."

Jonathan's first instinct was to answer the man's inquiries

directly. And then, prompted by his own curiosity, he reconsidered. "Why?" he asked finally.

Kincaid's opinion of Jonathan Dundee suddenly changed. He surveyed the man for a time, congratulating the lawyer's shrewdness in answering one question with another. Jonathan's directness had caught him totally unaware. For a brief moment, he considered lying to Jonathan, and then changed his mind. There had been a rumor of a romantic involvement between Jonathan Dundee and Regan, and only fragmented details about the disagreement that had obviously separated them. The next thing his detectives had discovered was that Jonathan was in Washington with a brand new wife, and Regan O'Rourke was no longer a part of his life.

Carefully watching Jonathan's face, Kincaid answered the lawyer's one-word query. "Regan O'Rourke was my mistress," he announced. "She has something that belongs to me, and I intend to have it."

Jonathan nodded his head. "Your son," he said, knowing from Kincaid's face that he had guessed correctly. "You want your son."

Jonathan's declaration brought a strange sense of elation to Kincaid. The detectives had told him that Regan's child was a boy, but somehow he had been afraid to believe them. But now, seeing the look on Jonathan's face and in his eyes, he knew at last that it was true. He had a son! The God that had stolen his legitimate offspring had failed to find the one that was conceived in sin! It was an omen, Kincaid thought, a sign from the heavens that he was forgiven. A measure of what had been taken from him was being returned, and he was being given another chance.

The door to Jonathan's office opened, the high-pitched objections of the clerk following the woman into the room, and both men turned. They were unable to conceal their joint surprise, an audible intake of air coming from both of them as Regan Dundee came through the door.

It took considerable time for all three to regain their composure. Years of memories assaulted Regan when she recognized Kincaid, and she was unable to stop the wave of physical weakness that swept her. He was an unwanted ghost from her past, and yet seeing him like this brought the bittersweet pain that always comes with the memory of a first love. *A lost love.* She held out her hand when he rose and moved across the room to meet her, ashamed at feeling a surge of electricity when their fingers met. He was, she noticed ruefully, as handsome and as self-assured as he was the first day they met.

Tactfully, she avoided his eyes, choosing instead to address Jonathan. "There's been an accident, Jonathan. Coop's been hurt." Her next words were carefully chosen, as much for her brother-in-law's benefit as for Kincaid's. "There seems to be some confusion as to just what happened. Marshal Dake is here. He's holding Coop at the jail."

Jonathan's mouth shut in a tight line. He knew from the look on Regan's face, from the things she had left unsaid, that there was more, much more. Grudgingly, he admired her self-control, realizing it was partly due to her reluctance to air the family's dirty linen in front of someone else. He slipped into his suit coat. "How badly is he hurt?" he asked.

Regan's answer was to the point. "There's a military doctor with him, Jonathan. He says that Coop will die if we don't get him out of the jail."

Jonathan nodded. "I want you to wait here, Regan, until I find out what has to be done."

For all their differences, Regan's respect for Jonathan's skill as an attorney—as an effective manipulator of the law—had never diminished. Still, she considered his words, more aware than ever that Kincaid was still in the room. "No, Jonathan," she said softly. "I'll wait for you, but I'll be at the house." She saw immediately that he was annoyed that she had not blindly acquiesced, and she could only shake her head when he repeated his orders with his eyes.

Disgusted, Jonathan left the room, sweeping past Regan without looking at her. He slammed the door with such force that the windows rattled within the frames. The sound was magnified by the tense silence between Regan and Jefferson Kincaid, and unable to stop herself, the woman reacted. It was as if she had been struck by lightning. There was a feeling that she was rooted to the place where she stood, unable to move, and yet her mind was filled with the terrifying need to flee. She could feel her heart beating, the sound roaring deep within her head and flooding her ears, and she stifled a strong urge to scream.

"Regan?" Kincaid said, his voice soft, filled with a mock caring.

Forcing a calm she did not feel, Regan answered the man. "I have to go, Jefferson," she said. She could no longer avoid looking at him. "Why?" she asked finally, knowing he would understand the question.

Kincaid remembered the woman's quick wit and felt a need to do something to appease her growing suspicion. "A coincidence, Regan," he lied easily. "I have business here." That much, he thought smugly, was the truth.

Regan absorbed the man's words, her concern about Cooper clouding her thinking. She accepted his words without argument. "I have to go."

Kincaid sensed the subtle collapse of the woman's reserve. "I can help, Regan. Please let me help." Hesitantly, he reached out to her, and then placed his arm around her shoulders. It was like turning back the clock, and the feeling within him was even stronger when his gaze was drawn to her mounded belly. She had been pregnant when he last saw her, too.

As if she read his thoughts, Regan pulled away. A shudder passed through her, and she shook loose of his fingers. "Just go away, Jeff. Please. Just go away." It was almost a prayer.

Kincaid remembered the last time she had said the same words to him. It was the morning he had told her about his wife, his sons. The same morning he had told her he could not—*would not*—marry her.

Kincaid watched as Regan left the room, staring hard into her wake long after she had shut the door and disappeared from sight. He wasn't going anywhere. Not now. And not without his son.

Chapter Six

Jonathan Dundee's arrival at the jail was heralded by a sudden and respectful hush that momentarily swept the crowd. They stood back, making a pathway for him, intimidated by his size and bearing and still in awe of his place in the community, despite his long absence in Washington, D.C. Jonathan was the flesh and blood embodiment of the deceased Malachai Dundee, and there was not one man in the crowd who did not remember—grudgingly or admiringly—the old pioneer. There had been a Dundee Transport for as long as there had been a Phoenix.

Jonathan was aware of the silence that greeted him and took advantage of it. He strode past the men, nodding to those he did not immediately recognize, and speaking with those he did. They returned his salutes, and their mood changed. The open hostility of only moments before became a guarded sympathy. Poor Jonathan, they thought. Cheated out of his inheritance by his father's breed get, and now this. . . . It was a shame, the disgrace the man had to face because of his brother. His drunken, murdering brother.

Marshal Dake was waiting at the door. He ushered Jonathan inside, his eyes sweeping the crowd. There was a wry humor in him as he assessed the fickle mood of the masses. "You ever think of running for office, Dundee?" he asked, shutting the door, knowing damned well the magnitude of Jonathan's future political plans.

Jonathan faced the lawman. "Why not?" he answered. He inhaled, ignoring Dake's sarcasm, and nodded toward the dark area beyond the office. "Are you filing charges, Dake? Or do you intend holding Coop until you can find something to arrest him for?"

Dake shifted his gaze to Bucky Conners and ordered him out of the room before answering Jonathan's question. The lawman's expression never changed, the mirthless smile pasted across his lips as if etched in granite, and his tone was the same when he addressed Jonathan as it had been when he sent Conners away. "How does *murder* sound? Just for starters. That should keep you busy enough while the powers-that-be look to the finer points of law." The marshal had played this game many times before. "Hell, before it's over, I figure there'll be a dozen attorneys sniffing at Coop's heels." He snorted, a vision of man-headed vultures fueling the natural contempt he had always had for lawyers. He could see them stripping the flesh from Cooper, scavenging on his body until there was nothing left of the man or his business.

Shaking his head to clear away the image, the lawman continued, his tone changing. "What we've got, Dundee, is a wrecked coach, a driver who in all likelihood was drunk on his ass, and at least two people dead." He paused, saving the worst for last. "Aaron Beitermann's son and daughter-in-law." There was no need to say more—Jonathan was well aware of the legislator's influence throughout Arizona, and his open antagonism toward Cooper Dundee.

Jonathan was quiet for a long moment as he considered the news. "What you've got," he began, pretending that it made no difference who it was who had died, "is a fistful of suppositions. I want Coop charged, Dake," he declared, calling the man's bluff, "or I want him released."

"Sure you do, Dundee," the lawman returned. He had not missed the fact that Jonathan had not asked to see his younger brother or, for that matter, asked about his injuries. "I'm going to charge him. And as far as I'm concerned, he's already under arrest."

"And bail?" Jonathan asked. "Who's going to set bail with the judge out riding circuit?"

Dake shook his head. "That's *your* problem, not mine." He stepped back, gesturing for Jonathan to follow him, and led the way back to the cells.

The sound of Cooper's labored breathing touched both men as soon as they stepped into the dark passageway. There was the stifling aroma of sickness filling the air, heightened by the wet rattle of Cooper's lungs as he struggled against the pain deep in his chest. Jonathan hesitated, steeling himself, and then moved through the grillwork to take his place beside his brother's bed. It struck him how sickness and death had their own peculiar aromas. Even impending death. "My God," he breathed, and was surprised at the unnatural loudness of his own voice.

Cooper Dundee's face was virtually unrecognizable. One eye was bruised and swollen shut, and the other covered entirely by a thick, blood-encrusted bandage. The color had washed from his normally tanned features, the startling whiteness of his skin emphasizing the purple bruises and the deep brown smears of dried blood caked atop countless abrasions. Unable to help himself, Jonathan reached out and touched his brother's shoulder.

There was a sudden flood of memories that washed through his very soul: memories of their shared and distant childhood and of the years that followed. A hundred times in anger, Jonathan had wished his brother dead. More, he had wished that Cooper had never been born. Those childish thoughts and wishes had remained with him into manhood, and for a moment, he was ashamed.

Cooper was his brother. The blood tie was there, no matter how he had tried to deny it. There was more. Deep inside, Jonathan felt a growing remorse. He did not *hate* Cooper, nor had he ever hated him. And now this . . . The extent of Cooper's injuries devastated him.

The guilt he felt overwhelmed him, and he spoke. "I want him out of here, Dake." He cleared his throat in a vain attempt to regain his lawyer's composure. "I want him out of here *now!*"

Dake was unmoved. He stood, leaning against the far wall, cleaning his fingernails with a small blade of his pocket knife. "You saw that crowd outside, Dundee," he said finally. "You may have a following in this town, but Coop . . ." The words drifted off as he indicated the man on the cot with a sweep of his arm. Dake knew that Cooper Dundee had never been fully accepted by the Anglos in the community. His part-Apache heritage had marked him from the beginning. He had been tolerated because the businessmen needed him, and that need would soon be gone.

"They've got him tried, convicted, and hung," Dake continued. "I let him out of here, we're going to have big trouble."

Jonathan knew that the lawman was talking about a lynching. His gaze swept Cooper's form as he pondered the man's words, his eyes finally settling on Major Stockwell.

The doctor, eyes on the floor, said quietly, "He'll die if he stays here."

Dake shrugged. He was not without compassion, neither was he a fool. "I can't grant any special favors to Coop just because he's your brother, Dundee." They were sparring again, feeling each other out, and the lawman knew it.

"House arrest," Jonathan suggested. He nodded at Major Stockwell. "Coop was carrying a military payroll and dispatches. He was carrying the mail." Clearly, Jonathan was thinking out loud, but not without a purpose. He was doing his best as an attorney to convince Dake of a need to compromise.

"And?" Dake asked, suspicious.

"Coop may be under the jurisdiction of the military, Ethan." He raised his hand when the man started to object. "Or he may be under your jurisdiction." He shook his head. "I don't know yet. And if I don't know, then *they*" —with a nod he indicated the unseen crowd still outside in the street— "sure in hell don't know. You can place him under house arrest."

Stockwell spoke up. "We can take him home and post a guard at the house."

Dake's brow knotted. "A military guard," he muttered. He didn't like the presumptuous interference of the military in a matter he was fully qualified to handle. He was a federal appointee, and if the military stepped in and took control, it would look like he couldn't do his job.

Jonathan sensed the man's hesitancy. "A civilian guard as well, Ethan, until Coop is well enough to . . ." He couldn't finish.

Dake scratched his neck, mulling Jonathan's proposal. "All right," he agreed. "But I'm in charge of the military and the selection of the civilian guards."

There was an audible rush of air as all three men exhaled. Each, for his own reasons, was relieved by the compromise. Dake would retain control, Stockwell would be able to provide better care for his patient, and Jonathan . . .

Jonathan would be able to resume his place as head of the Dundee family. Already, the wheels were turning as his earlier feelings of guilt and concern faded, and he was anticipating his future moves. *A blessing in disguise,* he mused. Now he would not have to follow through on his threat to sell Angela's share of the stage line. Instead, he would help his younger brother, and in exchange for that help, he would take back everything that rightfully belonged to him.

"I want to take Coop home right now, Dake," he announced without betraying his secret thoughts.

Dake nodded and then headed back through the office and out into the street. Jonathan could hear the lawman's words as he addressed the crowd. "Cooper Dundee has been placed under arrest," he announced, and there was a hearty roar of approval. "House arrest," he continued, raising his voice and proceeding without waiting for their response. "I'm going to need deputies," he declared. "Extra deputies to guard the Dundee house."

A dozen voices sounded. The loudest one belonging to Adam Babcock.

Regan watched from the front door of her house as Jonathan led the grim procession across the street. Two troopers bore the canvas stretcher, their matching footsteps as precise and perfect as those of two men marching across the parade ground at Fort McDowell. There was a gentle back-and-forth swing to the litter as the soldiers moved, as if they shared the pain of the injured man they carried and were genuinely concerned about his well-being.

Regan knew the reason for the troopers' concern and care. Major Stockwell marched along beside the recruits, gruffly ordering them to pay attention to their task and severely berating them when they did not. Midstreet, he stopped them, pausing to secure the blankets that covered Cooper Dundee's legs. Regan thought she saw a brief flash of metal, but quickly dismissed the vision as a trick played by her own mind and the terrible fears that had crowded her thoughts. Briefly closing her eyes, she willed the dark fears away. Cooper was her only concern now, and the rest did not matter.

Jonathan said nothing until he was inside the house. He held Regan in place, his hand on her arm, and waited until the doctor and the two troopers were in the front bedroom before he spoke. "The two passengers on the coach were Aaron Beitermann's son, Tad, and the boy's new wife. They're both dead, Regan."

She inhaled deeply, and her arms closed tightly around her own body. "He wasn't drinking, Jonathan. I don't care what Dake thinks or what he's been told. I *know* Coop wasn't drinking." Regan's gaze was fastened on the figures in the room just beyond the doorway. Unable to stand it any longer, she unwrapped Jonathan's fingers from around her arm and pulled away.

Unrelenting, Jonathan followed after her. "He's under arrest, Regan. The only way Dake would let go of him was for me to agree—"

"My God." Regan's sudden exclamation as she entered the bedroom interrupted Jonathan. She made no effort to hide her anger at the sight before her. The blanket had fallen away from Cooper Dundee as the two troopers and Major Stockwell placed him on the bed. Heavy leg irons bound his ankles, and a similar manacle dangled from his right wrist. One of the troopers was fastening the steel bracelet to the bedpost above Cooper's head.

Regan inhaled sharply. She had seen the shackles when Stockwell had stopped the two litter bearers, but had refused to believe what she had seen. The disbelief was in her voice when she was finally able to speak again. "Take them off," she ordered. "Dammit! Take them off!!"

Jonathan and the physician took her outburst for hysteria. Alarmed, they both moved to Regan's side. "Mrs. Dundee," Stockwell began gently. Paternally, he put his arm around her shoulder.

Regan wanted no part of the man's attempt at comforting. She turned away from him, backing away from both men until she again faced them. Her words were directed at Jonathan. "How could you?" she demanded. "How could you let them do this?"

Jonathan's face colored, and when he spoke, the words came through clenched lips. "You wanted him home, Regan. This was the only way Dake would let him go." He raised his hand when Regan started to argue. "There's more," he said. "There'll be guards. Dake is already making arrangements to deputize the men. They'll be staying here until . . ." He didn't finish.

Regan stared up into the man's face. "Until what, Jonathan?" she demanded.

Jonathan shook his head and refused to answer. Cooper was, in his opinion, a dead man. It didn't make a damn if it was the injuries that killed him or if he died at the end of a rope.

Regan was unable to control the anger that was clawing at her. She went to the front door and held it open, blocking the way when Marshal Dake attempted to enter. Her back to the lawman, she called out to her brother-in-law. "Get out, Jonathan." She half turned then, just enough so that she could see both Jonathan Dundee and the lawman. "Both of you. Get out."

Dake's foot was on the threshold, and he hesitated. Behind Regan, in the doorway of the bedroom, stood Major Stockwell. The expression on the physician's face matched the woman's. It was an expression of utter contempt. The lawman reconsidered his trespass and backed away. "My office, Dundee," he said curtly. "*Now!*"

Jonathan's mouth opened and then shut. He answered the lawman's request with a single nod of his head and then followed him out into the street.

Regan shut the door and then collapsed against the heavy wooden frame. Speechless, she watched as Major Stockwell took control of the parlor and gently ushered a curious Michael and a pensive Niña back into the kitchen. She stared after the man, finding something reassuring in the gentle tone of his voice as he spoke with the two children.

He returned to the parlor, a steaming mug of coffee in each hand. "I've sent your hired girl, Maria, to the pharmacy," he said gently. "As for the children . . ." He smiled and nodded toward the kitchen.

Regan shook her head at the proffered cup of coffee and then changed her mind. She felt ashamed of her earlier behavior, and even more ashamed that she was still standing in the parlor and not at her husband's side. And yet she could not bring herself to go into the bedroom.

It was the iron shackles and the two troopers, one on either side of the large double bed she had shared with her husband. There was something obscene in the way they stood beside the bed, as if they intended to spend the night watching.

Instinctively, Stockwell sensed the woman's hesitation.

He turned, facing the doorway to the bedroom, and issued a terse order. "I want those irons removed," he growled. "And then I want you to get out of here."

There was the subtle sound of booted feet against the wooden floor as both troopers immediately and automatically responded to his command, and then a quick halt as they reconsidered. The younger trooper had already unlocked the restraints and was still bent over Cooper's legs. Nervously, he cleared his throat. "But Marshal Dake, sir. He . . ."

"I'm the ranking officer here, trooper, not Marshal Dake!" Stockwell drew himself erect. Approaching fifty, he had never lost the military bearing that marked him as a professional soldier. "I gave you an order. I expect to see it carried out!"

The two soldiers moved, on the double, tripping over their own feet as they scrambled to release Cooper and get out the front door.

Using his foot, Stockwell kicked the door shut. He was smiling when he faced Regan. "Mrs. Dundee," he said, bowing at the waist and gesturing toward the bedroom.

Regan returned his smile and hurried through the door, half expecting the man to follow after her. She was surprised, and then relieved, when he shut the door after her and remained outside in the parlor.

She moved to the bed, quietly, knowing inside that the noise didn't matter. Cooper was beyond hearing now, his injuries and the drugs condemning him to some limbo between this world and the next. He lay there, silent except for the sound of his labored breathing, his face a ghastly gray against the white pillowcase and the stained red bandage that covered the right side of his face.

Regan dropped to her knees beside the bed. She reached out, her fingers closing around Cooper's right wrist. Carefully, holding her breath, she counted his pulse for a full minute as she marked the subtle rise and fall of his chest.

She felt as if she had lost control of her entire world and that there was nothing she could do to stop what was happening. Cooper lay before her, more dead than alive, and she was filled with a terrible sense of dread. She would lose him forever if the injuries did not heal and he did not get well.

There was another alternative, perhaps even more horrifying. Cooper could go to prison. She thought of him behind bars, confined in some dismal cage, nothing more than a number on a sheet of paper, dying by inches, locked away from everything he loved and everyone who loved him. For the first time in the long day, Regan began to weep, but she found only a small amount of release in the flood of tears.

There was a gentle knock at the door and then the rustle of starched cotton as Angela Dundee entered and moved across the room. Gently, she dropped to her knees beside her sister-in-law and took the woman in her arms, grateful that Maria had come to fetch her after going to the pharmacy. "He's going to be all right, Regan," she murmured. "Everything is going to be all right." Her own tears mingled with Regan's.

They held each other for a long time, each locked in her own thoughts. In the end, it was Regan who was doing the comforting. She patted the younger woman's head and felt her own strength returning as she consoled her.

"He's not going to die, Angela," she whispered. "I won't let him die." It was a promise she intended to keep.

Chapter Seven

Jefferson Kincaid stood at the window of his Phoenix hotel room. His own reflection stared back at him, and he made a silent appraisal of the image, as critical in his evaluation as he would have been in sizing up a total stranger.

He studied himself with smug satisfaction. The years had been kind, and his own diligence had paid off. There was none of the softness he observed in other men his own age or men who were even younger. His form was long and lean, with a sportsman's hardness to his arms and torso. Only a dusting of gray touched the dark hair at his temples, a gray that was enhanced by his steel-blue eyes. He was a handsome man, arrogant and proud of his looks. And he was aware of his weaknesses as well as his strengths. Only a fool ignored his own faults, he mused. Just as only a fool failed to observe and use the weaknesses and faults of his enemies.

He had chosen the suite at this particular hotel because of the panorama that spread out beneath the broad, wooden-railed porch. The wide veranda provided him a full view of both sides of the main street, and now, as he had done every morning for the past three weeks, he watched and waited.

Buildings on both sides of the street drew his attention. The jail and Jonathan Dundee's office were on the same side of the street as the hotel, the front doors of both buildings clearly visible from his window, and he diligently noted the comings and goings at both. He also watched the comings and goings at the Dundee Transport office, which was directly across the street from the hotel, as well as at the sprawling Victorian cottage, with its mock second story and intricate gingerbread, halfway down the block on the same side. His son lived in that house. His son, his ex-mistress, her husband, and the young daughter of a common whore. But not for long, he promised himself silently.

His thoughts were interrupted by a single knock on the door. Still at the window, he held his ground and called out, "Come in!"

Frank Gilman came through the opening, easing into the room with the quiet step of a man used to treading lightly. He was a short man, stoutly built, with a body devoid of flab, and somehow out of place in his role as Kincaid's manservant and driver. Still, there was a definite attitude of deference when he approached his employer. He stood, hat in hand, waiting for the other to speak before speaking himself.

Kincaid stared at the man. "Well?" he demanded.

"Adam Babcock," Gilman replied. He hesitated before continuing, wishing he had a drink and knowing that Kincaid was aware of his inner thirst. "He was the hostler at the New River station, before he hired on with Dake as a special deputy. Babcock's not his real name, Mr. Kincaid," he finished.

"I assumed as much," Kincaid responded. He was watching the other man's face. "What else?" he prompted.

"His real name is Adam Becker." Gilman's reply was concise, and there were no wasted words. "He worked for Dundee Transport up until about two years ago. And then he got himself into a bind. Cooper Dundee fired him." He didn't bother to tell Kincaid the reason for the man's dismissal, knowing it didn't matter. "Later, he tried to kill Dundee." Gilman inhaled, considering his own words as he said them. "He spent better than a year in Yuma." The thought of the prison caused him to shudder. Unaware of his own movement, he rubbed his arms, warming himself. "When he got out, he took an assumed identity and managed to get rehired without the stage line knowing who he really was."

"I want to see him, Gilman." Kincaid congratulated himself on his instincts. He had been suspicious of Babcock from the first time he had seen him prowling the street outside Dundee's house, just as he had been suspicious of the way the man seemed to share his secret enjoyment of Cooper Dundee's miseries. "Soon," he ordered.

Just as quickly, he changed the subject. "What did you find out about the boy?" he said, his voice softening.

The sudden change of direction in the conversation had no effect on Gilman. He simply followed Kincaid's train of thought. "The woman is keeping him close to home," he answered. "There's been trouble at school, and . . ." The words trailed off into an uneasy silence as he chose not to divulge what he had sensed when he observed the woman. She was suspicious of Kincaid's continued presence, just as she was wary of being watched.

"And?" Kincaid demanded. There was a subtle, harsh change in his voice, and his hand tightened around the neck of the brandy decanter he had just picked up.

"The other children," Gilman began, picking his words carefully. "They've been on the boy pretty hard about what his . . . about what Dundee did. The woman pulled him out of school. She keeps him off the street. Him and the girl." Gilman realized his mistake too late.

For a moment, it was as if Kincaid had not heard Gilman's reference to the little girl, almost as if it did not matter that she was still in the same house with the boy. And then, suddenly, Kincaid's smooth facade—the forced calm—was gone. "Trash!" he stormed. "My son is living in a house filled with human trash!" Without warning, he picked up the crystal decanter he had been fondling and hurled it across the room. Before the heavy glass shattered against the wall, a half dozen matching goblets were knocked to the floor at his feet. He continued his rampage, venting a rage that had escaped the dark corners of a mind that could no longer contain its madness, until there was nothing left within reach of his flailing arms that he had not destroyed.

Just as quickly as it had begun, the insane rage subsided. Gilman watched passively as the change occurred, no longer amazed by Kincaid's sudden transformations. He had witnessed these strange fits before. Too many times before.

Kincaid was smiling. He stood in the middle of the glittering pile of broken glass, oblivious to the devastation that lay at his feet. "And how *is* Cooper Dundee?" he asked, almost as if he really cared.

"Still in bad shape," Gilman answered. Already he was picking up the debris. "Estevan Folley is back," he announced matter-of-factly. Gilman was careful not to show any emotion when he spoke to Kincaid, fearful that he would be accused of taking sides. Worse, that his employer would suspect him of some insidious form of betrayal.

Kincaid laughed. He was opening yet another bottle of

liquor. "A mixed-breed, a woman, and now a greaser," he intoned, listing his adversaries. The arrogance in his voice betrayed his feelings of contempt for Estevan Folley and the others, and it was clear that he felt that none of the three—singly or together—was really worthy of his attentions or his efforts. He was used to much bigger game: combatants who offered some real challenge.

Abruptly his mood changed again, and he reconsidered. *Damn you, Regan*, he cursed silently. It had been three weeks since the accident—since he had first seen her—and not once had she visibly surrendered to the pressures that surrounded her. She moved through the streets, silently enduring the gossip and the whispered innuendos as she went about her business, ignoring those few foolish enough to confront her.

Her strength amazed him, and he fancied himself as the one who had endowed her with the grit and determination she was now displaying. She seemed able to do it all: to care for her ailing husband, to run what was left of the business, and to tend to the needs of her family.

And to keep me away from my son. Kincaid's eyes narrowed, and he returned to the multipaned door that opened onto his porch, staring into the windows of Regan's house. In his warped mind, he could see beyond the heavy draperies and into her very soul.

The single thought that constantly tormented and drove Kincaid was resurrected and filled his mind. *Regan was evil*. She had given herself, her body, to another man, and now she was trying to give away Kincaid's son, this time to the bastard she had taken as her husband.

He couldn't let that happen. Somehow, he was going to see the boy. And then, when the time was right, he would take him.

Regan suppressed a shudder. She stood in front of the oval mirror in the hallway, her back to the windows, and felt the uneasy skin-prickling sensation that came when she was being covertly watched.

It was a feeling that had become too familiar in the past weeks. She had developed a sixth sense about the people who passed by, instinctively knowing the ones who would

pause in their walking to stare at her back. Inevitably, it was
people she knew—or thought she had known. Acquaintances,
even old friends, would approach her, averting their eyes
until she passed, and then she would sense their prolonged
gaze, their righteous disdain. It was the same everywhere she
went.

It was something worse than contempt each time she
was at the bank to discuss the sale of her own business to her
associates in Chicago. She would overcome one temporary
obstacle only to find herself confronted by another. For some
reason someone at the bank was playing games. She just
hoped that now that Estevan Folley was back he would be
able to straighten things out and complete the sale, so that
she could circumvent the bank and its lawyers.

And there were times when she honestly felt that Jonathan was doing more harm than good. Though he had temporarily backed off on his threat to sell Angela's share of the
business, he was evasive about everything else—about Cooper,
about the charges that were being made against him, about
the transport line, and about what Jonathan expected to gain
when this was all over.

There was more troubling her as well. Deep inside,
Regan felt a terrible guilt that nagged at her until it had
become a raw wound within her heart. It was a guilt about
Michael's adoption, about Cooper's desire—out of love for
both of them—to make Michael his son. She had refused to
discuss the subject with him the very morning he had left for
Prescott, purposely putting him off until . . .

Until perhaps it is too late, she thought grimly.

Angry, Regan stared at her reflection, scolding herself
for the morose mood that held her. She braced herself,
stubbornly refusing to yield to the feelings of fear that threatened to consume her.

"This has got to stop, old girl," she said aloud, absently
tracing the worry lines that marred the forehead of her reflected image. "It's got to stop *now!*" Her mirror twin nodded
in agreement, and she laughed. Maybe she really was going
crazy, after all!

She heard the soft drag of leather against the hall carpet,
and then the thump-bump of Estevan's crutch. Another face
appeared in the mirror, behind her shoulder, and she smiled.
A flush of embarrassment flooded her cheeks, and the smile

grew. "You heard me." She said the words without turning around.

Estevan nodded. "I also talk to myself, Regan. Sometimes, I even answer." He laughed, and there was a brief flash of pain as he shifted his weight onto his bad leg.

Regan faced him then, painfully aware of the way they always seemed to speak in whispers even in the full light of day. "Don't rush it, Estevan," she scolded.

As if the pain were nothing, he shrugged. "I've got to start earning my keep, Regan," he half joshed. He was about to continue, only to be interrupted by the opening of the front door. His mouth shut in a tight line as he watched Marshal Dake and another man enter. He did not know what he resented more: the constant presence of the guards or the fact that the men Dake had hired came and went without observing even the simplest amenities, like knocking before entering.

Regan sensed Estevan's smoldering anger, and it matched her own. It took considerable effort to maintain a calm—a politeness—she didn't feel, but she somehow succeeded. "Marshal," she greeted.

Immediately, Dake took off his hat. He nodded at the bearded deputy that accompanied him and then at the door of Cooper's bedroom. "It's that time again, Mrs. Dundee."

She was tempted to let him suffer, knowing that he was aware of her true feeling about the way he had found it necessary to intrude in her life. But she could not. In spite of the circumstances, she could not truly dislike him. This was his job, and he was doing it the only way he knew how, trying hard to be fair to everyone.

Regan managed a smile for the lawman. "The traditional changing of the guard," she breathed. Without waiting for the man to respond, she led the way to the front bedroom.

The smell of sickness and infection filled their nostrils as they tiptoed into the room. Even the heavy scent of camphor and eucalyptus failed to mask the stench of damaged lungs and festering flesh.

White dominated the room: white sheets and pillow cases, a white bedspread that seemed to glow with a blue-white radiance that was a cold reflection of the filtered sunlight streaming through a narrow opening in the heavy draperies. Even the man in the bed was white, robbed of his natural coloring by the illness and infection that ravaged his too-thin body.

The inner pain that Regan felt each time she entered the bedroom never diminished. It was as if she had a raw wound deep within her that was horribly torn asunder and made worse each time she came through the doorway. It was a torment that matched the depth of her love for Cooper, and she could feel it to the very core of her heart.

Lovingly, she approached the bed, her fingers gently caressing the waxlike flesh on her husband's bandaged forehead. She whispered her morning greeting and kissed parched lips that no longer responded to her touch. "I'm here, Coop," she murmured. "I love you."

Estevan watched the tender exchange, a dull ache in his own chest as he forced himself closer to the bed. He reached out, touched Cooper Dundee's shoulder, and cleared his throat. "*Dios te bendiga, hermano*," he said softly. *God bless you, brother*.

Dake inhaled loudly, saying nothing and dismissing the guard who had spent the night in a chair beside Cooper's bed. He used his eyes to direct the deputy who had come with him into the seat that had just been vacated, and when the other man attempted to speak, silenced him with a stern look that would have routed the dead. And then he turned his attention to Regan and Estevan Folley. "Has Stockwell been here yet this morning?"

Regan shook her head. She was still beside Cooper. "There's been no change, Ethan." Her voice broke, and it took her a moment to compose herself. *Cooper's skin was so hot, so damned hot.* "He said that we were to call him only if there is some change," she finished.

When he dies, Dake thought darkly, his face clouding. Death—the strange mechanics of death—had been part of his life for more years than he cared to remember. He knew all the queer little ceremonies that accompanied a man's dying, just as he knew the peculiar dialogues and customs civilized men practiced in their fruitless attempt to defeat death. At the end of the rope or in his own bed, even the most practical man was foolish enough to try to hang on to something over which he had never had any control.

Cooper was dying. Estevan Folley and the woman might

not care to admit it, but Cooper was dying. And Stockwell had been too much of a milksop to tell them.

The lawman sighed, his eyes sweeping the man and the woman who kept the vigil beside Cooper Dundee's bed, and he found that he was as much a coward as the physician.

He felt a sudden need to make repent for the rude inconveniences he had forced on the woman and her family during the past weeks, and no longer giving a damn about the proprieties that normally governed him, he made his decision. "We're leaving now, Babcock," he said finally, addressing the deputy who perched in the chair beside the bed.

Babcock had been leaning back in the chair, and he came forward suddenly. The quick shifting of his weight caused the chair to slam hard against the bare wood floor with such force that it scraped across the planking. The screeching sound of wood against wood shattered the silence and muffled his single oath.

Dake crooked a finger at the man, silently ordering him out. From the beginning he had harbored a dislike for the deputy without really knowing why, and now, seeing the look of open defiance on the man's face, the simple dislike became a strong sense of revulsion. "There aren't going to be any more guards, Babcock. You can tell the others. And you can turn in your badge." For the first time in weeks, Dake felt in charge.

Babcock's anger peaked, and forgetting where he was— *who he was pretending to be*—he stalked across the room. He was abreast of the lawman when Dake started out the door, and they collided. "You can't fire me, Dake. Goddamn it! You can't!"

Dake grabbed the man, one hand on each shoulder as he spun him around and shoved him through the doorway. "The hell I can't!" Still pushing, Dake propelled the man out of the room and into the hallway. He paused just long enough to shut the door behind them.

Estevan stared after the pair. He had the bothersome feeling that, sometime long ago, he had witnessed the same scenario, Babcock momentarily seeming strangely familiar. As if . . .

"Estevan." Regan whispered the man's name, and the quiet desperation in the single word was more alarming than if she had shouted.

The floorboards beneath Estevan's feet began to tremble, and there was a sudden clattering of metal and wood as the big bed began to shake with a terrifying force that rattled the glasses on the small nightstand. Cooper bolted upright in bed, his body rigid as a great spasm of pain took him. His mouth opened, and he gasped for air, his nose and lips turning deep blue as his lungs rebelled and refused to work. There was a wet rattling deep in his chest as he struggled against the congestion that was suffocating him, and he tried in vain to cough. The sudden, sharp pain in his bandaged ribs paralyzed him.

Regan was already on the bed. She thumped hard at Cooper's back, between the shoulder blades, and then with Estevan's help forced Cooper back down. "We've got to turn him on his side, Estevan," she ordered. "This way! Turn him this way!"

Estevan obeyed, struggling to pull the pillows from beneath Cooper's head and shoulders. He flung the heavy feather cushions aside, swearing at their bulk and then changing his mind as he jammed them against Cooper's back and shoulders.

Regan was on the other side of the bed. She moved with a cold efficiency that belied her inner panic. Cradling Cooper's head in one hand, she used the fingers of the other to probe the depths of his throat in an attempt to force a cough and clear his lungs. Stubbornly, he fought her, gagging and then trying to pull away, and just as stubbornly, she held on.

Time was their enemy. Cooper's face had taken on a bluish tinge, the flesh around his nose, mouth, and eyes a deathly dark blue. He was sweating profusely, his cotton nightshirt already soaked and robbing him of all body warmth. Still, the phlegm blocked his lungs, and he could not breathe.

Regan's fingers probed more deeply. She was crying, more in frustration than in fear, and the words came as one with her tears. "You're not going to die, Coop! Damn you! *You're not going to die!*"

As if he heard her, Cooper began to respond. He no longer struggled against her fingers, yielding instead to the natural need to vomit. Quickly, Regan withdrew her hand, tenderly wiping his face as his lungs began to clear. There was a great deal of phlegm, and then a frightening show of blood.

The wet rattle subsided, and his color gradually began to

return to normal. He was breathing laboriously now, but he was breathing. And he was cold. He began shivering, the fever that had ravaged his body was now gone and the profuse sweating chilled him. Again, the great bed began to shake.

There was a light rapping on the door, and then a gentle whoosh as the door swung open. Michael stepped silently through the opening, his eyes widening in fright as he watched the massive bed tremble. "Regan?"

She answered him with a feeble smile meant to reassure him and a gentle command carefully worded in an effort to protect him from her own fear. "Go get the doctor, Michael. Go find Major Stockwell." She breathed a silent prayer when he obeyed.

Quickly, Regan pulled Cooper's wet nightshirt away from his body, grateful when Estevan lifted Cooper upright and held him until she worked the garment free from his limp arms and over his head. Efficiently, she rolled up the damp shirt and dropped it onto the floor at her feet. And then, hurriedly, she began to undress herself. "Take your clothes off, Estevan," she ordered, avoiding his eyes. "We've got to keep him warm!" Totally naked, she slipped into the bed and beneath the covers, reaching out to take her husband in her arms. She held him, molding her pregnant body to his as best she could as she enveloped him in her warmth. "You listen to me, Cooper Dundee," she whispered. "You're going to get well. Do you hear me? *You're going to get well.*"

Silently, Estevan Folley, as naked as the day he was born, slid into the bed on the other side.

Chapter Eight

Angela Dundee stood dutifully at her husband's side, her cheeks a bright pink as she resolutely held her tongue. Her silence was only temporary. As soon as the door to the law office reception room closed and Jefferson Kincaid was gone, she surrendered to the mixed feelings of anger and disappointment that she had previously kept to herself. "I don't like that man, Jonathan. And I resent the fact that in spite of what I've told you, you've invited him to dinner again." She was silent once more, trying very hard not to yield to Jonathan's eyes.

He stared at his wife, silently, like an angry father who had been embarrassed by the bad manners of a recalcitrant and ungrateful child. "He's an important man, Angela," he began. He raised his hand to stop his wife's intended protest and continued, "Jefferson Kincaid has power"—his fist closed and he held it before the woman—"in the palm of his hand. Here. In California. But most of all, Angela, in Washington. He's a valuable friend. And I intend to *keep* him as a friend!" There was something final in this last declaration, and it was clear that as far as Jonathan was concerned, their argument was ended.

Angela was having none of it. Filled with dread, she had silently watched as Jonathan aligned himself with a man who had the very essence of evil about him. A man, she was sure, who used people as callously as she had seen him use his wit and his money. This time it was Angela who raised her hand to silence her husband. "I want the truth, Jonathan. No more lies, no more evasions. I want to know why Jefferson Kincaid is here. And why, every time I walk into a room—into this office—and the two of you are together, you change the subject and start discussing the weather."

Jonathan's expression was one of injured innocence. He reached out with both hands, tilting his head as he softly massaged the woman's straight shoulders. She yielded to his touch, almost melting beneath his fingers. "Jefferson Kincaid and I were simply discussing business, Angela. A *man's* business," he cajoled. There was something smug in his tone.

Angela's body tensed, and she pulled away. She hated the patronizing way Jonathan talked to her when he wanted to avoid a conversation and the demeaning way he dismissed her as nothing more than an empty-headed wife. A *decorative possession*, she thought bitterly. And she had allowed it to happen—because she loved him. She still loved him, as intensely as she had in the beginning, but it was no longer enough.

"He's Michael's natural father, isn't he?" she asked finally.

For a long moment, Jonathan Dundee was silent. He inhaled, taking a deep breath, and he could feel his entire body shaking. "A clever guess, Angela? Or have you taken to listening at keyholes?" His attempt to hide his vexation failed, and there was something more than husbandly disapproval in his tone.

Angela chose to ignore her husband's righteous consternation. "I'm not a fool, Jonathan. And I don't need to eavesdrop. It's all those dangling conversations, the bits and pieces I've overheard each time I came into the room." She paused briefly and then lifted her head to stare directly into her husband's face. "Why didn't you tell me, Jonathan?"

Jonathan could not endure her direct scrutiny. He averted his eyes, answering her question with a harsh question of his own. "Why didn't *Regan* tell you?" he mocked. "After all, you've become such good friends, Angela, such confidantes." He disapproved of the women's rekindled friendship, and that disapproval was evident in his sarcastic tone. "You'd have thought, during one of your little womanly chats, that Regan would have confided in you. *Trusted* you! Well?" he demanded, not really expecting any response.

Jonathan had not asked any questions Angela had not asked herself. "Regan is a private person, Jonathan, and I respect that. Right now her main concern is Coop, and all the things that have happened: the accident, the problems with

the bank." She paused before going on, cautiously weighing
each word before she spoke. "The difficulty she's been
having selling her business." Again she hesitated. "I think
that Jefferson Kincaid has been interfering in Regan's affairs,
Jonathan. Worse, I think you've been helping him."

The strained silence confirmed her suspicions. She bit
her lower lip, hating herself for the sudden need to cry and
for the fear she felt deep inside her chest. "You're Coop's
lawyer, Jonathan." *His brother*, she chided silently, afraid to
say the words.

Jonathan's lips were closed in a tight line, and there was
a stubborn set to his jaws. He shook his head. "Not anymore,"
he declared quietly, and it was as if he was responding to the
woman's thoughts as well as her words. His fingers closed
tightly around Angela's arms, just above her elbows, and he
held her fast. "I had hoped to tell you this later, under more
pleasant circumstances, in the hope that you'd share what I'm
feeling and be happy for me. I'm going to be appointed
attorney general, Angela. Frémont owed Kincaid a favor.
And now *I* owe Kincaid a favor. As for Regan . . ." He
shrugged his shoulders. "Kincaid isn't interested in Regan or
in causing her any grief. But he *is* the boy's real father,
Angela, and he expects Regan to acknowledge that."

"Coop is Michael's father now, Jonathan." She knew that
her husband was well aware of the depths of Cooper's feeling
for the boy. Suspicious, she continued, afraid that she already
knew the answer to the question she was about to ask.
"There's more, isn't there? *You* intend to take Dundee
Transport."

"What's left of Dundee Transport," Jonathan answered.
There was no need for pretense any longer, and he felt
strangely relieved. But he still could not face his wife directly.
"I've done everything for Coop that could be done, Angela."
That much, in fact, was true, and his conscience was clear.
"There isn't a man, under the circumstances, who could have
done more. He's under house arrest. He's at home. The
charges are going to be reduced to manslaughter, and he
won't be tried for murder. He'll be granted a change of
venue." Feeling less guilty and even a bit proud, he continued,
"I'll be in a position to see to it that he only serves a short
time. A year, two at the most. But he'll be *alive*."

Angela was shaking her head in disbelief. "And what will

he have left when it's over?" The thought of Coop in prison for any length of time terrified her even more than the chilling reality of a hanging.

Angry, Jonathan shouted his answer. "His wife! His wife and the child she's carrying! Which is a hell of a lot more than *I* had left when he took the line!"

Unable to restrain herself, Angela tore free. She lashed out at her husband, striking him across the mouth with the flat of her hand. The force of the blow came from deep within and was driven home by an inner pain more intense than her feeling of love. "You had *me*, Jonathan! And my one-third interest in the line and the home ranch!" A sudden wave of calm swept Angela, and she felt dead inside. "I won't let you do this. Not to Coop. And not to Regan."

Jonathan's fingers were pressed against his lower lip. A small cut burned at the corner of his mouth, and he could taste the salty warmth of his own blood. "You're my wife, Angela," he whispered ominously. "My *wife*! You'll do as I say, *when* I say!"

She backed away. "Not anymore, Jonathan. *Not anymore!*" And then she was gone.

Michael's heart pounded in his ears in cadence to the thump of his running feet as he raced in search of the army doctor, Major Stockwell. He raced down the boardwalk, the tears that stung his eyes blurring his vision as effectively as the panic that clouded his thinking. Old memories, only recently buried, filled his mind with all the terror of a horrifying nightmare—a nightmare that had once been a sickening reality.

He was reliving the past. The panic and terror he felt were the same feelings he had experienced when he lived with his parents—*the people he still believed were his parents*—in the house on officers' row at Fort Whipple.

They had died in that house. He had seen the look of death on their faces and had smelled the stench of their dying. It was the same look and the same smell he had seen and felt inside Cooper and Regan's bedroom.

Unsure of his direction, he kept running. Hoping Marshal Dake could help him find the doctor, Michael tried the marshal's office first, and when there was no response from within, he turned to the only open saloon that faced the main street. He barged through the door, colliding with the swamper. "Marshal Dake," he panted, trying hard to see over the man's shoulder. He kept bobbing up and down, checking the backs of the men who lounged at the bar. "I need to find Marshal Dake!"

"What you need, boy, is to get your fanny out of here!" Roughly, the sweeper ushered the boy out through the door. "And stay out!" he ordered.

Michael faced the street, his chest rising and falling rapidly. He couldn't stop himself from crying, angry and frustrated at his failure in finding Dake or the doctor and unsure of his next move. The early morning traffic had already begun, and the streets and walkways were filled with people hurrying about their own business with no time or inclination to help an obviously truant child.

A brief flash of blue and yellow on the opposite side of the street captured the boy's attention. Thinking it might be the uniform of Major Stockwell, he dashed into the roadway, unmindful of the traffic.

Jefferson Kincaid had just stepped out of Jonathan Dundee's office. He paused at the doorway, shielding his mouth with his cupped hands as he lit a tailor-made cigarette, satisfied that—in spite of Angela's untimely interruption—the meeting with Jonathan Dundee had gone well. A thin haze of blue smoke lifted into the air above his head as he inhaled deeply, anticipating his next mission.

Glancing into the busy street, he saw the boy. He recognized his son as soon as he saw him. There was a cold rush of panic as he realized what he was seeing, and then he sprang into immediate action.

Michael was midstreet. He had carelessly plunged into the roadway without looking, narrowly dodging a heavy farm wagon. The tail end of the vehicle brushed his shoulder, spinning him around and directly into the path of a briskly moving buckboard.

The horse was wearing blinders, its side vision obstructed by the leather rectangles that protruded from the sides of the headstall. The animal sensed the boy before he saw him. Panicking, the big gelding reared up on its hind legs, its front legs slashing the air in front of him.

Kincaid raced into the street, grabbing the boy and

picking him up in one smooth motion. He held him, pressing the boy's head against his chest to protect him from the front feet of the rearing animal, and then neatly pivoted out of the way.

Michael's breath and tears were warm against Kincaid's chest, and the man held him for a time before setting him down on the boardwalk. Already he was thinking of ways to further ingratiate himself to the child. And then he was aware of heavy breathing above and behind him. Frank Gilman stood at his employer's shoulder breathing hard, his round face red from his effort.

"I saw him from the hotel," Gilman panted. "Is he all right?"

Kincaid nodded. He had left Gilman at the hotel attending to the piddling chores of a bookkeeper. "Get the buggy, Frank," he ordered quietly. His hand was firmly clasped around Michael's upper arm.

He waited until the driver was gone. "Are you all right, boy?" he asked.

Michael's head bobbed up and down. "Yes, sir," he whispered. He could feel his heart beating within his chest, as if the skin around his ribs was too small. And then he remembered the reason for the careless risk he had taken. "Coop," he breathed, more to himself than to the man. "I got to go, mister," he panted, still out of breath. "My pa . . ."

Kincaid's face darkened and then relaxed as he gained control of his emotions. "Cooper Dundee," he said easily, forcing a smile for the boy's benefit.

Again, the boy's head bobbed in a quick up and down nod. "I have to find the doctor." The old panic was pushing at his chest again, and the words poured out in a chorus of sobs. "I tried to find Marshal Dake so's he could tell me where the soldiers are." Michael was pulling away from Kincaid's fingers even as he said the words. "Major Stockwell . . ."

Gently, Kincaid grabbed the boy's shoulders, measuring his touch and keeping it light. "I sent my driver for my carriage," he cajoled, stroking the boy's hair. "I can help you find Dake and the major," he lied.

Michael considered the man's words. There was no one to advise him, no one else who had even tried to help. Looking up, he studied the man's face and tried to place him.

Kincaid sensed the boy's wariness. "You've probably seen

me with Jonathan," he said, nodding in the direction of
Jonathan's office. "We're great friends," he went on, searching the street for a sign of his driver and visibly relieved
when he spied the team of matched grays rounding the
corner. "And he is Cooper's brother," he continued. To settle
the matter, he gave the boy a quick man-to-man hug, his arm
loosely around the youngster's shoulder.

"Michael?"

Angela Dundee approached the man and the boy from
behind. She reached out, tapped the boy's upper arm, and
called his name again. "Michael?"

"Angela!" The boy turned and buried his head in her
skirt. She held him, staring over his head and directly into
Jefferson Kincaid's coldly brilliant blue eyes. The impact of
what she saw, a myriad of intense emotion, stunned her, and
she was momentarily speechless.

When she recovered, her attention was solely on the
boy. Bending her knees, she gracefully lowered herself until
she was eye to eye with the youth. "What's wrong, Michael?"
she asked quietly.

He took her hand, not minding at all that it was pressed
against his cheek. "Coop." His lower chin trembled, and he
bit his lip before continuing. "I can't find the doctor, Angela."

The woman nodded her head. "We'll find him, Michael.
You and I."

Kincaid's voice cut into the momentary silence between
the boy and the woman. "I offered to help," he said. The
words were flat, emotionless, and it was clear that he was
struggling to stay in control. "I sent for my driver." Even his
movements were carefully measured, as if his body required
a separate order for each emotion, and there was a stiffness in
his gesture as he pointed to the curb. "I can help the boy find
Stockwell."

Angela pulled herself erect. "I think not, Mr. Kincaid,"
she said softly. The firmness of her refusal did not escape the
man.

He stared at her, his eyes narrowing. "Your *brother*
could be dying," he said, knowing full well what the impact
of the words meant for the boy and not caring. "Or haven't
you considered that?"

Angela was as surprised by her own reply as was the
man. "There are things worse than dying, Mr. Kincaid. And I

think you are the kind of man who understands that." She left the rest unsaid and turned back to Michael, taking his hand.

He rebelled, still dwelling on Kincaid's final words about Cooper and what could be happening. "The carriage," he argued. "We can do it faster if we use his carriage!"

Angela felt herself giving in to the boy and was aware of Kincaid's eyes. He was smiling—sneering—at her. "Michael," she began, purposely averting her eyes and concentrating on the child.

The boy didn't respond. She felt him tear from beneath her fingers and watched helplessly as he bolted away. "The doctor," he yelled over his shoulder. He stabbed the air with his arm, pointing the way, and began to run.

Angela started after him, relieved to see Major Stockwell's distinctive light-gray campaign hat moving above the heads of the shoppers that crowded the sidewalk, no longer afraid when Michael disappeared among the people. The sudden tightening of a man's strong fingers on her wrist stopped her and held her back.

Kincaid dug his fingers into the woman's wrist just above her gloves, his nails penetrating the skin. "You shouldn't have interfered, Mrs. Dundee," he murmured harshly. "You're going to regret having interfered."

One by one, Angela began to peel the man's fingers away from her arm, her eyes wide as she met Kincaid's gaze. She felt herself completely powerless to turn away. It was as if they were alone in the middle of a deserted street, the cold power in his eyes and his touch frightening.

Kincaid's features were predatory, and there was a chilling gleam deep in his eyes that the woman could only equate with the feral hunger for violence she had seen in the desert birds of prey that beguiled their victims and then devoured them. It had never occurred to her until now that Kincaid would actually consider kidnapping Michael. She had thought that the man was simply taking advantage of an existing situation, diverting the boy, keeping him from finding the doctor until it was almost too late, only to appear at Regan's doorstep like some knight in shining armor.

Angela realized then just how naive she had been, how blatantly foolish. She had underestimated Kincaid's capacity for cruelty. He would have been content to let Regan's husband die, and while he was dying, steal her child. "You were going to take him," she rasped, finally recovering her voice. "You were going to let Coop die and then steal Michael!"

Kincaid relaxed his hold on the woman, and then, aware of the people that bustled around them, drew her close once again. "The boy is *mine!*" The words came from between his clenched teeth, and even his breath was frigid. "I intend to have him, and the rest be damned!"

Regan pressed her naked body against Cooper's chest, shivering as she felt her own warmth being drained by the coldness of her husband's flesh. The fierce trembling had subsided, and she thought that his breathing was easier now, more regular.

"It's working, Regan." Estevan Folley's muffled voice sounded from the other side of the bed. His own body was tightly compacted against Cooper's spine and not without pain. His unhealed leg was tangled in the heavy, damp blankets that covered the three of them, and the pain was in his voice.

Regan was silent a moment, and then there was a soft rustling as she arranged the sheet around her upper body. Clutching the linen with one hand, she rose up and peered across Cooper's bandaged head. "Are you all right, Estevan?" she asked.

The man felt awkward, embarrassed—and foolish. He looked at the ceiling, and then the wall, and finally at his best friend's wife. "I'm fine, Regan," he lied.

Regan's brow knotted, and she started to speak. And then the bedroom door opened.

Major Stockwell entered the room, Ethan Dake and Michael following on his heels. The physician's greeting was as genteel and correct as it always was. "Mrs. Dundee. Estevan." He paused only long enough to feel Cooper's forehead, and then made his diagnosis. "Fever's broke."

Dake was still in the doorway, having already herded Michael out of the room. Now he was standing, mouth agape, staring in disbelief at the bed. He'd seen many things in his life, but never had he seen anything like what he was seeing now. *Hell*, he thought silently, feeling old. *There is a whole generation of people under the age of thirty-five that is going to hell in a handcart, and these three are probably going to lead the way.*

Stockwell had finished his examination. He straightened, shaking his head as his fingers lingered on Cooper's forehead. "I didn't think he had a prayer," he admitted, for the first time actually voicing the doubts that had plagued him from the beginning. His eyes met the woman's, and he smiled. "You did the right thing," he said softly, nodding at the bed. "The important thing was to clear his lungs and not let him take a chill once the fever dropped. You'd make a fine nurse, Regan."

Regan returned the man's smile and crooked a finger, inviting him closer. "Somehow," she whispered, "I don't think Marshal Dake agrees with you."

Stockwell's booming laughter erupted and filled the room with a sound that had been absent too long from the entire house. He winked at the woman and turned to leave. "It's the results that count, Mrs. Dundee, not the method!" Still laughing, he shouldered his way past the lawman and out into the hallway.

Dake followed after the man, grabbing his arm. "And what the hell was that supposed to mean?" he demanded. His normally stoic composure was all but gone.

Stockwell faced the marshal. "You've got to get your mind out of the bordellos and into the sickroom, Ethan." The physician's gray eyes were dancing. "It was to keep him *warm*, Ethan. He's still too damned sick for an orgy."

Dake's bad temper had returned with a vengeance. "And a trial, you old quack! Is he still too damn sick for a trial?"

The major was laughing again. Nothing Dake said, or could say, was going to set him off. He waved the man away without answering him and set off to find Michael. They met in the kitchen doorway. "He's going to be fine, Michael. Coop's going to be just fine." It was so good not to have to whisper anymore, or to scold the children when they did not.

Inside the bedroom, behind the closed door, Regan and Estevan heard the man's words and silently rejoiced.

Estevan was the first to speak. "I'm not one to complain, Regan," he began. "A man would have to be a *fool* to be here like this and complain." He laughed softly. "But don't you think we should get dressed?"

Regan felt the same giddiness, the welcome sense of release, and began to giggle. "I might look," she teased.

"Not me," Estevan promised solemnly.

The silence returned, and the room was quiet except for the sound of their measured breathing. Already, the damp sheets were growing cold, and Regan was aware of their coldness. "I've got to change the sheets, Estevan. And we'll need more blankets." She felt the bed move as he nodded in agreement, and then the bed swayed again as he sat up and pivoted to swing his legs over the side. She discreetly turned her head.

Estevan dressed in silence, his back to the woman, aware of her presence as she moved from beneath the blankets. He suppressed a smile, still filled with the capricious good humor of only moments before, and was sorely tempted to peek.

He didn't have to. His gaze was caught by the dim reflection in the oval mirror that hung on the wall in front of him. Unable to resist, his eyes lingered on the muted image as he visually explored the woman's naked shoulders and back. From the rear, there was no hint of her pregnancy, only a subtle softening of the curves at her waist and hips. Estevan smiled and looked away. *You're a lucky man, Cooper Dundee,* he thought silently. *One hell of a lucky man!* When the time was right, he turned, facing the woman, and barely managed to hide his smile.

"Estevan?" Regan stared across at the man, puzzled, and then dismissed the confusion. She already had a set of fresh linens from the dresser in her arms, and she nodded at the bed.

Together, they changed the sheets, carefully shifting Cooper from one side of the bed to the other. It took both of them to unfold and arrange the quilted spread Regan had taken from the storage chest.

The movement, the comforting warmth of the fresh blankets, roused Cooper from his long slumber. Cautiously, he rolled onto his back and rejoined the world of the living. He was hungry, as well as keenly alert and filled with an incredible false sense of well-being. It was as if he had simply awakened from a long nap.

"Regan," he whispered. His physical senses were slowly returning and he felt the pain. He called out to his wife again, louder. "Regan."

Regan's face lit up, the worry lines on her forehead and at the corner of her eyes fading. She smiled, bending to kiss his cheek, and silently cursed herself when she was unable to stop the tears.

Cooper's stomach growled loudly, and the sound made the woman laugh. He patted his flat belly. "I'm starved," he croaked. His mouth felt as if it were lined with batting. "And thirsty!" The scent of Regan's hair filled him with a different kind of hunger, and he reached up to pull her close. "And . . ." His kiss was long and surprisingly passionate.

Estevan took his leave, quietly letting himself out. He had the definite feeling that before Cooper came looking for the food and drink, Estevan would have time to raise the calf and cure the meat.

Chapter Nine

Regan was at the kitchen table, stirring an unwanted cup of coffee that had already grown cold, grateful for the welcome quiet and the opportunity to talk. Angela Dundee was sitting in the chair directly across from her, silently waiting, her eyes filled with the questions she had tactfully never asked.

Absently, Regan tapped her spoon against the rim of the cup. "It's true, Angela," she said, her voice soft. "Jefferson Kincaid is Michael's father." She was speaking in whispers again, as she had done when Cooper was still deathly sick and the quiet was necessary. Only this time it was because she didn't want Cooper to hear what they were discussing. "It was all so long ago," she began, the bittersweet memories evoking a gentle laughter. It was as if she were talking about another person, some awkward and unsure child-woman she had known a long time ago.

"And . . . ?" Angela prompted. Reassuringly, she placed her own hand on Regan's.

"I was in *love*," Regan declared grandly with a great sweep of her arm. The smile was still there, but the humor was not. "I was such a fool," she breathed, shaking her head. "He was married, Angela. He had a wife, two sons, and a whole different life a thousand miles and a thousand days away from where we were. I was fifteen," she continued. "Dirty, hungry, scared to death, and totally flattered by the attention of a man who was so much older and so much wiser. I didn't know he was married, Angela. I was stupid enough to believe that *I* was going to be his wife."

Suddenly, her reflective mood changed, and she was angry. "Why now, Angela? Why did he have to come here now? And what in God's name could he possibly want here in Phoenix?"

Nervously, Angela withdrew her hand. "Michael," she said finally. "He wants Michael."

Regan stared across at her sister-in-law. "You can't be serious!" She knew otherwise when she saw the haunted look far back in Angela's pale eyes.

Angela nodded. Her next words came slowly, and they were filled with a mixture of shame and disappointment. "He told Jonathan that Michael was the reason he had come to Phoenix. I didn't know, Regan!" she said, fearful that her friend would be angry with her. "Not in the beginning. And then, today . . ." The thought of Jonathan and the things they had said to each other came back to torment her, and for a moment she weakened. As much as she disapproved of Jonathan's relationship with Kincaid, she still loved him and did not want to betray him. And then the anger returned.

"I think that Jonathan and Kincaid are responsible for the difficulty you've been having arranging the sale of your business through the bank, Regan. Jonathan for his own reasons, and Kincaid . . ." She didn't really understand all the things that motivated Jefferson Kincaid, but she did know that he meant to have the boy. "Kincaid wants Michael," she finished. She had already decided against telling Regan everything that had happened when Michael was searching for Major Stockwell. There was, she rationalized, no reason to cause her friend even more alarm than what she was already feeling.

Regan was stunned. It had never occurred to her that Jefferson Kincaid would consider claiming a child that had been an embarrassment to him. She shook her head at the notion, her mind a jumble of disjointed thoughts that had no clear meaning.

As if to remind her of one more awesome responsibility, the child within her womb stirred. *Coop's child*, she thought. The much-wanted baby that she had forgotten in these past weeks. Her life had gone on, one day at a time, and the changes that had occurred in her body had been marked simply by a loosening of the cotton sashes on the long shifts she wore. Nothing more.

And the rest of her life? It seemed to be tumbling down about her like loose shale beneath the feet of a stalled mountain climber. Selfishly, she had hoped that, when Cooper was well, they would be able to pick up all the pieces.

But not this. With all of Cooper's problems, she could not bring herself to tell him about Jefferson Kincaid. He had enough to deal with now without having to contend with problems she had created before she ever knew him. She reached out, taking Angela's hand in her own and holding on with a determination that was in her words. "I'm not going to tell Coop about Kincaid. I want you to promise that you won't tell him, either."

"Regan . . ." Angela shook her head, certain that Regan was making a big mistake.

"Please, Angela," Regan implored. *"Please."*

The intensity of Regan's words reached out to Angela, and she nodded her head in reluctant agreement. She was about to speak when she heard the whimpering cries of her infant. She watched as a sleepy Niña carried the baby into the room, and the mood of both women changed. "He's hungry," she said, taking the child from Niña's arms and watching as the young girl padded back down the hallway to her room.

Regan smiled. She touched the baby boy's head and felt the softness of his curls. "You'll be staying here, Angela?" she asked.

Already, Angela was nursing the child, a soft blanket discreetly hiding her breast. "Just for a while, Regan, if it won't cause any inconvenience for anyone." She smiled. "Until Jonathan . . ." The words faded with the smile.

Regan understood fully. She could only hope, for Angela's sake, that Jonathan would have sense enough to realize just what he could be losing.

Cooper sat upright in the bed, a thick pile of heavy feather pillows nested at his back. It had been a long day, filled with the in-and-out traffic of the curious and the genuinely concerned, and the big room had seemed to shrink with each arrival. Dake had come, of course, and the army physician, Major Stockwell. Also Angela and the baby, with Jonathan conspicuous by his absence, and two of the retired hands who had worked for the transport line when Cooper was just a boy. And now it was Michael's turn. A smile tugged at the corner of Cooper's mouth.

The boy sat at the foot of the bed, facing him, his legs crossed Indian style, his fingers picking at the knotted yarn on the quilted bedspread. He was scrubbed and combed and wearing a clean nightshirt, all ready for bed. "And then she hit me," he said, pointing to the tip of his pug nose as he told Cooper the why and how of his first meeting with Niña. "Hard."

"Is that why you brought her home?" Coop teased. "Because she could beat you up?"

"Ha!" Michael snorted. "I'd have punched her back," he declared, "if she hadn't been some dumb old girl!" In spite of himself, the boy was laughing, too. And then he turned serious. "Her ma left her," he said finally. "And Bucky Conners was going to put her in jail. But Regan stopped him." He had almost forgotten how Regan had saved them both.

"And Niña's been here ever since," Cooper said, his eyes on the boy's face.

Michael nodded. His brow furrowed, and he suddenly looked like a little old man, deep in thought. "We could keep her, Coop," he said finally, his voice soft. He chose his words with a great deal of caution. Regan had warned him about upsetting Cooper, or about causing him an unnecessary worry. There were a lot of things Cooper didn't remember, and the not remembering made Michael mad. Still, Michael had to try. "You could adopt her. When you adopt me," he finished quietly, dropping his head.

Cooper reached out, his hand cupping the boy's chin, understanding his hesitation. It never failed to amaze him how much his life had changed since Regan and Michael had become a part of it. With the exception of his mother, there had never been anyone he was really sure of, anyone who loved him in the way God intended for a man to be loved. *No one that had ever made him feel so much a man.* Gently, he lifted Michael's head. "I haven't forgotten, Michael," he said softly. "Not that." They had talked about the adoption only a short time before Cooper's accident.

Michael stared up at him. "I was so scared, Coop," he whispered. "When they first brought you home, and then today . . ." There weren't enough words to tell Cooper just how afraid he really was.

"Me, too," Cooper said. He wrapped his arms around the boy, not caring about the dull pain in his chest that increased as they shared a hug. He felt Michael's shoulder pressing against his ribs and reluctantly let go, his hand still resting on the boy's shoulder. "It's going to be all right, Michael," he promised. He tapped the underside of the youngster's chin with his bent thumb and forefinger.

"So you think we ought to keep her?" Cooper grinned, deftly changing the mood and returning to their earlier discussion of Niña. He wanted very much for the boy to smile again. "You know," he joshed, "I used to bring home puppies and kittens. But I never once brought home a little girl!" In spite of the pain deep in his ribs, Cooper laughed, and Michael joined in.

Estevan Folley stood in the doorway. He felt a small twinge of jealousy, seeing Cooper and the boy together. In spite of everything that had happened, Cooper was a fortunate man. In the past two years he had built himself a real home and had surrounded himself with a family that loved him. Estevan could not help but envy the fullness he sensed in his friend's life. Feeling the intruder, he cleared his throat and then spoke. "Is this a private celebration, or can anyone join in?"

Cooper's arm was still draped around Michael's shoulder. "Always room for one more, compadre. Isn't that right, Michael?" he prompted, giving the boy a quick hug.

The boy shrugged, a mischievous fire lighting his blue eyes. "Maybe," he said, turning to Estevan. "You got something good to eat?" Since Cooper's recovery, his own appetite had rivaled the man's.

"What I've got," Estevan started, easing down onto the bed, "is a message from Regan. Something about how it's an hour past your regular bedtime, and there still isn't any kindling in the wood box."

Michael made a face. "And she wants me to fill it *now?*" he complained.

"Right now," Estevan answered. He lifted the boy up off the bed and set him on his feet. When Michael hesitated, he gave him a light swat on his rear end to help him along.

The two men were silent for a time, waiting until they were both sure that Michael was gone. Cooper was the first to speak. "And now, *hermano?*" he asked.

Estevan hesitated before answering, sorting out his thoughts and putting matters into their proper order. He knew that Cooper was aware of the real purpose of this visit, that he had not come just to fetch Michael. They had been friends too long for either of them to indulge in the polite amenities that were normal between a lawyer and his client. And that's what Estevan was now: Cooper's attorney. What existed between them at this particular moment was a real need to sort out all the facts and to have a serious discussion of all the problems that lay before them.

Estevan began, slowly. "I talked to Jonathan this afternoon. He's not going to represent you, Coop." The next part was difficult. "Frémont's appointed him attorney general. As it stands now, Jonathan will excuse himself from actually participating in anything that has to do with your case. There's going to be a hearing," he continued, "probably before the week is out. Aaron Beitermann's attorney is pushing for a quick trial."

"For a quick hanging," Cooper interrupted, his tone rueful. He was quiet a moment, his fingers rubbing at his temples. His jaw tightened, and he stared straight ahead, cursing himself. He had worked the thing over in his mind, again and again, from the first moment he regained consciousness, and it was always the same. "I don't know what happened, Estevan," he said finally. The words didn't seem right. "I don't know *how* it happened. I keep trying to piece it together. Everything. From the time we left the way station, until . . ." The words faded into silence again, and he felt the nausea deep in his belly as he remembered the sensation that had gripped him when the coach went over the cliff.

That was the last thing he remembered. That and the screams of the horses. *And the high-pitched wail of the young woman.* The same primal fear filled him again, and he felt a cold sweat on his back and at his armpits.

"I remember the sounds," Estevan breathed. It was as if he were reading Cooper's mind, and he closed his eyes for a moment. "They all think you were drunk, Coop," he said finally. "Beitermann. Dake. Even Jonathan."

Cooper's head came up, a flush of anger sweeping him. His temper had become a real problem since he had regained his senses, and he was having trouble keeping it under control.

"That's a lie, Estevan!" he snapped. "Goddamn it! You know that's a lie!"

The Mexican nodded. "I know you weren't drinking, Coop. So does Regan. But you can count on one finger of one hand the number of people in this town who believe you were sober. Who *want* to believe you were sober," he finished, trying to make Cooper understand.

Cooper lay back against his pillows. His whole body seemed to shrink, and the gauntness returned to his face. "Jesus Christ, Estevan," he whispered. "It's like the whole world has gone crazy." He was quiet again, trying harder to fit the pieces together as he forced himself to remember the accident.

There had been no warning, no hint that anything was wrong. The trip had been routine, boring almost, tedious in such a way that he had even been sorry that it was necessary for him to make the drive. Only the fact that Estevan was with him had made it seem like it was in the old days when he had been driving full time. He had even been grateful to find two unexpected passengers waiting for him when they reached the station north of Phoenix.

It was coming back to him now, bit by bit, but with a startling clarity that surprised him. He could even remember the narrow ribbon of white lace that trimmed the new Mrs. Beitermann's spring frock. *But not her face*, he realized, suddenly confused.

"Dake's been pretty thorough collecting evidence," Estevan announced, his voice cutting into Cooper's memories. He chose not to tell Cooper about the investigation at the site of the accident or the circuslike atmosphere that had prevailed when the crowd of sightseers got out of hand and overran the canyon during their grisly search for souvenirs. "He's taken statements from the stationmaster, Bragg, and from his wife. And the hostler—Babcock."

The mere thought of the hostler triggered the same aggravating gnawing at the back of Estevan's mind that it always did, and he closed his eyes briefly to drive the disquieting sensation away. He chose his next words with great care. "They all made a big thing out of the brandy you gave everyone at the station," he continued. He chose not to say anything about the broken flask that was found in Cooper's back pocket.

Cooper laughed. It was a harsh sound, without humor. "I bet," he said. "Of course, no one remembers that the only thing I drank while I was there was water." His brow knotted, and without realizing it, his fingers dropped to his chest. He recalled the smell now, and the wet cold of alcohol that had mingled and grown even colder with the sticky wetness of his own blood.

There was a momentary surge of panic, and he grabbed Estevan's arm, his fingers digging into the man's flesh so hard that Estevan instinctively pulled away. "You were with me," Cooper said, half rising up from the pillows. "The whole time?"

Estevan nodded. "You weren't drinking, Coop." He was sorry that he had to tell his friend something that he should have known for himself.

Cooper exhaled, unable to shake the feeling. There had been times, when his drinking was out of control, that he could not remember what he had done, where he had been, not even how he had gotten from one place to another. Days—weeks at a time—had become nothing but big black holes in his life. He started to speak, found that his mouth was dry, cleared his throat, and began again. The dryness was still there. "What do we do now, Estevan?"

"Fight them," Estevan answered. "But not here." He paused for a moment, letting the words sink in. "It's going to be expensive, Coop. There's going to be a change of venue." Silently, he wondered why Jonathan had been so thorough with a job that didn't really mean a damn to him, and why, for that matter, he had been so cooperative when he turned over Cooper's file. And then he knew. There were few places of any consequence in Arizona where the Dundee name was not known. Regardless of the place, the case would be well publicized, and Jonathan would be lauded for his fairness to the public as well as for his impartial treatment of his own brother.

Cooper was painfully aware of Estevan's prolonged, silent thought without fully comprehending the reason. "The military," he suggested, grabbing at straws. "Why not leave it to the military?"

Already Estevan was shaking his head. "Two dead civilians," he answered. He changed the subject. "We can drag it out—use the law itself to delay everything until peo-

ple forget." The hesitation came again as he attempted to find
the proper words, and he raised his hands in a gesture of
futility.

"We need to buy some time, Coop," he declared. "And
that's what's going to cost."

"How much money, compadre?" Cooper asked the question in a subdued tone, his voice not much above a whisper.
"And how much time?" When Estevan tried to answer, he
waved the man's words aside. "I'm about this far," he said,
measuring a minute space with his thumb and forefinger,
"from going under."

Estevan exhaled slowly, his lips pursing as he emitted a
low whistle. "I knew things were tight, but . . ." He was
remembering the patched and mended harness. Unable to
finish, he shook his head.

"I've kept the bills paid," Cooper said. "And I've managed to set some money aside." He forced a smile. "We were
going to expand the line. Invest in more equipment so that
we could haul more freight." The strained laughter came
again, edged with a poorly subdued dread. "I've got two
notes at the bank." He glanced at the calendar that hung on
the far wall, silently cursing the time he had lost. *Three
weeks had been torn out of his life, and he could remember
none of it!* None of it except the pain. "Both of them are due
on the first."

"Ten days," Estevan figured aloud. He grimaced, struggling with his crutches as he stood up, his leg asleep. The
pins-and-needles prickling extended from his little toe to his
crotch, and he swore. Stubbornly, he began to pace, thumping up and down the room in an effort to regain the feeling in
his bad leg. "What are your chances of getting the bank to
extend?" he grunted.

"About as good as a snowball's chance in hell," Cooper
answered honestly. The lack of well-wishers from among his
business acquaintances during the long day had convinced
him of that. He forced himself upright, pivoting until his legs
dangled over the edge of the bed, and then he clutched at his
stomach when he suddenly felt dizzy. "Give me a hand," he
said.

Estevan considered Cooper's request. "You sure?"

Cooper nodded. "I sure in hell can't do anything for
myself in here," he declared. The nausea still dogged him,

and it took considerable time, even with Estevan's help, for him to get up on his feet.

Together, the two men moved up and down the narrow pathway between the bed and the far wall. There was an awkward pause each time they attempted a turn, the tangle of feet and Estevan's crutches becoming a Chinese puzzle at the end of each round.

In the end, Cooper surrendered. He lowered himself back onto the bed, wiping the sweat from his forehead with the back of his hand. He was trembling, like an old man who had been too long in the sun. The feeling of helplessness overwhelmed him, and it was made worse by the fleeting glimpse of a seemingly unfamiliar face in the mirror that hung above the dresser. It took a little time before Cooper realized that the stranger's face was his own.

"My God," he murmured. It was the first time he had seen himself as the others saw him.

He was, strangely, clean shaven. The absence of whiskers surprised him, and he touched his chin, startled when the mirror image did the same.

There was nothing familiar about his face. The long weeks of illness had washed the color from his cheeks, and there was a jaundiced hue to his skin that emphasized the dark hollows beneath his eyes—*eye*, he thought, correcting himself.

Numbly, his hands touched the gauze bandage that still covered his right eye. He braced himself and then, resolutely, untied the single knot above his ear. Methodically, he began to unwind the thin gauze.

"Coop . . . !" Estevan's hand darted out as he tried to stop his friend, and was savagely knocked away.

There was a tense silence as Cooper continued his grim chore. He leaned forward, staring into the glass with such intensity that Estevan audibly sucked in a lungful of air and held his breath. Horrified, he watched as, layer by layer, the thin cotton was peeled away, until it was gone.

Cooper's right eye was swollen shut, a thick layer of yellow matter caking the dark lashes and gluing the upper and lower lids together. And still there was pain, an incredible amount of pain, deep within the damaged eye.

A jagged, red line marred the skin below the eye, a finger-thick furrow slashing through the ridge of flesh above the cheekbone. It seemed to cut a path that led to the exact center of Cooper's eye, and he traced the line with one finger, unable to believe.

There was a macabre curiosity in Cooper Dundee's movements. A single finger crawled across the wound with a will of its own, moving slowly toward the damaged eye with a strange purpose that the man did not fully comprehend. It was as if he had no control over his own hand, and he watched in the mirror, dumbfounded as his fingers explored first the scab, and then the orb.

Physically shaken, Cooper turned away from the mirror. The vision continued to haunt him. He could still see his own fingers forcing the matted lids apart, exposing the eye. *What had once been an eye.*

"For God's sake, Coop." Estevan reached out, his fingers groping for the man's shoulder. The pain that marred Cooper's countenance and distorted his features was something more tangible than the physical hurt caused by his wounds. There was an inner, spiritual torment in his face that showed the profound mental anguish the man was experiencing, and the depth of his fears.

"You should have let me die!" Cooper raged. Fleetingly, he touched the bandages on his broken ribs as his hands traced the other injuries on his too-lean form. The feel of his own body was foreign to him, and he was filled with disgust at his weakness. *"You should have just let me die!"*

Estevan said nothing for a long time, unable to find the words. He could understand what Cooper was feeling, but that didn't stop him from hating the man's sudden surrender to his own weakness and his indulgent wallow in a pool of self-pity.

"Sure," he drawled. "We could have let you die. What the hell. Regan and the boy could have handled it." Grinning, he went on, purposely baiting the man who sat before him on the bed, wanting desperately for him to fight back. "She's quite a lady, Coop! I bet there's a dozen men out there who'd jump at the chance. *I'd* jump at the chance!" He leaned forward, his tone confidential. "You were sick a long time, Coop. It gave me the opportunity to see a lot of Regan." He laughed at his own wit, purposely allowing his tone to convey a double meaning. "To see things in her I never saw before."

He whispered the next words directly into Cooper

Dundee's right ear. It was a graphic description of Regan. *The naked backside of Regan Dundee he had seen reflected in the bedroom mirror.*

Cooper's reaction to Estevan's few whispered words was astounding. He rose up from the bed, totally oblivious of the pain that tore through his body. "You bastard!" he roared. *"You bastard son of a bitch!"*

Estevan Folley was doubled over in unrestrained laughter. Awkwardly, the crutches giving him a real problem, he backed away from the bed.

Cooper stumbled after him, his hands groping for his best friend's neck. Estevan's growing laughter only increased his rage, and he cursed again. "Hold still, damn you!"

Estevan ducked and, using one crutch as a pivot, spun away. He thumped across the wood floor, stymied for a time by an unwieldy doorknob, and then bolted into the kitchen.

He was still laughing when he came through the doorway. "He's going to be fine, Regan!" he announced proudly, moving quickly down the hallway. *"He's going to be just fine!"*

Cooper came through the bedroom door, unmindful of the fact that he was wearing nothing more than the bottom half of his summer long johns. He paused, just long enough to point a finger at his wife. "I don't suppose, Mrs. Dundee," he thundered, "that you'd care to tell me just how he" —Cooper jabbed the finger in the direction of his fleeing houseguest— "happens to know that you have a birthmark? And just *where* it happens to be?"

Regan was on her feet, her mouth open and cheeks flushed. It suddenly occurred to her how Estevan would know, and she cursed herself for having forgotten the mirror. Angry— but even more amused—she swept past her husband, intent on being the first to reach Estevan Folley.

"You *looked!*" she accused, feeling Cooper's breath on her neck as he followed after her. She couldn't stop the laughter. "Damn you, Estevan! *You looked!*"

Chapter Ten

Adam Babcock stood in the large sitting room in Jefferson Kincaid's hotel suite. His eyes were busy exploring the room, taking note of the various personal items that stood out from the less elegant accoutrements furnished by the hotel. The setting made him keenly aware of his own grubby appearance, and he felt ill at ease.

The cold gleam of glass and silver was everywhere. A crystal decanter filled with an amber liquor and topped with a heavy, ornate stopper sat on the desk in the center of the room, four matched tumblers in a precise circle at its base. There was a silver humidor on the desk as well, along with a matching set of implements for the experienced cigar smoker. *Even silver toothpicks*, Babcock snorted, feeling a jealous disdain.

He had no idea why Kincaid had sent his man, Gilman, looking for him. The only reason he had agreed to come was the twenty-dollar gold piece the driver had given him. Absently, he reached inside his vest pocket to fondle the coin and wondered if he had made a mistake. It was unnerving, standing alone like some naked fool in the middle of a hotel room, waiting for a man he didn't even know.

Kincaid sensed Babcock's discomfort as soon as he came into the room. He said nothing, continuing the silent game of nerves as he poured himself a drink. And then, purposely, he stood with his back to the man, watching Babcock's face in the mirror above the mantel and draining his glass before turning around. "A drink, Mr. Babcock?" he asked amicably. "Or perhaps something to smoke?"

Babcock responded in the fawning manner Kincaid anticipated. He nodded his head and accepted the glass and then helped himself to not one, but several cigars. "Working man doesn't have many chances to enjoy a really good smoke," he observed jovially. He made a big production out of sniffing the pilfered cigars, as if he actually knew the difference between a good smoke and a piece of wild hemp, and stuffed them into his vest pocket.

Kincaid lit his own cigar, pressed the match out between his thumb and forefinger, and took his seat behind the desk. "You need a job, Babcock," he said finally, coming directly to the point. "I know that Dake has fired all his extra deputies. It stands to reason, if you aren't working for him, you might consider working for someone else. For me," he said, enjoying the game.

Babcock helped himself to a second drink and then sat down without being asked. The liquor was potent, and it was working. He felt a warm flush spreading over his body, a warmth that was already eating at his brain. He felt cocky enough to put his feet up on the desk. "What makes you think I *need* a job?" he asked slyly.

Kincaid's smile almost reached his eyes. "Because Gilman only had to give you twenty dollars to get you to come," he answered. "He'd have paid five times that if you'd been smart enough to hold out for the price." Kincaid grinned. He reached out and knocked Babcock's booted feet off his desk.

Babcock was confused by the man's admission and angry with himself for being such an ass. "I don't want to work for you, Kincaid," he declared pompously. "I don't *have* to work for you!"

Kincaid shrugged. "And I thought you wanted to get even with Cooper Dundee."

Babcock was unable to hide his surprise at the man's quiet declaration. "I only wanted to see him pay for what he did to that young woman and her husband," he lied sanctimoniously.

"You wanted to see him dead!" Kincaid retorted. He leaned back in his chair, his eyes boring into the man, and continued. "I wonder what Dake would think about that 'accident,' Babcock, if he was smart enough to realize that you were the last man to work on that coach."

Babcock was feeling even more uncomfortable than before. He tried to meet Kincaid's cold scrutiny and failed. "Ain't no secret that I worked at the way station," he murmured.

Kincaid nodded in agreement. "No." He inhaled, purposely prolonging his speech in order to study the man's face even more closely. "But I'd be willing to gamble that Dake doesn't know that you worked for Dundee Transport at another time." He knocked the ash off the end of his cigar and studied the burning tip for a time before continuing. "Two years ago. At the station north of Casa Grande." There was a sureness in his voice that gave a ring of authority to his words.

"That's a goddamned lie!" Babcock sputtered. He was sweating, and he tugged at his collar in an effort to improve his breathing.

"I don't like being called a liar, Babcock," Kincaid replied. His voice was ominously quiet. "You're going to work for me, starting now. For fifty dollars a month and expenses."

"Go to hell, Kincaid!" Babcock stood up suddenly, not giving a damn about the man's offer of wages that were twice what most men could hope to make. He slammed his fist onto the desk and then turned and headed for the door.

Kincaid let him go—until the man's hand closed around the knob and he started to open the door. "Becker!" he called loudly. "Adam *Becker!*"

It was as if Babcock had been hit squarely between the shoulders. He visibly shrank, and his whole body sagged as he leaned against the door and gently eased it shut. A considerable amount of time passed before he composed himself and was able to turn around. He started to speak and then, seeing the look on Kincaid's face, stood mute in the knowledge that there was nothing he could say to convince the man that his suspicions were untrue. "What do you want, Kincaid?" he asked resignedly.

"*Mr*. Kincaid," the other answered. He wiggled a finger at the subdued man who stood before him, and beckoned him to come back to the desk. "Don't bother sitting down," he ordered. "You aren't going to be here long enough to get comfortable." Already, he had removed from a drawer and spread before him a folder holding the documents from Yuma Prison that Frank Gilman had secured, and he turned it around so Babcock could see. "You're going to help me destroy Cooper Dundee, Becker. And when the time is right, when *I* say the time is right, you're going to help me take back my son!"

"Your son?" Babcock's eyes were still on the papers on Kincaid's desk.

"The boy," Kincaid said impatiently, angry when he could see that the other man didn't comprehend. "Regan Dundee was my whore," he intoned, his voice growing colder. "And she had my child. *I intend to have him!* And you're going to help me."

Babcock was shaking his head. His planned revenge against Cooper Dundee was already succeeding without Kincaid's help. He'd be a fool to involve himself in an insane scheme to kidnap some child. But then he reconsidered. Kincaid could expose him. Panicked, he stared again at the folder that was now closed and tucked firmly beneath the man's arm. *Dead men can't tell tales*, he thought grimly. Covertly, his hand slowly moved toward his holster.

Kincaid stared up into Babcock's face and smiled, amused that the man could be such a naive fool. "Frank," he called softly.

There was a sound at Babcock's back, the gentle whisper of a door being opened, and then the cold sound of metal working against metal. *The sound of a weapon being cocked.* Hands frozen at waist level, Babcock half turned and found himself staring into the barrel of a large-bore pistol. The bedroom door at Babcock's back was now standing open, and Kincaid's driver was standing at the threshold.

Aware that Babcock was again watching him, Kincaid tapped the folder of documents from Yuma Prison. "Now, you try anything like that again," he said, nodding at the man's holster, "and Frank"—he smiled at his driver—"is going to hand deliver your prison records right into Marshal Dake's lap. What do you suppose he'll think when he finds out who you really are and realizes that you were the last one to work on the stage—to grease those wheels—and the first one to come upon the accident?"

"Hell, that ain't no proof!" Babcock stammered, sweating profusely.

"But this is," Kincaid replied with a smug grin. He reached into his pocket and pulled out a palm-sized metallic object, which he placed on top of the desk. "It took my men quite some time, but they finally found it. This lug nut came off a hundred yards ahead of the accident. You loosened that wheel, Becker. You killed those people. If Dake gets wind of what happened, you'll hang, and Cooper Dundee will be in the crowd that sends you off."

Babcock's right hand was trembling. His eyes on the grease-smudged lug nut, he wiped the sweat from his nose and struggled to clear his throat. Thoroughly humbled, he said, "What do you want me to do, Mr. Kincaid?"

Jefferson Kincaid smiled. "Be patient, Mr. . . ." the pause, like the sarcasm, was intentional, "Mr. Babcock. You must learn to be patient!" He found the man's complete capitulation extremely satisfying—and made all the more enjoyable by the fact that Babcock had so easily caved in to some flimsy evidence from Yuma Prison and a twenty-five-cent lug nut Frank Gilman had purchased at the hardware store.

Masking his own relief that his hunch had been correct, Kincaid's smile broadened. He intended to take even more enjoyment from the total destruction of Regan and Cooper Dundee.

The man stood before the desk in the Dundee Transport office, hat in hand, struggling to find the words that would let him speak his piece and still maintain some of his dignity. "I'm sorry, Mrs. Dundee," he began finally. "I been with the line for more'n ten years, and . . ." His voice failed him, and he shook his head.

Regan sat back in her chair, wishing for some relief from the headache that had plagued her since early morning. *And now this*, she thought angrily. *One more driver giving notice and asking for his final pay.* "I don't suppose there's anything I can say that will convince you to change your mind, is there, Mr. Thompson?" she asked quietly, not really expecting any answer.

"No, ma'am," the man answered. He considered the woman's plight and genuinely felt sorry for her, but it was not in his power to give her what she needed. His own shame made him attempt an explanation. "I ain't no coward, Mrs. Dundee," he started, his voice lowering. It was as if he were afraid that someone would hear him, and the words came in a hoarse whisper. "You know I got a family. I been *told* to quit, Mrs. Dundee. That if I wanted to see my family again, I'd best quit my job and get out." He shook his head, his sense of self-preservation taking hold again and diminishing his pride. "I'll need my pay," he said gruffly.

Regan nodded her head and again felt the throbbing pain at her temples. This wasn't the first time she had been told the same story in the past weeks. Over and over she had heard the tale, the men telling her about the mysterious someone who came to them threatening their own lives, or the lives of their families.

One of the drivers hadn't listened. Dake found him dead in an alley behind the stock barns, gutted like a pig.

Reluctantly, the woman took out the company check book. The dwindling balance shrunk another hundred dollars as she wrote the draft, and she paused for a moment to inhale and regain her composure. "It's all right, Mr. Thompson. You aren't doing anything that I wouldn't do myself under the circumstances."

The driver took the check, embarrassed by the woman's words. It would have been easier if she had yelled at him or if she had cried. But there was nothing—no sign of weakness—and it made him ashamed. Without another word, he turned on his heel and left.

"Regan?" Angela entered the office by the back door, a dinner tray balanced against one hip. She had seen Thompson leave and knew from his stiff posture and stride that something was wrong.

Regan forced a smile. "We've lost another driver, Angela." Thompson had been slated to make the early morning run south to Casa Grande, and his quitting presented her with yet another problem. She laughed, but it was a hollow sound without humor. "At this rate, I'll be driving the stages myself!"

"We'll hire other drivers, Regan," Angela announced firmly, not doubting for a moment that Regan was serious. She placed the tray on the desk, directly in front of the woman, and removed the cloth. "Eat," she ordered.

"We can't hire any more drivers, Angela, at least not here in Phoenix," Regan said. She toyed with the food, not really caring if she ate or not. "I've already tried," she said tiredly. Her ad in the *Gazette* had run for over a month now, and there had not been one response.

Angela stared across at her sister-in-law, sorry that she could not help. "I was at the bank this morning, Regan," she began softly. She shook her head, more angry with herself than she was with her husband and genuinely ashamed for being so gullible. "I was going to write a draft on the account Jonathan and I have, to get some money to help with the expenses. But Mr. Hancock"—she could still see the bank president's face—"informed me that my name is no longer on the joint account. He said that if I needed any money— beyond my *allowance* for day-to-day expenses—I'd have to ask Jonathan."

Her face colored as she remembered Hancock's smug attitude as he conveyed the message from Jonathan. The little man had enjoyed his role of emissary. There was something sickeningly patronizing in the way he delivered Jonathan's words.

She continued, her voice trembling as she repeated what she had been told. "Jonathan told Mr. Hancock that he was going to indulge me and that he was going to allow me to stay here with you until . . . *until I came to my senses!*" Growing even more angry, she swore. "Damn him!" The rage she was feeling swept her, and she was cursing herself as well.

Angela's brief outburst, her use of profanity, evoked heartfelt laughter from Regan. It was so unlike the woman. Regan was still smiling when she waved Angela's murmured apology aside. "It's all right, Angela," she laughed, grateful that her friend had cared enough to try. "But you know that Coop would never have accepted the money."

There was a stubborn set to Angela's chin. "Coop wouldn't have had to know, Regan, and neither would Jonathan, if he'd just left things as they were!"

The two women were silent for a moment, and then Regan began to speak, her voice soft, reflective. "You still love Jonathan, don't you?"

"I've always loved Jonathan," Angela answered. In spite of herself, she felt a sudden need to defend her husband. "It was so different, Regan, when we were in Washington and when the baby was born. It wasn't until he decided to come back here, to Phoenix, that things changed again. It's as if . . ." She gave up, unable to explain about her husband what she could not understand. "I love him," she finished.

"First love," Regan said, her voice strangely remote. "It's like that when you fall in love for the first time."

The screen door behind them slammed, and Cooper Dundee and Estevan Folley came into the office. "And the second time?" Cooper asked, aware of nothing more than the final few words that had passed between the two women.

Regan turned in her chair. She smiled up at her husband, amazed and grateful at the change that had occurred since he had recovered.

Cooper's face had lost the gaunt look of sickness that had marred his fine features. Now, having regained most of his weight and even some color from the rare times he was able to walk in the sun, the wild handsomeness was back. Even the black leather patch he now wore over his right eye did not detract from the fineness of his face. It gave him, she thought, the exciting look of an adventurous rogue.

Silently, she breathed a prayer of thanks, grateful that, for whatever reason, Dake had not chosen to put Cooper back in jail the moment he had recovered. She smiled, tilting her head to accept the kiss Cooper had aimed at her cheek and moving so that their lips would meet.

"The second love," she whispered when they parted, "is the best love."

Angela overheard and felt Estevan's gaze on her. She faced him, surprised and sorry at the hurt she saw deep in his eyes. Knowing better, she chose to believe that it was his broken leg that caused the pain. "I've got to go back to the house," she said, averting her eyes and picking up the dinner tray. "The baby . . ."

Regan stared after Angela, aware of the subtle, awkward exchange between Estevan and the woman. Silently, for Estevan's sake, she wished that things were different and Jonathan no longer existed. And then, torn by her feelings for both Estevan and Angela, she felt ashamed and shook the dark thought away.

"Sometimes," Cooper breathed, staring after his younger sister, "I wish . . ."

Estevan interrupted him, laying his hand on his friend's shoulder. "Don't say it, Coop." He smiled. "She loves Jonathan. If I didn't believe it before, I . . ." Momentarily, he was at a loss for words, and then he spoke again. "All you have to do is watch her with the baby," he said softly, "or see the look on her face when she's looking out the window waiting . . ."

". . . waiting for Jonathan to come and drag her home," Cooper finished. He made no effort to hide his disgust, finding himself at a loss to understand Angela's romantic fantasies about a man whose main interest in life was his own selfish ambitions.

Regan toyed with the idea of telling both men about Jonathan's latest maneuver at the bank, and then, prompted by the inborn loyalty of one woman to another, decided against it. "Business or pleasure, gentlemen?"

"A bit of both," Estevan answered, smiling down at her. "I filed the adoption papers, Regan," he said softly, inwardly pleased with himself as much as he was pleased with Regan for her recent change of heart and her eagerness—in spite of her initial fear that Michael would find out the truth—to please Cooper.

He raised his hand when she started to speak, anticipating her question. "We won't need any birth certificate for Michael. The government—the army records from Fort Whipple—will back up our claim that he was your brother's child." Wisely, he shrugged his shoulders, leaving the rest unsaid.

Cooper was at the window, his back to his wife. "It's going to be all right, Regan." He wanted to reassure her and to let her know that he understood her reluctance to tell Michael the truth about his birth, but the words didn't come. The only thing that mattered, he told himself, was that now—after all this time—the proper papers had been filed and the boy would soon be theirs.

"How long?" Regan asked when she found her voice. She had been terrified that some official document recording Michael's birth would be required. *The same document that named Jefferson Kincaid as her son's father.*

"Six months," Estevan replied, wishing that it did not take so long. "Maybe less, if I can manage to pull a few strings."

There was an audible whoosh as the woman exhaled and a louder sound as she clapped her hands together in an expression of relief and joy. "Well," she smiled, smacking her hands together as if she were ridding her palms of a layer of dust, "so much for the pleasure! And the business?" she teased, feeling better than she had in a long, long time.

Cooper was still at the window, and he answered her without turning around. "I've got the money for the bank, Regan," he said. "The two thousand dollars we need to cover the interest payment and an extension fee on the notes." His tone was subdued.

Regan's gaze shifted from her husband's back to Estevan Folley's face. *Where?* she asked silently, using her eyes. When Estevan shook his head and did not answer, she guessed. "You've sold the Morgan," she said softly, thinking of the bay stud Cooper had imported from the East to breed with the Dundee mares. When Cooper didn't answer, she knew that she had guessed right.

She rose up from her chair and joined Cooper at the window, her arms going around his neck. "I'm sorry, Coop."

He kissed her. "We'll get him back, Regan," he promised, knowing it was a lie. He had let a local stockman handle the sale and knew nothing about what had transpired beyond the fact that the buyer had paid in cash. He pulled Regan close and held her for a long, long time.

"Regan! Coop!" Breathless, Angela came through the back door, her face flushed. It was obvious from her color and her breathing that she had been running. She composed herself and said, "Bucky Conners was just at the house. He's taken Niña."

Thinking of her son as much as she was thinking of the little girl, Regan inhaled sharply. "He can't," she declared angrily. "He has no right!"

"Her mother's back," Angela answered. "She was with him." She shook her head. "Niña didn't want to go, Regan. And Michael . . ." There were no words that would adequately describe the desperation she had seen in Michael's face.

Already, Regan and Cooper were on their way out the door. "Lock up the office for me, Estevan," Cooper shouted over his shoulder.

Perplexed, Estevan Folley watched after his friends. He had seen a quick flash of anger in Cooper's face that he hadn't seen in a long time, and it troubled him. "Coop!" he yelled.

Cooper and Regan hurried down the back alley that led to their home, neither of them speaking. They had almost reached the back porch when Michael came running down the stairs. He bypassed the woman, going directly to Cooper, his arms locking around the man's waist. "They took her, Coop!" He was trying very hard not to cry. "Mr. Conners and

Dotty! Get her back, Coop! *Please!* You've got to get her back!"

A dark form appeared in the doorway, blocking out the light from the kitchen. It was Ethan Dake, and there was little doubt why the lawman had come. "Let it be, Dundee," he ordered.

Cooper led his wife and the boy up the stairs. "You know what happened, Ethan?"

Dake backed into the room. "Conners was just doing his job," he said simply. "The girl's mother came back," he finished.

"Just like that," Cooper said. There was a definite edge to his voice. Ignoring the lawman, he bent down, until he was eye level with the boy. "I want you to tell me exactly what happened, Michael," he said softly. This time there was only love in his voice—love and a genuine concern for the youngster that stood before him.

"We were getting ready for bed," Michael answered. His own nightshirt was stuffed into his pants and he was barefoot. "Mr. Conners came, and that woman, Dotty. She said she was taking Niña back to Clancy's," he sobbed. "They didn't even let her get dressed."

Cooper stood up, his hand still resting lightly on Michael's shoulder. "Regan," he said finally, struggling to keep the anger he felt from spilling over into his voice. The woman understood at once. Gently, she took Michael's hand and led him down the hallway to the front part of the house.

Cooper waited until he was sure the boy was out of earshot. "What's going on, Ethan?" he asked quietly. Already, a fire was building in the pit of his stomach.

Dake lowered his head, choosing his words carefully. "Dotty got back two days ago, Coop." He lifted his hand, stopping the question before it came. "This afternoon, she was knocking on my door, looking for the girl." Frustrated, he threw up both hands in a gesture of confusion.

"Two days," Cooper echoed. The woman had been gone for two months. Behind him, he could hear Estevan and Angela. They came up the porch stairs and into the kitchen, and he moved aside so that they could pass him. He felt the air stir as Angela moved past him on his blind side, and knew when the subtle rush of air ceased that Estevan had chosen to stay by his side. "Have you got any idea what's going to happen to Niña if she stays with her mother?" he asked. "What her life is going to be like if she stays on at Clancy's?"

Dake nodded his head. "The kid belongs to her mother, Dundee." He considered his next words and then decided it was best to get it all out in the open. "You may as well know. Rumor is, Clancy's arranged an auction," he said, wondering how the old pimp had known Dotty and the girl would be back. "High bid takes the girl for the night." It made him sick having to say the words and even sicker to know that he was powerless to stop any of it. "For Christ's sake, Dundee, what the hell do you expect me to do? The kid belongs to Dotty! If she took it in her mind to rent the girl out to some pig farm, there isn't a damned thing I could do to stop it."

"Estevan?" Cooper asked without looking around.

There was a soft sound as Estevan took a deep breath. "By the time we filed papers, Coop, or convinced Dotty to give her up . . ." The hopelessness prompted him to make a remark that, without his knowing, was strangely prophetic. "It's the same thing with Michael, Coop. If something happened to Regan before the adoption is approved and the boy's real father turned up to claim him, you couldn't do a damned thing legally but stand back and watch."

"Legally," Coop repeated, and both men instinctively knew what he was thinking.

Dake shook a finger at the younger man. "You listen to me, Coop, and you listen good. I've stuck my neck out for you. By rights, soon as you were on your feet, your ass should have been in jail. For the woman's sake—and for the boy's—I let it slide. That could all change, son. Quicker than you could ever know."

Cooper smiled. "I'm thirsty, Estevan," he said, as if he hadn't heard one word Dake had spoken. "Thirstier than I've been in a long time." Already, he was heading out the door.

Dake started after him. He thrust out a big hand, catching Cooper's arm and pulling him up short. "I won't let you do it, Dundee," he warned.

Cooper suddenly turned, his right hand balled into a tight fist. He hit Dake, hard, a stunning, calculated blow to the man's temple. The hit was completely unexpected, and the lawman, carried forward by the force of his own stride, went down to his knees. Cooper hit him again, a wicked but measured blow to the back of the man's neck with the side of his hand. Dake collapsed at his feet.

"Sweet Jesus," Estevan murmured.

"We're going to Clancy's, Estevan," Cooper said. "We're going to find Dotty. And then we're going to bring Niña back home." He stepped over Dake's prone form and headed out the door.

Jefferson Kincaid was seated at a table in the front of Clancy's bordello, his eyes locked on the open door. A glass of whiskey sat before him, untouched, one finger of his right hand making a wet circle around the pitted rim.

"How do you know he'll come?" Adam Babcock asked the question in a low voice that was already whiskey hoarse.

"He'll come," Kincaid declared. His eyes narrowed, and a sardonic smile touched his lips. He found it immensely satisfying, the way he controlled and manipulated the lives and fortunes of the people around him.

Babcock followed him about like an obedient dog. And Frank Gilman. He thought of his driver, of the years the man had served him, and the smug smile grew.

Gilman had stolen from him—had embezzled a thousand dollars that he had used to buy his wife's younger brother out of trouble with a Barbary Coast gambling house. Kincaid used the threat of prison and exposure to bind the man to him. *Twelve years,* he thought. Gilman had been his personal servant and bodyguard for twelve years. The thought prompted a mirthless chuckle. At most, Gilman had faced a five-year prison sentence, and yet, out of love for his wife and daughters and a sense of pointless pride, he had placed himself in bondage for twelve.

It would be the same with Jonathan Dundee, Kincaid reasoned. The man was guilty of no crime, but he was filled with ambition and a need for recognition. To win the attorney's allegiance, he had simply dangled a different kind of carrot in front of the man's nose. Instead of fear, he had used the promise of political power and had offered the man the opportunity to regain control of Dundee Transport.

Kincaid was enjoying his role as a malevolent god. Through his effective use of others, through the raw power of his wealth, there were few lives in this uncivilized hole he had not covertly touched—from the president of the bank to the whores in this very bordello.

And all for one purpose. To punish Regan. Kincaid's face hardened as he thought of the woman, and a strange fire smoldered deep within his blue eyes. In the past weeks, his obsession to punish her had grown even stronger. She was with him constantly, in the dark, secret corners of his mind. It was more, now, than the fact that she had stolen his son.

He had been the first man to bed her. She had belonged to him, totally. And although Regan had lacked the breeding to be anything more than his mistress, he had been generous enough to allow her that much, and to offer her so much more. She could have stayed with him, traveled with him to all the places his wife would not go, but she had refused. And then she had left him.

And had taken a bastard as her husband. He thought of them in bed together and hated them both.

A properly respectful nudge from Babcock roused the man from his dark musings. "Cooper Dundee," the man muttered and rose up from his seat.

Kincaid reached out and pulled Babcock back into his chair. He watched with great interest as Cooper Dundee, followed by Estevan Folley, entered the room.

Cooper was aware of the many eyes that followed him as he strode across the bare floor. He moved with the easy grace that had marked him before the accident, as if he had come to this place seeking the same thing every other man who was here was seeking. And in a way, he was.

"Where's Dotty, Mick?" he asked amiably when Clancy came forward to greet him.

"Busy," the man answered. "You lookin' for a drink, Dundee? Or you stickin' to the story that you're still dry?"

Cooper forced a smile. "I'm still dry, Mick," he replied. "I asked you where Dotty was."

Clancy moved behind the bar, and his right hand disappeared. "I told you," he growled. "She's busy."

Cooper made a point of putting both hands on the bar. "I've got a proposition for her," he began.

Clancy laughed. "You and a hundred other men!" He used his left hand to grab a bottle from the back bar and placed it before Cooper and Estevan Folley. "Drinks are goin' for a buck apiece tonight," he announced. "You don't drink, you don't stay for the . . . festivities."

Estevan plunked down a coin and took the bottle. "We want to talk to Dotty about the little girl, Clancy." He made no effort to appeal to the man's better side. Mick Clancy didn't have one.

The pimp shook his head. "You ain't got a leg to stand on, counselor," he said with authority. "Dotty works for me, and startin' tonight, her brat's goin' to finally start earnin' her keep. You want the girl, you bid for her. Just like the rest."

Estevan reached across the bar, his hand closing around Clancy's collar. He was surprised when Cooper pulled him away. "We'll bid, Estevan," he said quietly. "Just like the rest."

Chapter Eleven

The bordello was blanketed in a thick blue haze, the air heavy with the acrid smell of smoke and sweat. Men crowded three deep against the bar, and there was not one empty seat at the ragged scatter of extra tables that had been brought into the long barroom from the rooms upstairs.

Cooper Dundee and Estevan Folley sat at a small table in a rear corner of the room, their chairs wedged uncomfortably against the walls. They were so close that their knees touched.

Cooper poured a drink for his friend, aware of the way Estevan was massaging his stiff leg. "It's not going to be much longer," he said apologetically.

Estevan nodded without speaking. He picked up his glass and gulped the whiskey down in a single swallow. "Clancy's got more help behind the bar," he observed through clenched teeth. He watched as a quartet of big men took their places, surveying their unfamiliar faces and trying to place them. Cooper Dundee's scrutiny was just as intense.

The bordello had been their playground, in their not-so-distant and not-so-innocent past, a place they had come to as boys in pursuit of their manhood—or at least what a boy perceives as his manhood.

Cooper suppressed a chuckle. He toyed with the up-ended glass that sat before him and lifted his gaze to find Estevan's eyes returning the look, and he knew that his friend was sharing the same thought. "You ever wonder," he began, "just how many times when we were growing up that we got our asses thrown out of here?"

Estevan smiled, and the lines that pain had drawn around his mouth eased. "About as many times as your father came here and dragged us out by the hair." He grinned and laughed aloud, remembering the times that Malachai Dundee had tried to impress on them both the difference between *being* a man and *acting* like a man.

"Malachai," Cooper breathed. It had been a long time since he could think about his father and not feel pain and a great sense of emptiness. "You know, compadre," he confessed, the smile growing, "I don't think I would have even come in here that first time if he hadn't told me I couldn't."

Estevan stared across at his companion. In only a few words, Cooper had summed up the one flaw that had plagued him all his life: the strange, inborn need to defy authority, to challenge the rules. As a boy, it had been manifested in a need to test his father—and later, Estevan realized for the first time, to test and challenge Jonathan. It was a sobering thought for the young attorney, and he started to speak.

Cooper touched Estevan's arm. "It's starting."

Estevan's gaze followed Cooper's, his eyes locking on the narrow back door that led to Mick Clancy's private office. It opened just enough for Clancy, with considerable effort, to squeeze through. He pulled the door shut behind him, as if he were hiding some treasure, and raised his hands and voice at the same time.

It was a formal occasion, and Clancy had dressed the part, the three-piece dark suit he wore his idea of stylish attire. His uplifted arms exposed the circle of sweat that had already begun to form at the armpits of the tight Prince Albert jacket. "Time for one more round, boys!" he shouted. The beer, like the watered rotgut, was going for a dollar a glass now, and the businessman in Clancy prompted him to push his wares.

"We've had enough to drink, Clancy!" a voice shouted. "More'n enough!" another answered. A swell of bass and tenor grumblings echoed the same sentiments. "We want the girl!"

It became a chant—a suddenly obscene and tuneless chorus of pagan voices. "We want the girl! We want the girl!"

Cooper visibly tensed. He rose up out of his chair, staring over the heads of the other men and seeing nothing. The chanting demands were diminishing, replaced by those in the front rows with a series of shrill whistles and hoots. He could see the upper part of the door to Clancy's office as it swung open a second time, and then a brief flash of Dotty's bleached blond hair. And then he saw the child.

Niña had been placed on the bar. She stood, swathed in a garish black velvet cloak that covered her body, her small face pale above the dark fabric. Her auburn hair, which Regan Dundee had kept braided, was curled and piled on top of her head, copper-penny red beneath the lantern light.

Her face had been made up, pink rouge coloring cheeks that fear had robbed of their natural color. Bright red gloss highlighted her lips, her innocent baby mouth purposely outlined to form a provocative pout. It was the same with her green eyes. The skillful trickery of experienced hands had painted and shadowed them to look larger, deeper. The effect was stunning: The once childish face, smooth and without blemish, was now the face of the woman Niña would become. She was beautiful.

A beefy hand reached out, grabbing at the heavy cloak. Terrified, Niña backed away, but Clancy caught her and held her in place. Using a hickory ax handle as a club, he beat the impatient drunk's hand away. "Not yet, friend," he warned. The four similarly armed bartenders moved in to back him up.

"Ten dollars!" a voice called. There was a restless murmur as other men dug into their pockets to count their money. The less fortunate backed away from the front of the room, drowning their sorrows in one more glass of expensive beer. "Ten dollars!" the voice repeated.

Clancy laughed. "Not even for the first peek!" Holding on to the little girl's arm, he forcefully guided her down the length of the bar, spun her around, and then made the promenade in the opposite direction. When he turned her to face the crowd, the cloak swirled out, exposing Niña's slim ankles and a portion of her bare calf.

There was a brief silence, more grumbling, and then another voice lifted over the din. "Fifty dollars!" A flurry of hushed "damns" and "goddamns" followed the bid.

Clancy greedily considered the man's words. "A drop in the bucket," he snorted. The crowd was larger than he had anticipated and, from the way money was being spent, more prosperous.

Cooper swore softly and watched as George Hancock, the president of the Stockman's bank, shouldered his way through the crowd. The banker stood in front of Clancy, sure that he had won the prize when no one else matched his bid, and reached out to take the girl's hand.

Clancy stopped him, his massive fist closing around the banker's fat wrist. "You bid fifty, Hancock," he grinned. "I'll raise you five and keep her for myself," he challenged.

Hancock took a long lingering look as he dug into his fat wallet for more money. "Then let's get on with it," he groused. He fingered the cash he held between his fingers and made another bid. "Sixty," he snorted, waving the money beneath Clancy's nose.

Cooper was on his feet and at the end of the bar. Estevan Folley was beside him. He was staring at Cooper in unabashed awe, surprised at the man's control, and puzzled by the unusual calm. "Coop?"

"Seventy," Cooper Dundee said, shaking his head at his friend. He was staring straight ahead at Clancy and the banker, watching their faces as he made his bid. When Clancy hesitated, he urged him on. "You heard the man, Mick. Get on with it." Cooper was smiling, and his voice was soft, almost jovial. But both hands were in plain sight and tightly clenched on the edge of the bar.

Clancy returned the smile, and there was almost as much sincerity in both his eyes as there was in Cooper Dundee's one. "She was at your place for over a month, Dundee," he breathed quietly, winking. "Isn't any chance that you already know what she's worth . . . ?" The change of expression in Cooper's single eye stopped the man midsentence, and his attempt at bawdy humor died.

Hancock took advantage of the silence to make another bid. "A hundred," he said, thinking of the little girl's smooth skin. He was sure, knowing Cooper's financial woes as well as the finances of the others who crowded the room, that the bid would go unchallenged.

There was an anticipatory hush. Not one man in the room was prepared to spend that kind of money, even for the privilege of a first-time romp.

"*Five* hundred," Coop declared loudly. He patted the bulge inside his vest pocket.

Hancock's slack mouth opened and then shut. "The cash," he sputtered, feeling cheated. "Make him show the cash!"

Already, his gaze on the crowd, Cooper was counting out

the bills. Five crisp one hundred dollar bills. He kept a balled fist on top of the stack, but allowed Clancy to ceremoniously ripple the edges.

"U.S. greenbacks," Clancy announced. "As fresh and as clean as the girl."

Cooper's gaze locked on the banker's face. Ceremoniously, he thumbed through the stack of bills beneath his hand. "The bid is five hundred," he repeated, his voice rising slightly. Without looking at the money, he fanned out the proper number of bills in a half circle on the bar.

Clancy reached out, his fingers lovingly caressing the cash. "Well, Hancock?" he asked, grinning.

Angrily, Hancock shook his head. "Maybe you were right, Clancy," he sneered. "Could be Cooper already knows what the girl has." He forced a laugh, trying to maintain his pompous sense of importance. "Damaged goods," he snorted. "Only a fool would bid on damaged goods!"

Estevan inhaled sharply and instinctively grabbed at Cooper's arm. To his surprise, there was no familiar feeling of tenseness in the muscles beneath his fingers. Cooper simply brushed his hand away.

"Let it go, Hancock," Cooper smiled coldly, keeping his words private. "Before *you* end up a piece of damaged goods they'll have to scrape up off the road with a spoon." His smile grew as he watched the fat man recoil and back away. Turning, he faced the other men who were still crowded against the bar. "The bid was five hundred," he declared loudly.

Clancy took up the cry, ever hopeful. "Five hundred!" he parrotted. "Do I hear six?" The only response was the restless shuffling of feet and a chorus of discontented grumblings.

Jefferson Kincaid had watched the proceedings with the detached interest of an amused god. "Give Dundee his moment of glory," he whispered to his driver, Frank Gilman. Then, when he thought the time was right, he tapped the man's arm. Once, with one finger.

Gilman stood up. "One thousand," he announced.

The temporarily disenchanted bar patrons, many of them already on their way out the door, stopped. En masse, they turned around to watch.

Cooper searched the crowd, his gaze settling on Gilman.

He didn't recognize the man or his companions. "Twelve hundred," he countered.

"Thirteen," Gilman shot back after only a moment's hesitation.

Grimly, the two men continued bidding, increasing the bids by fifty dollars each time. The room had grown completely silent except for the quiet sobbing of the little girl.

"Two thousand," Cooper said finally. There was a cold knot at the pit of his stomach, and he was beginning to regret he had chosen this way to settle matters.

Gilman played his part well, just as he had done when Kincaid had him locate the girl's mother and pay her to take back Niña, and again when he'd been sent to purchase Cooper Dundee's Morgan stud for exactly two thousand dollars. He waited for a long time, until he felt the familiar, covert tug at his coattail. "I yield to the gentleman," he murmured, bowing.

For a time, the entire room had seemed to hold its breath. There was an audible rush of air as they all exhaled.

Clancy waggled a finger at Cooper and then spent a long time counting through the second stack of bills. "Done," he said finally. He turned, holding up the money and waving it at the crowd, at the same time dismissing his extra barmen with a subtle nod. And then, wanting to please the crowd—and to inspire their inner thirst for his more tarnished whores—he grabbed at the little girl's cloak, preparing to yank it off.

Cooper grabbed the man's wrist. "She's mine," he said. "Bought and paid for." Still holding on, he lowered his voice. "I want a receipt, Clancy. Just to keep things nice and legal." Purposely, he dug his fingers into the long tendons on the underside of the man's wrist. "Estevan," he called softly. His voice rose only slightly, but his tone was completely changed. "Get Dotty."

The woman was behind the bar, a tray of glasses in her hands. She looked first at Clancy and then at Cooper Dundee and his lawyer. "I got nothing to do with this," she whimpered.

"You do now," Cooper answered harshly. "Tell her to get her ass over here, Clancy. Now."

Clancy stared into Cooper's face. The man's earlier calm—his amicable control—was gone. What remained was some intangible menace that fired Cooper's good eye and turned it the color of green ice. He had seen that look only once before: when he was running guns to the *comancheros* in Texas and tried to up his price. In the end, he gave the guns away. It was a small price to pay for his life.

"Dotty!" he croaked. The word came out in a hoarse, barely audible whisper. "Dotty!"

The woman heard the panic in his voice and responded. She shook so hard that the empty glasses on her tray rattled and tipped off the edge. It didn't matter. She stepped over the broken glass and hurried to Clancy's side.

Estevan Folley had a pad of paper lying flat on the bar. He was writing fast, nodding his head as Cooper spoke. When he was finished, he turned the paper around for Cooper to see, reading aloud in a soft voice that was meant for no one else to hear. When he was done, Cooper took the document and shoved it, with the pen, in front of Clancy and the woman.

"This is how it's going to be, Mick," he breathed. "You take a thousand. You give Dotty the rest. I *keep* the girl." His voice lowered again, more ominously than before, and the man and the woman were forced to move forward so that they could hear. "You're going to get on a stage, Dotty, and you're going to leave. And you aren't *ever* coming back! You're going to sign this," he finished, tapping the paper with his finger. "And Clancy's going to witness it."

Forgetting his earlier panic, Clancy swore. "Like hell!" It was bad enough, Cooper Dundee trying to keep the little girl, but to lose Dotty, as well. . . . It was like having two of his girls out with a case of the itch. Worse, it was like having them dead. "No!" he exclaimed.

Cooper increased his hold on the man's wrist. "Don't be a fool, Mick," he smiled. "Rumor is, you're taking bets that I'm going to hang for what happened when the coach went over that cliff." He couldn't bring himself to mention Tad Beitermann and his wife, and he forced the horror of the memory away. "I can only hang once," he reasoned. "Doesn't make a damn to me if I hang for two or hang for three. . . ." he lied.

Clancy believed him. He lifted his hand to take the pen and make his mark. And then he shoved the paper in front of Dotty. "Sign it," he ordered gruffly.

The woman looked at the paper and traced the words

with one finger. Slowly, she read the words, one by one. "She's mine," she whined softly, looking up at Cooper and Estevan. Crocodile tears began to trickle down her cheeks, washing away the thick layer of powder and rouge.

Cooper was unmoved by her crying. He pulled a stack of bills out of Clancy's fist, folded them, and stuffed them down the front of the woman's dress. "We had some good times, Dotty. There was a time when I even liked you," he admitted truthfully. And then his voice turned hard again. "She doesn't mean a damn to you, Dotty. You stay here with her, or you leave with her, it'll always be the same. First time you get thirsty," his fingers touched her lips, "first time you have a need for a new dress," his hand drifted down her neck to the lace collar of her new gown, "you'll sell her to get it." Hoping there was something decent left within the woman, he spoke again. "Let her go, Dotty."

The woman's head snapped up. "Why?" she demanded coldly. "She ain't no different than me, no better!" She gestured toward the entire room with her outstretched arm. "It was good enough for me, for my old lady. It'll be good enough for her!" she shrieked spitefully.

Estevan was behind the woman. He put his arm around her waist, almost affectionately, and whispered in her ear. "You sign the paper," he breathed, nuzzling her neck, "or so help me God, I'll spend the rest of my life looking for something in the law that will put you *under* the jail."

The woman froze. In the past, Estevan Folley had gotten her out of more than her share of scrapes, from something as minor as a drunk and disorderly to a more serious charge when she had knifed an overly attentive cowboy. "She ain't no better," she sobbed bitterly. And then she signed.

Cooper picked up the paper, reread it, and handed it back to Estevan. He knew that what they had done was only marginally legal. Just as he knew that neither Clancy nor the woman would ever have the courage necessary to do any more than hate him.

Dotty pulled away from Estevan, her head held high and her clenched fist knotted at the bodice of her dress where Cooper Dundee's money lay nested between her breasts. She never looked back, not even when the child called after her: "Mama?"

Cooper reached up. He gathered the child into his arms,

careful to keep the cloak wrapped around her small body. When he turned, he searched the near-empty room, seeking out the stranger who had bid against him and had known just when to stop. The man and his companions were gone.

Silently, he headed toward the front door, grateful that Estevan was at his back. He said nothing to the child that was nestled in his arms, aware of the warm wetness of her quiet tears against his shirt.

When they were outside, he set her down on the walkway and felt her tense beneath his fingers. It occurred to him then that she was still terrified—worse, that she was terrified of him and what he might do to her. He was, after all, the man who had bid for her. *Just like the others.*

Gently, he guided her to the small horse trough in front of the building and, using his handkerchief, began washing her cheeks. Bit by bit, the layers of face paint washed away, and with it, the haunted look of premature age.

She was becoming a little girl again. The trembling was subsiding and the quiet sobs becoming more infrequent. She was still mute, watching Cooper's face and wanting desperately to trust him.

"Michael's waiting for you, Niña," he said softly, wanting to reassure her. "And Regan." He dabbed a little harder at her lips to get rid of as much color as he could. Satisfied, he stood up and once again pulled the cloak tightly around her. "We're going home, Niña," he said, picking her up. When he touched her, she was still rigid. "And this time you're going to stay. Nobody," he promised, "*nobody* is ever going to take you away again."

Niña collapsed against the man's shoulder. She put her arms around his neck and held on, tightly, her head pressed against his chest. She could still hear her mother's bitter rantings.

Cooper kept walking, thinking how incredibly light the child was. He was startled, then relieved, when Estevan came up beside him. Estevan touched the girl's cheek, concerned at her silence. "How is she?"

Cooper shook his head. Together, they mounted the front steps. Estevan opened the screen door, and before he could open the other, found Regan and Angela already there. He backed away, letting Cooper and the child inside, and did not follow.

Regan reached out, taking the child in her arms. Seeing the traces of makeup, she frowned, inhaling deeply as she unwound Niña's fingers from around the dark cloth. The child's near nakedness appalled her, and she understood without being told a part of what must have happened. Without saying another word and with Cooper close behind her, she turned and headed down the hallway to the bedroom Niña shared with Angela and the baby, pausing just long enough to call out to Michael and summon him from his room.

Cooper touched her arm and bent his head to whisper in her ear. "Clancy had his auction, Regan. I spent the two thousand."

Shocked, Regan's eyes widened. And then she nodded tersely in a gesture of immediate forgiveness and acceptance. "I don't care, Coop," she said truthfully, pulling the child close and stroking her hair with a back and forth sweep of her chin. "I wouldn't have cared if it had been twice that." She lifted her head just long enough to look at her husband and smiled. "I didn't think it was possible to love you more than I already do," she said strongly.

She placed Niña on the bed without removing the cloak and pulled the blankets up around the little girl's neck, moving aside to let Michael sit down, and then she was in Cooper's arms. The kiss said even more than the words.

Estevan had returned. He stood in the doorway of the bedroom and cleared his throat. "I don't want any arguments, Coop." He placed a folder against Cooper's chest. "I want to buy in," he said.

Cooper's fingers moved to where the packet lay against his shirt. He knew without looking that the two thousand dollars he needed to meet the payments at the bank were inside, and his first instinct, goaded by his foolish pride, was to refuse. He changed his mind. "You could be buying a big piece of nothing," he warned.

"I don't think so, Coop," Estevan answered. He put out his hand.

Cooper accepted the gesture, knowing the handshake would be more binding than any written document. Even the thank you wasn't necessary, but he said it anyway. "*Gracias, hermano.*"

Angela was in the room, already in her nightclothes, and her spontaneous good humor roused them all from the awkward and embarrassing emotional impasse. "Dundee and Folley," she said, laughing, writing the letters in the air before her with a grand sweep of her hand. "Or perhaps, Folley and Dundee!" Mindful of Michael and the girl, she led the way out of the bedroom and down the hallway to the front room. "I know," she teased. "We'll change the name altogether! Dundee, Folley, Dundee, and . . ."

"Dundee," a voice murmured from behind. It was a summons, not a suggestion.

Cooper turned to face the sound. Ethan Dake stood before him, one hand working a still-sore jaw that felt out of place. The other was behind the man's back, wrapped around a shot-filled sock the lawman, out of habit, always carried in his front pants pocket. "I owe you one, boy," he said, gesturing for Cooper to come closer.

Cooper complied, his chagrined laughter almost boyish. "I'm sorry, Dake," he said. He pointed at the man's jaw. "About that," he went on, intending to explain what had happened at Clancy's bordello, "and . . ."

He never got the chance to finish. Dake's concealed right hand shot out with the speed of a striking rattler. He connected squarely with the button of Cooper's chin. Cooper went over and back, and it was all Estevan could do to catch him and attempt to break the fall. "Not one word, counselor," Dake warned when Estevan started to speak. He bent down and hoisted Cooper onto his broad shoulder, "not unless you want to join him."

Estevan stepped back, shaking his head. "I've got a feeling he's going to need me more out here," he declared, raising both hands in a gesture of submission. He had no choice but to watch as the lawman carried Cooper Dundee out the front door.

"Estevan!" Angela fumed, outraged when the man did nothing but stand mute. "Do something!" she demanded.

Estevan shook his head. "I can't do a damn thing, Angela," he said harshly. "Not until tomorrow morning." With that, he took his leave.

Hands on her hips, Angela stared after him. "I can't believe he said that," she said wonderingly.

"He's right, Angela," Regan said quietly. "I'm going to bed."

Puzzled, Angela stared after her sister-in-law. She couldn't understand the woman's sudden passivity any more than she comprehended Estevan's. Not to be put off, she followed the woman down the hall, startled to find the door to Regan's bedroom already shut when she reached the room. She started to knock and then, realizing that Regan and Estevan were right, changed her mind.

Tomorrow, she mused. A wave of pessimism washed through her, and she grimly wondered just how much more grief another tomorrow could bring.

Regan was up before the sun. In truth, she had never slept. She changed clothes, pausing a long moment to stare at the unmade double bed as she struggled to fit into the divided riding skirt she had worn before her pregnancy. She was surprised and then fleetingly concerned when she was able to adjust the leather laces at the waist and make it fit, and then laughed at the fullness of her belly beneath the once-loose gathers below the belt. With both hands, she measured her stomach, intrigued at the compact ball that encompassed the entire world of her unborn child. She stood for a time, her hands in place, and tried to remember the last time she had felt the baby move.

Stubbornly, she refused to yield to the somber possibilities, silently wishing she could remember what her body had been like when she was pregnant with Michael. *It's normal*, she told herself. She was slim, slimmer than most women, and more prone to show. *Seven months*, she reasoned, squinting in the dim light to read the calendar that hung on the back of the door. *At the most, I am only seven months along.*

She sighed, rubbing at the dull ache in her back, and continued with her dressing. She would need a second pair of socks, a coat, gloves, and of course her boots. Methodically, she put them on.

The sound of her boots across the carpeted floor seemed louder than normal, and she paused at the door to pull them off. And then, carrying them, she eased open her door and padded softly down the hall to the kitchen.

Every sound seemed magnified in the silent house. Regan heard the flutter of a mourning dove's wings, and then the scratching of the bird's toenails as it grappled for a perch on the back porch roof. Even the simple chore of stirring the fire created its own unique sound. As quietly as she could, Regan continued with her morning chores. She cursed the necessity, but knew that before the long day was over she would be grateful for the strong black coffee she was brewing.

She left the house, carrying extra coffee in the small container she normally used for cream, and started down the alley. The morning air was colder than she had anticipated, and she felt a twinge as a chill coursed through her body.

There were few signs of life on the streets, and for a moment Regan feared that her single remaining employee—the young man who tended the stock—would not be awake. Worse, that when she reached the barn he would not be there.

Her worst fears seemed to be coming true when she approached the barn. The coach stood in front of the big double doors, dew glistening on the leather driver's seat and the empty traces. *Please, God,* she begged, ashamed at how much she had been asking of Him in the past days.

Straining against the weight of the hanging doors, she forced them open, first one and then the other. "Martin!" she called out for the hostler. "Martin!"

The young man stumbled out of his room, wearing nothing but his long johns. Red faced, he disappeared back into the room, and when he reappeared, he was stuffing his shirttails into his still-unbuttoned trousers.

"Damn, Miz Dundee," he breathed. "You scared the livin' hell out of me."

"I want you to harness the team, Martin," she ordered, averting her eyes for the young man's sake.

He was visibly shocked. "You ain't got no driver," he declared, as if she didn't know.

"*I'm* going to drive, Martin," she announced curtly. She had made her decision the night before, when Dake had taken Cooper to jail.

The hostler started to argue and then changed his mind. He was her employee, not her keeper, he reasoned as he set about his business.

Efficiently, Regan helped him. She moved quickly, her nimble fingers rivaling the more experienced youth's as they secured the harness. When they were finished, he stood back, not knowing if he should offer her a hand up or not.

She lifted her skirt, bracing herself against the body of

the coach, and then felt a hand on her arm. Grateful, she assumed it was the young man, but when the expected boost didn't come, she turned to face him.

"You can't do this, Regan." Angela tugged at her sleeve, holding her back.

Regan eased back down onto the ground. "I don't have any choice, Angela," she breathed. "Coop's in jail, and even if he wasn't, Dake wouldn't let him drive. And Estevan has a broken leg."

"And you're carrying Coop's child," Angela retorted. She took hold of Regan with both hands, shaking her. "You could lose the baby, Regan!" The woman's answer surprised and shocked her.

"Then I'll lose the baby, Angela," Regan answered.

Stunned, Angela retreated a full pace. "You know what this baby means to Coop, how much he wants a child!" She was remembering Cooper and the way he played with her little boy—the way he had fussed and coddled and changed dirty diapers as if he had been doing it all of his life. *He had paid more attention to the infant than Jonathan had.*

Regan cleared her throat and took a deep breath in an attempt to compose herself. "We can have more children, Angela. But there won't be another transport line if we don't honor our contracts. There won't be a ranch at Casa Grande," she finished.

Angela was still appalled by the woman's seeming coldness. "Jonathan will lend you the money."

Regan shook her head. "No, he won't, Angela. And you know that," she chided.

"Then let Jonathan have what he wants, Regan," Angela argued. She still could not face the fact that Cooper would choose to let Dundee Transport perish before he would allow Jonathan to be in control again, any more than she could face knowing that Jonathan would not help unless Cooper gave in to his demands. "Please!"

Again, Regan refused. "I won't do that to Coop," she said quietly. "I won't let Jonathan do that to Coop!" She put her hand on Angela's arm. "You're not to tell Coop or Estevan where I've gone, Angela. Dake isn't going to let Coop out of jail, and there's nothing Estevan can do to help. Not this time. Promise me you won't tell!"

Angela was shaking. "You had this planned all along,"

she accused. "This is why you didn't even try to argue with Dake last night! Damn you, Regan," she swore. And then she hugged her.

Subdued, Angela watched as Regan climbed up into the box. As angry as she was, she could not help but admire and envy the woman's determination and strength. "You be careful, Regan," she shouted. She watched after the coach until it disappeared around the corner and onto the main street.

Chapter Twelve

Dotty stood on the covered walkway in front of the Dundee Transport office, waiting, a single small valise in her hands. Hung over and without makeup, the long years at Clancy's bordello showed clearly on her face. And yet she was not old.

She had been barely fourteen when Niña was born. Now, at twenty-six, time was catching up with her. Here she was, a second-generation whore with no last name that she could remember, with another one-way ticket out of another town. The money in her suitcase that Cooper and Estevan had given her did little to console her. She thought of the men, of the fact that they were responsible for her having to go somewhere new, and hated them both.

Regan saw the single passenger waiting for her and, unaware that it was Dotty, was disappointed that there were not more. Carefully, she guided the team up beside the platform, stopping the coach so the door was just the proper distance from the edge of the porch. The two women recognized each other at the same moment, and it was visibly awkward for both of them.

Regan was the first to speak, and for some reason, it seemed important that she remain civil. "Dotty." She smiled pleasantly.

Dotty read Regan's smile as one of smug self-righteousness, as if they had been to war and Regan was the victor. "You seem surprised, Mrs. Dundee," the woman drawled sarcastically. "Like you didn't know that your husband and his lawyer told me to leave town." Knowing full well the troubles that plagued the line, she continued, goading the woman,

136

"Tell me, your regular driver sick? Coop still not able to drive?"

"For now," Regan answered calmly. She continued to smile at the woman. "This is a *family* business, Dotty. We all do our part."

Dotty nodded her head. She had still made no effort to board the coach. "Must be why you had Coop buy the kid," she observed. "If you can't hire help, then you buy it. Or make it," she finished, shading her eyes with one hand to get an even better look at the woman in the box. The anger she felt toward Cooper Dundee was now directed at his pregnant wife.

In spite of herself, Regan held her temper. A wry smile touched her mouth, one eyebrow arching as she contemplated the sour beginning of what she had hoped would be an otherwise uneventful day. "I have a schedule to keep, Dotty. If you intend going anywhere on this coach, you'd better get in." It was becoming more difficult to remain civil, and Regan had to force the smile. "If you'd please, ma'am," she added graciously, remembering her scriptures: *A soft answer turneth away wrath.*

The woman on the walkway had little knowledge of the Bible and even less desire to make peace. But she knew she had lost the skirmish. Finally speechless, she reached up to open the door and then reconsidered. Inspired, she stepped away from the coach. "I've changed my mind, Mrs. Dundee." She smiled pertly. "I don't think I'll be leaving, after all." *At least, not yet,* she finished silently.

Regan was actually relieved. Absently, she called out to the team, urging the horses into a brisk walk and finally a gentle trot. Dotty watched after the coach, elated with herself and the idea that was forming in her mind. She was going to leave, all right, but in her own good time. And when she did, it would be with more than Cooper Dundee's thousand dollars.

She was going to take back her child.

Jefferson Kincaid watched from the shadowy doorway of his hotel as the big Concord rumbled up the street. He withdrew further into the darkened portal as the coach passed

by, tipping his head to light a small cigar and hiding his face
with his cupped hands.

He was surprised, then elated, to see Regan in the
driver's box. The simple fact that she was there told him that
his brief reign of terror among the drivers had finally reached
fruition.

"Regan," a nearby voice whispered. Jonathan Dundee,
who had been on his way to his office, was on the walkway in
front of the hotel. He stopped midstride to stare after the
coach, his voice filled with shocked disbelief as he whispered
the woman's name.

"It would appear," Kincaid began, pausing to puff harder
on the dark-papered stogie and making what seemed to be
idle conversation, "that things at Dundee Transport are even
worse than you suspected."

Jonathan nodded without speaking, his lips compressed
in a tight line. "No drivers," he said finally. "They don't even
have any drivers!"

Kincaid smiled, amused by the man's impotent anger.
"Your brother is back in jail," he said, watching Jonathan's
face. He waved toward the street with the cigar. "Gilman saw
Dake carrying him out of the house last night, a short time
after that fiasco at Clancy's bordello."

The grimace on Jonathan Dundee's face was made worse
by Kincaid's last declaration. He'd heard about the auction,
well after the fact, and could not even begin to understand
what had possessed Cooper to bid on a child that was destined to be a whore. *Two thousand dollars*, he thought bitterly.
For the mixed-breed get of some common slut. And with
Regan's blessings. "This has got to stop," he breathed, more
to himself than to Kincaid.

Kincaid laughed aloud. "Hell, Jonathan, you can't control your own wife," he said, tempering the slur with laughter
and a brotherly smack on Jonathan's stiff back. "How do you
intend to control your brother's?"

Jonathan felt a need to vindicate himself. "I *let* Angela
stay at that house," he announced, "in order to give her a
chance to come to her senses!" He truly believed what he
was saying.

Kincaid brightened. He followed along beside when Jonathan began walking, his arm still around the man's shoulders
as he offered a comrade's good advice. "You could talk to

her," he cajoled. "Now, when Regan and Coop are both gone."

Jonathan pulled up short. "And you could talk to the boy," he observed slyly, proud of himself and his insight.

Kincaid's eyes narrowed, the smile somehow failing to touch anything more than the corners of his mouth as he nodded in agreement. "Good idea," he murmured, as if Jonathan really had been the first to have the thought. He gave the attorney another hardy slap between the shoulder blades and stuck out his hand. "You first, my friend," he grinned, gesturing toward the Victorian cottage at the far end of the street.

He waited until Jonathan was on his way and then walked hurriedly back to the hotel. He was going to do more than *see* the boy. Finally, after all the long days of waiting, he was going to have his son.

And my revenge, he mused coldly. After all the long years of searching, he was going to have his revenge.

Angela stood in the front doorway of Cooper and Regan's snug house, feeling the fool. Her hand was pressed against her own chest, just to the left of the hollow between her breasts. In spite of herself, she felt the familiar swelling of her heart that had come when she first saw Jonathan crossing the street, and she wanted desperately to have the strength necessary to close the door and refuse him.

He stopped her. Without even realizing how close he had come to being turned away, he was at the door and through it.

"I don't want to talk to you, Jonathan," she whispered, unable to meet his gaze.

He shook his head at her words, already sensing her weakness. Without saying anything, he took her in his arms and kissed her, the warmth becoming a real passion and a strong physical need. When their lips at last parted, he kept her locked within his arms. "I want you to come home, Angela," he said gently. "Now!"

The unintended harshness of his final word restored some of Angela's resolve. "And if I do, Jonathan?" she began. "What will you do for me if I do?"

Puzzled, Jonathan tightened, then loosened, his grip. "A

new gown!" he said finally, as if a new dress was what she really wanted. "Some new furniture!"

Angela's anger was returning. "And money, Jonathan. Will you also give me back my share of the money?"

He stared at her, openmouthed. There wasn't a woman in the world, in his opinion, who understood the real truth about what money represented. "I've always given you money," he said paternally. "As much as you've needed, and *when* you needed it."

She laughed. Money for dresses or to furnish the house. *To embellish his belongings,* she thought dryly, *so that he can present the proper image.* "I need five thousand dollars," she said quietly, "to reinvest in Dundee Transport."

Jonathan was aware of other people in the room and looked up to see Michael and the little girl from the bordello. Regan's hired girl, Maria, was with them. "I have no intention of discussing our personal business in front of Coop's hired help. Or in front of those children."

Angela bristled. Maria had Angela's son in her arms. "And *our* child, Jonathan. I suppose you have no intention of discussing this in front of our child, either."

Jonathan's face colored as he realized his mistake. He hadn't even asked about the boy. His pride had prevented even that. "Angela," he pleaded.

Something pathetic in his voice appealed to Angela's compassionate nature. "Take the baby into the kitchen, Maria," she instructed, her voice soft. She anticipated Michael's question even before he asked. "You and Niña can go outside, Michael." She smiled and canted her head, shaking a finger at them both when the light in their eyes warned her of an abundance of exuberance about to spill over into the morning quiet. "You're to stay close to the house," she ordered. "No wandering off and no mischief!" Both children flashed a "who, me?" grin, and then they were gone.

"And now, Jonathan," she breathed, her expression changing when she turned to face him.

Jonathan Dundee inhaled. There was something in his wife's face that he had never seen before: a strange determination that made him uncomfortable. *Regan,* he reasoned. She had been with Regan much too long.

* * *

Dotty watched as the two children played. The resentment swelled within her soul as she heard their laughter. It was the same feeling she had experienced the night before, when Cooper and Estevan had stolen her child away.

Her security. Niña was the ace in the hole she had kept, just as her own mother had kept her. *Until there was a need for more money than a shopworn whore could make on her own.*

Resolutely, the woman made her way to where the children were playing their quiet game of marbles. She had already been to the mercantile, and a bag of long licorice sticks and giant jawbreakers was clutched firmly in her hand. Nonchalantly, she approached the pair, knowing they did not see her. "Hi, baby," she greeted.

Niña, like Michael, was hunkered down over the crude circle they had toed into the dirt. Startled, she let the big glassie roll uselessly away from her slack thumb, and for a moment she froze, staring at the gaudy patent-leather slipper that was directly in front of her. "Mama?" she breathed timidly.

Dotty smiled benignly. "I wanted to tell you I was sorry, baby. About what happened last night. Clancy made me do it," she lied. As proof of her repentance, she proffered the sack of candy with one hand, helping the child rise with the other.

Michael stood up and brushed off his knees. There was a belligerent set to his small jaw, and he protectively moved in front of Niña, shaking his head at the bag of sweets. "That's a lie," he said, shoving the candy away.

Dotty's smile disappeared, her nostrils pinched white above her tight lips. "Oh?" she said. "And what makes *you* so damned smart?"

"Coop!" the boy answered. "And Regan. I heard them talking, after they went to bed."

Dotty cut the boy short. "And just what else did you hear, little man?"

Michael's fingers wrapped around Niña's small hand, and he was still standing in front of her. He bit his tongue, stopping the words that almost escaped his mouth, choosing the new ones with greater care. He wasn't going to say anything that would hurt Niña. And he wasn't going to let Dotty say anything that would cause her pain, either. "You signed a paper," he began carefully, "saying that Niña could live with us. Forever," he finished.

Dotty stared down at the boy, surprised at his sudden show of maturity. She knew, if he had eavesdropped on Cooper and Regan, that there was much more he could have said if he had chosen to do so. "I was forced to sign that paper," she said, struggling to remain in control of her emotions. She smiled then and tugged open the small purse that dangled from her left wrist. A large roll of bills was nested at the bottom of the bag. "They gave me money, and now I'm going to give it back," she intoned. "I love you, baby," she crooned, reaching out to touch Niña's pale cheek. "I want you to come away with me."

Michael turned to face Niña, still protectively holding on to her hand. He saw the single tear rolling down her face and stopped it with one finger. Too well, he understood what she was feeling. She wanted to believe Dotty. More, she wanted to belong—to really belong—to someone who was a part of her. *Just as he wanted to belong to Coop.*

Dotty saw the exchange between the two youngsters. Impatient, and afraid she was losing ground, she threw down the useless bag of candy. With the same hand, she reached out and grabbed Niña's arm. "You're coming with me!" she hissed. "You're mine, damn you, and you're coming with me!" She was behaving like a fishwife haggling over a piece of meat.

The look of sad confusion that had marred Niña's face turned to a look of horror. She began to scream, clawing at Dotty's arms in a frantic attempt to break away. "No, Mama! No-o-o!!"

Jefferson Kincaid stood in the center of his sitting room, snapping orders to his driver and a sullen Adam Babcock as the two men packed his belongings. "I want you to arrange for a wagon, Gilman, and then Babcock"—he jabbed a finger at the bearded man, who was securing the top of a wooden crate—"can follow with our things and make the proper connection with the Southern Pacific at Casa Grande. You'll be joining us in San Francisco, Babcock."

Babcock's jaw tightened, and he mouthed a surly reply.

"San Francisco," he agreed. He had already resigned himself to a long term of servitude in Kincaid's employ.

Kincaid ignored Babcock's grim mood, intent on his own fastidious preparations for the trip south to the railroad at Casa Grande. It would all be so easy now, he thought smugly. With Cooper Dundee out of the way and Regan Dundee on the road heading south, everything was falling into place. *Just as he had planned, right from the beginning.* He would simply take Michael, and once he had him . . .

Babcock finished sealing the crates, securing the last lid with a final, vicious stroke of the heavy hammer. The noise exploded within the room like a shot, rousing Kincaid from his dark reveries. And then, expectant, Babcock stood back, waiting for the mandatory ceremony. It was like that with Kincaid. If he had learned nothing else about the man, he had learned this: There was nothing that Kincaid did without some grim, tutorial ritual.

Frank Gilman, Kincaid's driver, was busily making notes on the small, wire-bound notebook he always carried. Purposely, he counted the collection of wooden boxes, aloud, more for Babcock's benefit than his own. Quietly, he made a verbal inventory, pointing to each crate as he listed the contents for his employer. "The silver," he said, pointing to the first. "China and crystal," he continued. There were four more boxes, and he noted each one accordingly. Linens, clothing, leather-bound books, and Kincaid's collection of private papers.

At his employer's direction, he had saved the smallest for last. It was an ivory inlaid case, three inches thick and slightly more than a foot square, with a silver handle. "Your papers, sir," he finished, tapping the case with his pencil.

Kincaid took the case, his eyes on Babcock's face as his fingers closed around the handle. "This one goes with me," he smiled. "As always." Inside were the files and documents Frank Gilman had collected regarding Babcock and his years as Adam Becker, along with a palm-sized lug nut from a stagecoach—Kincaid's hold for eternity on Adam Babcock, body and soul, if it so pleased him. "You've taken care of the bill?" Kincaid asked Gilman.

The driver nodded. "And sent for the coach." Already, Gilman was putting on his gloves.

"You'll come with us, Babcock," Kincaid ordered.

The request—the order—surprised the burly man. Mouth agape, he stared across at his employer. "For what?" he managed to gasp finally.

"To help take the boy, you fool!" Kincaid snapped. "And to take care of anybody who might get in my way!" He turned on his heel, knowing there would be no further argument, and led the way out through the door.

Estevan Folley stepped out of the rundown cantina into the dusty street and was temporarily struck blind by a morning sun that burned as bright as the fires of hell. The blaze of blue-white light that tore through his eyes and into his brain was almost as intense as the *mezcal*-primed flames that burned deep in his gut. Unsteady on his feet, he clutched at the fire in his belly with one hand and his cane with the other, appearing to be intoxicated, when in truth he was stone sober.

Not that he hadn't tried to get drunk. He'd spent the entire night in pursuit of that particular kind of folly, and now, in the bright, merciless light of day, he was sorry he had not succeeded. "You're going to pay for this," he breathed, admonishing his shadow as if it were a younger brother who had publicly misbehaved.

It had been a long night for the attorney. His feelings of frustration had driven him out of the Anglo bordellos and into a place where he could think and feel in his native Spanish. But even here, in the faded, familiar grandeur that had once been the center of the old Phoenix presidio, the answers he had sought had not come.

"Coop," he breathed finally, and there was a note of apology in his voice. He genuinely felt that he had failed his best friend at a time when the man needed him most.

Limping badly, Estevan thumped his way down the boardwalk, his mind busy. Nothing made any sense. Not the accident, not all the things that had happened since the accident. Bits and pieces of the puzzle spread before him, as they had through the long night, and still none of the pieces fit.

And yet they must. In his orderly, attorney's mind he began to catalog what he recalled, until a single common factor began to appear. It was a face: the same face that had

plagued and teased his mind for the past weeks like a hair
tickling at the back of his throat that he could not dislodge.

A bearded face. The dark, somehow familiar countenance he had seen . . . *where? And when?*

It came to him as he hurried down the street. It was the
face of the hostler, the man he had seen at the way station
north of Phoenix, smearing grease on the rear wheel of the
coach in the brief hours just before the accident. The same
laughing face he had seen later, in his dream, in the wide-
awake nightmare that tortured him after his long climb out of
the canyon. And again, at Cooper's bedside, the day Cooper
almost died.

And one more time. He had seen that dark face only the
night before, in Clancy's bordello. *At the same table with the
man who had bid against Coop for Niña.*

His memory came alive, each spark of reminiscence
firing another until he remembered it all. Becker. The face
he remembered belonged to Adam Becker.

A flurry of angry, forgotten words came back to him, the
same words he had heard almost two years ago at Becker's
trial for attempting to murder Cooper Dundee.

*You're a dead man, Dundee! When I get out, when I
come back, you're a dead man!*

Chapter Thirteen

Dotty's fingers were knotted tightly in Niña's hair, the child's twin pigtails coiled tightly in the palm of her right hand. She shoved the child against the wall of the building, holding her firmly in place as she addressed the young boy who was pulling at her arm. "You let go of me, boy," she rasped, breathing hard as she tried to restrain her daughter and at the same time ward off Michael's blows. When the boy ignored her, she yanked at Niña's hair, hard, until the child cried out in pain. "I mean it!" To emphasize her threat, she made the little girl cry out again.

Michael backed away, his hands balled into tight fists at his sides. He wanted to run, to find help, but was desperately afraid to let Niña out of his sight. "Let go of her," he demanded. "Just let go of her!"

Dotty smiled icily and shook her head. "No." There was something haughty and cruel in her expression, and she was filled with a sense of power. Niña trembled beneath her fingers, and Michael . . . The woman's smile grew as she considered the boy.

Michael was a problem she had not anticipated, at least not in the beginning. She hadn't even considered that the boy would be with Niña, simply assuming that he, like the others of his species, would lose interest in her daughter when her newness as his playmate wore off.

But she had been wrong. The boy was persistent. And he was beginning to be a real problem. Somehow, she had to get rid of him. If she left him behind, if she failed to silence him, he could spell trouble. He could run straight to the law. Worse, he could run to Cooper. *Or Estevan*, she realized, steeling herself against the chill that swept her body as she remembered the way he had threatened her the last time she had seen him.

Michael stared up at the woman, watching her face. He saw a myriad of emotions wash across her features and struggled to understand them. And then the color drained from her cheeks, her eyes closing briefly as she struggled to suppress a shudder. It was the one thing Michael was able to understand: fear. And there it was, just for a moment, etched clearly on the woman's pale face.

Michael charged the woman, using her brief moment of vulnerability to catch her off guard. He rammed his head squarely in the soft hollow beneath her breasts, in the small area unprotected by bone or muscle. "Run, Niña," he shouted. "Run!"

Dotty doubled over in pain, her hands clutching at her stomach as the wind was knocked out of her. Quickly, Niña tore away from her and, with Michael following close at her heels, began to run.

"Damn you!" Dotty croaked. She forced herself erect, intent on pursuing the pair, and lifted the hem of her skirts as she sprinted after them.

Michael urged Niña on with panted words of encouragement, falling behind her as he slowed down to look back over his shoulder. Dotty was gaining on them, running with surprising agility and closing the gap between them. When the boy turned his head a second time, his feet became tangled, and he fell.

Dotty shrieked victoriously and abandoned her pursuit of her daughter. She focused totally on the boy now, skidding to a complete stop and using the momentum of her own stride to tackle Michael as he tried to get up. She straddled him, grabbing his arm and forcing it behind his back, and then she yanked him to his feet. The pressure of her grip increased as she forced Michael's hand and arm upward against his spine. "Call her back!" she ordered.

The pain in Michael's arm and shoulder was excruciating, and he was unable to stop the tears. And still he refused to obey. "No!"

There was more pain as the woman assaulted Michael a second time. "I told you to call her back!" she hissed. Again the boy refused to do as he was told.

Niña came to a jolting halt at the end of the alley.

Without turning to look, she knew that Michael was not behind her—more, that he was in trouble. *That he needed her!*

Pivoting, she spun around, the fear that had masked her face dissolving in the wake of a terrible anger. Michael was hurting, and her mother was responsible for his pain. Enraged, she screamed out at the woman—"Mama!"—and the single word was more ominous than a stream of angry threats.

Determined to find help, Niña turned and ran, spurred on by her own anger. She sprinted out of the alley, heading for Marshal Dake's office and unmindful of those she passed in the street.

Kincaid was the first to see her. She was coming straight at him, her small arms pumping furiously as she ran. There was a feral grace in her flight—not the scared running of a deer, but the determined race of a hunting animal. Bending down, Kincaid reached out to her. "Whoa, little one!" He smiled, sweeping her up off the ground.

Startled, the girl froze. And then she stared into the man's smiling face. *He is the one,* she thought, remembering. *The one Michael pointed out to me. The man who saved him from the runaway horse.* "Michael," she panted. She turned her body away from him and pointed at the mouth of the alley. "Dotty has him, and she's hurting him!"

Kincaid set the child down, keeping hold of her hand as he raced down the walkway. "Gilman," he called softly. "Babcock!" The two men obediently followed after him. Together, they turned the corner, just in time to see Dotty deliver a vicious cuff to the side of Michael's head.

Like a striking snake, Kincaid charged the woman and grabbed her arm. He pulled it up and back, slowly, his fingers biting into the tendons at her wrist and stopping the flow of blood to her fingers. He said not one word, conveying more with his eyes than he could ever convey with his mouth.

Michael broke away from the woman, dodging under her upheld arm and disappearing behind the man to the place where Gilman stood waiting with Niña. And still, Kincaid did not release his hold on the woman. He kept pulling her arm upward and back, towering over her as he forced her against the wall of the mercantile and covered her with his body. Only then did he speak, his voice a soft, ominous whisper as

he breathed the words in her ear. "You're filth, bitch! How
dare you touch my son!"

Mouth agape, Dotty stared up at the man, unable to
understand his words, but thoroughly understanding his anger.
And then she began to whimper. "My girl," she cried. "He
was botherin' my little girl. . . ."

"Liar!" Kincaid hissed, slamming her upraised arm against
the rough siding. This time the woman's tears were real.

Dotty's arm was a sickly blue white, and her elbow stung
with the prickling pain of a thousand small needles. "I just
wanted my kid," she confessed. "Just the girl!"

Kincaid released his hold and smiled benignly at the
whore. "And the boy? What would you have done with the
boy?" There was a strange lightness in his voice, as if the
woman's answer had satisfied and interested him.

Dotty's mood changed. She stood, her back against the
building as she rubbed her arm. Something in Kincaid's face
told her that they were kindred spirits and that he would
understand. "I only wanted the girl," she explained. "Just my
girl." Coyly, she reached out, fingering the lapel of Kincaid's
jacket. He was, after all, just a man, and like any other, he
had his needs and his weaknesses. Besides, she had seen him
at Clancy's, covertly directing the bidding against Cooper
Dundee for her daughter.

The thought inspired her, and she moved in such a way
that her hip brushed directly against the man's groin, at the
same time raising her knee ever so slightly to caress his inner
thigh. "I want my daughter," she breathed, batting her eyes.
"For the same reason *you* wanted her." She had assumed that
he had bid for her not so much for his own pleasure, but for
the price the child would fetch in other, richer markets.

Kincaid continued toying with her mind. "And the boy?"
he persisted.

Dotty turned her head only slightly, eyeing Michael.
"He's nothing to me," she admitted truthfully. She giggled,
and her laughter was filled with malice. "Nothing but trouble.
Like Coop," she went on, her voice a mocking singsong.
"Just like his step-daddy!"

Kincaid was smiling, but the grin reached no farther
than the upturned corners of his mouth. The remarks about
Cooper and Michael only fueled the insane rage that was

working on his tormented mind, and his mood became more sinister.

"You were going to take him," he accused. "Turn him over to some pig-farm dandy to play with, while you pocketed the money." The thought of his son as the plaything of some vile pervert filled him with even more rage. "*I'm* taking the boy." He smiled coldly. He touched the woman's cheek with the palm of his hand, gently, and then turned the caress into a sharp, flat-handed slap. "And the girl," he finished, his voice soft. "I'm also going to take the girl." He had no interest in the child for herself: it was simply to spite the woman, and to insure his own safe departure with his son. Besides, the child seemed to amuse Michael, and all growing boys needed at least one toy.

"No!" Dotty grabbed Kincaid's arm, rubbing her face with her free hand as she clung to his sleeve with the other. "Goddamn you, *no!*" When he did not respond, she continued ranting, making threats that fell on deaf ears. "I'll set the law on you," she screamed. "I'll . . ."

Kincaid unpeeled her fingers and tore away from her, ignoring her empty promises. "Babcock," he said, nodding at the woman. As the man passed him, he quietly issued another order. "Get rid of her."

Babcock stopped cold. "What the hell . . . ?" He read the man's face and couldn't believe what he saw. Not that it bothered him: It was just that there was no need. "Jesus," he argued. "You can pay her off!"

Kincaid never even looked back. "I said to get rid of her." And then, his voice rising and filled with good humor, he put out his arms to the two children who stood in the shadows against the wall. "Michael," he smiled. "We meet again."

Gratefully, Michael stepped forward, remembering his manners. He extended his hand, the way one man would offer his hand to another. "I want to thank you, Mr. Kincaid. Me and Niña."

Kincaid laughed and accepted the boy's hand. "Time to take you home, Michael." He smiled easily. His face lit up, as if he had just now thought of his next suggestion. "We'll use my carriage," he cajoled. "Take a short ride to give you some time to tell me just what happened. I'll explain it to your aunt," he continued when the two children seemed reluctant. He guessed at the reason for their hesitation and knew from their faces that he was right. "And I'll see to it that you don't get into any trouble for running off and playing where you shouldn't," he promised. Still grinning, he led the boy and Niña out of the alley.

Estevan Folley cursed his own lameness as he stomped up the boardwalk. He had abandoned the crutches only a week before, depending now on a stout oak cane that stubbornly refused to behave like a good third leg. The narrowed tip of the stick caught in yet another knothole, throwing him off stride, and he swore again. *"Maldito sea!* Dammit!"

Determined, Estevan continued on, heading for Marshal Dake's office. It was still unclear in his mind what he would tell the lawman or how, for that matter, he would make himself understood. Mentally, he prepared himself for the marshal's arguments, playing both parts in a silent scenario that could very well determine the course of Cooper's life.

His first move was to convince Dake that Babcock was, in reality, Adam Becker. It seemed absurd now, when he considered his arguments, because the Adam Babcock that Dake had hired as special deputy was so unlike the Adam Becker he had arrested only two years before for attempted murder. Already, he could hear Dake's incredulous laughter, and the man's snide remarks inferring that Estevan was just one more shyster clutching at straws in a grandstand play to save a client's neck. Just as he could hear the lawman's complaint that Estevan was trying to make him look like a fool. That was the hardest part—convincing Dake and at the same time keeping him from feeling the dunce.

Anxious to see the lawman, Estevan stepped down from the boardwalk and into the alleyway. He took the familiar shortcut, a narrow corridor leading from the old presidio to the back alleys of the Anglo section of town.

Silently, he moved through the shadows, relieved that the worn pathway made his going easier. His pace increased as he marked off familiar back doorways, and he stared ahead to the junction where the alleyways intersected. *A right turn,* he calculated mentally, reminding himself that the route he was now taking was the reverse of the one that would have— via the main street—led him directly to the front door of

Dake's office. He stifled a laugh. Back alleys and back doors: the hallmarks of a true shyster! Dake would be the first to remind him.

It was then that he heard the voices, low and incoherent, the soft rumblings of a man and the panicked pleading of a woman.

Instinctively, Estevan flattened himself against the wall. The sun was behind him, and his silhouette stretched out before him, long and lean, reaching almost to the corner of the building and dangerously beyond. Holding his breath, he listened, an uneasy feeling deep in the pit of his stomach as he heard the unseen woman's whimpering pleas.

"Let me go," she whined. "For God's sake, let me go!"

"Can't," the man mumbled, as if he were trying to convince himself. "Goddamn you, I can't! You were going to call the law," he accused. There was the muted sound of a scuffle, and more cries from the woman. Her voice rose until it was a shrill scream. The noise ended abruptly. "Shut up!" the man ordered gruffly.

Cautiously, Estevan slid along the side of the building. When the woman cried out again, he hefted his cane like a club, and hurriedly scooted around the corner. "Let her go!" he ordered.

Babcock, his back to Estevan, did as he was told. He released his hold on the woman, both hands against the wall on either side of her head as he held her in place with his chest. Estevan moved behind the man. "I said to let her go."

Stealthily, Babcock's right hand crawled down the weathered siding to disappear between his body and Dotty's. He remained in place above the woman, as if he had not heard Estevan's voice, until his fingers closed around the haft of the knife that was buried in Dotty's stomach. And then he turned, the knife firmly clenched in his fist, the blade still wet and dark with the woman's blood.

Estevan saw the brief flash of sun against the sharp blade. Intuitively, he backed away, forgetting his lame leg and going down to one knee as Babcock charged.

Babcock rushed the fallen Mexican, leaping into the air, both feet off the ground as he attacked. Instinctively, Estevan dropped all the way to the ground and rolled away. Babcock landed belly down in the dirt, momentarily stunned by the impact.

Estevan's crippled leg hampered his agility. Rising on one knee, he groped in the dirt for his cane, relieved when his fingers closed around the smooth oak. He lifted the staff, gripping the end with both hands as the man charged again.

Babcock's voice lifted in a guttural cry of victory. Still clutching the knife, he thrust out his hand, now aiming for Estevan's exposed throat. "You're dead, greaser!" he roared.

Estevan braced himself. Off balance, his lame leg extended in front of him, he was unable to use the cane as a club. He gripped the stick with both hands and, just as Babcock lunged, rammed the nub firmly into the ground. And then he feinted to the right, pushed the cane slightly forward, and held on.

Too late, Babcock realized Estevan's purpose. He dropped the knife, both his hands going immediately to his genitals as he collided midair with the heavy carved crook of the cane. With an agonizing howl of pain, Babcock collapsed writhing in the dirt at Estevan's feet.

Quickly, Estevan leaned forward and pulled Babcock's revolver from its holster. He cocked the piece, ramming the cold barrel against the fallen man's temple, and whispered in his ear, "*You're* dead, gringo!"

Babcock froze. Estevan's tone, more threatening than the pressure of steel against his skull, convinced him that he was going to die. "No," he begged.

Grimly, Estevan laughed. His eyes swept the alley, falling at last on the still form of the dead whore. A dark brown stain below the woman's breasts marked the place where Babcock's knife had penetrated her dress, the woman's pale fingers knotted prayerfully against the wound. It struck him then how much Babcock's mewling plea for salvation sounded just like Dotty's own pathetic cry for mercy. The man deserved to die.

Resolutely, Estevan took control of his emotions, his years of training as an attorney forcing a calm he did not feel. In the end, common sense prevailed. Dead, Babcock was no good to Cooper and his defense. Shaking his head, he uncocked the pistol and pulled the weapon away from Babcock's sweating ear. "Get up," he ordered.

Babcock did as he was told. Still clutching the soreness between his legs, he rose.

The attorney was on his feet, the pilfered revolver firmly

clenched in his right hand. "We're going to see Dake," he breathed, pointing the way with the pistol's barrel. When Babcock hesitated, he recocked the piece. "Don't even think about it, Becker," he grinned coldly, reading the man's mind and purposely using his real name. Thoroughly defeated, Babcock turned around. The game was over, and both he and Estevan knew it.

Together, the two men trudged down the alley, toward the main street and Dake's office. They rounded the final corner, Babcock stumbling as he stepped up onto the walkway. He caught a fleeting glimpse of Kincaid's carriage coming toward him, hesitated, and then felt the harsh pressure of the gun against his spine as Estevan urged him on. There was another fleeting moment of hesitation as he saw Kincaid's face at the buggy's window. A false sense of hope for deliverance swept him and just as quickly died.

Kincaid's unforgiving gray orbs bored into Babcock's own, his lips compressed in a tight line as he followed the man with his eyes. Gilman, perched on the driver's seat, seemed to sense his employer's mood, and the team slowed.

Unable to stop himself, Babcock turned his head, feeling the coldness of Kincaid's scrutiny as their eyes met for a final time before Kincaid moved beyond his line of vision. And yet he knew that the man was still watching him.

Puzzled, Estevan stared at Babcock's back. He had witnessed the exchange between Babcock and the man inside the carriage. Slowing down, he fell even farther behind his prisoner, half turning to catch another quick glimpse of the unfamiliar carriage. When he turned back, Babcock was a full length ahead of him. "Becker!" he called out.

From behind Estevan, the explosion of a handgun shattered the morning quiet. Openmouthed, Estevan watched as Babcock rose up on his tiptoes, the man's shirt suddenly billowing out around a small, craterlike indentation beneath his right shoulder blade. The pea-sized hole seemed to smoke, and then it grew, the bright red of fresh blood flooding the thin chambray as Babcock fell forward and collapsed onto the boardwalk in front of Dake's office door.

Estevan sprinted forward, the drawn pistol still in his hand but pointing downward. As if with a will of its own, his finger tightened against the trigger, and the gun discharged into the wooden walkway. Cursing, he dropped down beside

abcock, his free hand on the man's jugular as he searched
r and found a pulse, and then he felt the pressure of strong
ngers on his own neck. Dake's right hand reached from
ehind Estevan's back to snake past his ear as the lawman
renched the pistol away from his clenched fingers.

Even before he turned, Estevan addressed the lawman.
It wasn't me, Ethan!" When there was no response, he
:ood back up, slowly, careful to keep his hands in full view.
There was a carriage . . ." When he turned to face the
.wman and to point the way, there was nothing in the street
ut a diminishing cloud of dust.

Dake said nothing. He hefted the pistol he had just
aken from Estevan and raised the barrel to his nose. The
.eat of the steel and the pungent smell of powder did little to
ppease the lawman's suspicions. "Inside," he ordered.

Estevan exhaled, his eyes closing briefly. "He's still alive,"
e breathed, aware of the crowd that had gathered. He
tared up at the lawman, repeating the words, this time using
he wounded man's name. "Becker's still alive."

The attorney's words startled Dake, the man's brows
notting as he contemplated their meaning. And then he
odded matter-of-factly, as if he wasn't really surprised after
ll. "Find Stockwell," he barked, watching as Bucky Conners
isappeared into the throng of milling onlookers. "And then
ou," he ordered, pointing at two of the townsmen, "help get
.im inside!"

Kincaid braced himself as the carriage lurched forward
nd the horses broke into a smooth run. He sat directly
cross from a terrified Michael and Niña, seemingly oblivious
f their presence as he stroked the still-warm pistol.

He seemed to draw strength and an almost carnal satisfac-
ion from the weapon, and there was a dreamlike vagueness
ɔ his eyes. And then his expression changed. "Fools,"
ie muttered, his right hand encircling the long, engraved
•arrel of the custom-made gun. He worked the pistol up and
lown in a series of abrupt thrusts as he spoke. "I've sur-
ɔunded myself with a bunch of fools."

"Becker," he intoned. "And your mother." He nodded
iis head, appearing to look at both youngsters at the same
ime as he continued speaking. "That whore," he breathed.

"Dotty," Niña whispered shamefully. She reached out to Michael, grateful when she found his hand searching for hers.

"Your mother," Kincaid repeated. This time his eyes, like his words, were solely for the boy. "Your mother—a whore."

Stubbornly, not understanding, Michael shook his head. "My mother was a *lady!*" he argued. "She . . ."

". . . is a whore," Kincaid finished blithely, using the present tense. And then his voice turned cold again. "Regan is your mother," he explained impatiently. "And *I* am your father."

Michael's mouth opened and then shut, noiselessly. When he regained his voice, his tone was as cold and as argumentative as the man's. "My father and mother are dead." It was the first time the boy had ever said the words, and they hurt. He needed something to take away the pain. "Regan is my aunt, and Coop is going to be my pa."

Kincaid bolted forward in his seat. "Never!" he declared. *"Never!"* And then, realizing that he had frightened the boy, his mood changed. "That's why I came to Phoenix," he smiled. "For *you,* Michael. Because I wanted to find you! She stole you away," he went on quickly, nodding his head up and down at the same tempo at which his hand was still moving on the barrel of the pistol. "When you were just a baby. And then she *gave* you away to her brother." Kincaid sighed. "Like some damned puppy she didn't want anymore."

He paused, just long enough to reach out and touch the boy's face. "It's not your fault, Michael," he cajoled. "She could have kept you. I offered her everything!" he lied, insanely unaware of his deception. "Money. A fine house. *You* could have had everything!"

Michael stared across the small space that separated him from Kincaid. He couldn't believe what the man was saying, and yet he knew that Kincaid had no reason to lie.

Small mysteries came back to haunt the boy. Questions he had asked his parents when he was little—questions that they had laughingly avoided. *Where did I come from, Mama?* And when his baby sister was born. *What was it like when I was born? When I was a baby?* He shut his mind against the doubts. "You're lying," he whispered, his voice growing louder. *"You're lying!"*

Kincaid just smiled and shook his head. "You were six

months old, Michael. Regan handed you to her brother, walked out the door, and never once looked back." He inhaled. "Think about it, Michael. Until your—" Kincaid hesitated, and his hesitancy somehow made the word vile "—*parents* died, you didn't even know you had an *Aunt* Regan."

That much was partially true. Michael's eyes fluttered as he fought back the tears. Until the day she came for him at Fort Whipple, he had never once seen his aunt.

Confused, feeling betrayed, Michael sank back into his seat. There had been questions, he now realized, that Cooper had never answered, either. Questions about why, at first, Regan wouldn't even talk about the adoption—and later, the questions he asked when she suddenly changed her mind. And yet he didn't want to believe the things Kincaid was saying.

It was as if the man could read his mind. Kincaid touched Michael's face again, caressing his cheek with the fingers of his left hand. "We're going to find Regan, Michael. And then you'll see." With his free right hand, he continued to stroke the barrel of the pistol, as if he found strength and comfort in the feel of the cold metal and a perverse sense of excitement.

"She'll tell you the truth, Michael. I'll *make* her tell you the truth."

Michael shook his head. He wanted no part of this man or the stories he was telling. "She's not my mother," he declared, pushing Kincaid's hand away from his face. "Damn you! *She's not my mother!*"

Kincaid was beyond hearing. The thought of finding Regan possessed him fully. Michael and Niña were already becoming vague entities that he was willing into nonexistence until finally, he was alone with his dark fantasies and the long-barreled Buntline pistol.

He thought solely of Regan and the long days and nights they had spent together when they were lovers. He had loved her passionately, and she had dared to leave him. *She had dared to give herself, her body, to another man.*

Kincaid's fingers closed in a tight fist around the barrel of the Buntline. Regan had betrayed him. She had made a mockery of his love. He was going to find her, and when he did, she was going to die.

Chapter Fourteen

Regan stared into the vast reaches of the desert south of Phoenix, the roadway stretching like a straight ribbon into the wavering horizon. Patches of nonexistent water shimmered deceptively in the occasional low spots, and even the horses seemed to be fooled by the mirages as they increased their pace as if in anticipation of cool drink.

The woman called out to the animals, using her voice and a steady pressure on the lines to slow them down. Already, the heat from the climbing sun was taking its toll, a white foam beginning to form a crazy-quilt pattern on the glistening, dark bay hides.

She had made good time. One change of horses had already been accomplished, and the outbuildings of the next way station were plainly in view up ahead. "One more river," she sang aloud. "One more river to cross." And then she laughed, remembering the wild tales of stage drivers driven mad by the desert and the sound of their own voices.

Her laughter was cut short, and she inhaled sharply at a sudden pain in the small of her back. Already, she had lost count of the number of times the dull ache had returned. She told herself that it was nothing. After all, it had been almost a year since she had ridden up top on a coach, and her body had simply grown soft in all the wrong places.

She forced herself not to think of the pain, concentrating instead on the miles that still lay before her. The next stop would be brief, with no delay for passengers or pickups of mail—a mere pause as the hostler changed horses and performed the customary maintenance. And then she would be on her way again to the important connection at Casa Grande. *And the linkup with another driver,* she rejoiced. She refused to face the possibility that there would be no relief driver.

Gradually, of their own accord, the team slackened its pace even more, without any restraint from Regan. Creatures of habit, the big dray animals knew that their run was over and that water and grain was waiting. They loped easily into the station yard, coming to a halt directly in front of the door, and whinnied in greeting to the four-horse hitch that already stood waiting.

Gratefully, Regan eased herself down from the box, slipping as she groped with her toe for the rungs of the front wheel. A strong arm reached up to catch her, and she felt herself lifted down to the ground.

The young hostler let go of Regan, unable to conceal his surprise. "Mrs. Dundee," he breathed. And then he bowed graciously at the waist, sweeping the wide-brimmed sombrero from his dark head.

"Tomás," she said amicably. "Thank you." Her fingers lingered on his arm longer than she intended. "Water, Tomás," Regan said softly. "I could really use a drink of water."

Sensing the woman's weakness, the young man kept a steadying hand on her arm. Gently, he led her to the sparse shelter of the covered doorway, still holding on as he offered her a gourd full of air-cooled water. "You shouldn't be driving, señora."

A wave of nausea swept over the woman, and she inhaled deeply in an attempt to ward it off. "I have to make the connection at Casa Grande," she whispered. In an attempt to reassure the youth, she forced a smile and silently requested another drink with a subtle nod toward the clay urn.

Tomás shook his head. His unabashed awe at the woman's courage—at what, in her obviously advanced condition, she had already accomplished—showed plainly on his smooth face. "You should rest, señora," he admonished her. "I'll take the coach on to Casa Grande, Mrs. Dundee." He made another small, polite bow as if he were wrong to be so forward. And then, fervently, he made a second solemn declaration. "I'll take it beyond Casa Grande, if that's what you need!"

Gratefully, Regan closed her eyes. She knew now, from the continuing pain in her back and the duller pain between her legs, that she could not afford to let her pride rule her

head. Casa Grande seemed a million miles and another world
away. There was no way, feeling as she did, that she could
make the drive aboard the big Concord. "I'll need to use the
open coach for the drive back to Phoenix." She could not
conceal the desperation in her voice when she said the final
words.

Tomás nodded, knowing that it would be futile to argue.
She would, at least, be at the reins of a smaller, lighter
vehicle in which she could make better time. "The tele-
graph," he said finally, already heading into the corral for a
second fresh team for the woman. "I'll send a wire to the
office in Phoenix as soon as I reach Casa Grande!"

Regan could only nod her head. The pain in her back
was slowly crawling around her side to her lower belly. *Not
now, God*, she begged. *Please, not now.*

Adam Becker lay face down on a cot in the same cell that
had only recently been occupied by Cooper Dundee. Stockwell
was attending him, and in a tight circle around the bed stood
the others: Marshal Dake, Estevan Folley, Jonathan, and
Cooper Dundee. Each held his breath as the physician listened to Becker's heart. When he straightened, he was shaking his head, and it was obvious from his face that Becker was
dying. "You can turn him over now," he advised, somehow
reluctant to let the man die while staring into the filth on the
jailhouse floor.

It was Estevan and Jonathan who turned the man onto
his back, and they were both surprised to find that there was
no evidence of an exit wound on the man's front. Stockwell
volunteered the answer to their question before they could
ask it. "The bullet hit the sternum," he said guardedly,
pointing to his own chest. "Ricocheted off the bone and then
angled down. He is drowning in his own blood, and there
isn't a damn thing I can do to stop it."

Jonathan and Estevan exchanged a brief glance, neither
one speaking. Estevan had already told both Dake and the
elder Dundee what he had discovered about Becker's true
identity, as well as the other things he could only surmise.

"Conjectures," Jonathan finally said. "All you've given
me so far is a bunch of theories about what *could* have

happened. I need a statement, Estevan. Even if it wasn't Coop who was involved, I'd still need a statement."

Estevan nodded, knowing that what Jonathan said was true. "Then get your statement, Mr. Prosecutor," he goaded. He made no effort to hide the sarcasm.

Jonathan touched Becker's shoulder. "We know, Becker," he began, taking great care as he chose his next words. "There's no point now in going on with this farce. Two years ago, you swore that you were going to get even with Cooper Dundee when the law sent you to Yuma. The accident, Becker . . . is that how you planned to take your revenge?" There was no response, and Jonathan continued. "Talk to me, Becker," he urged.

Stubbornly, Becker shook his head. The fool was talking to him as though he were going to die! "Go to hell," he mumbled defiantly. "You and the greaser can both go to hell!"

Stockwell watched the exchange between the lawyer and the injured man. He cleared his throat and shouldered his way between Jonathan and Estevan, sick to the core of his soul over the magnitude of Becker's vendetta. Two people had died in that canyon accident, and Cooper Dundee had been needlessly maimed for life.

And then there was Dotty, he thought grimly. The dead whore Dake had sent him to examine in the dark alley behind the office. Bending down, the doctor searched Becker's countenance for some sign of remorse and genuinely thought he had found it. "For the good of your eternal soul," he begged, "tell the truth. Now, before it's too late." Becker's reply was immediate and profane.

Estevan swore and rose up to follow a stiff-backed Dake past the physician and the others and out through the open cell door. "What now, Dake?" he asked, discouraged.

The lawman snorted. "You don't really expect Becker to give Jonathan a statement?" he asked incredulously.

Estevan nodded. "He's dying," he answered, as if it made a difference.

"And he hates Coop's guts!" the lawman retorted. Dake was silent for a long moment, rubbing his chin and half-sitting on the edge of his desk. The whole time, his gaze was locked on the four men who still remained inside the cell: Stockwell, Becker, Jonathan, and Cooper.

Cooper was quiet—too damned quiet, the marshal mused. For the first time since Dake had dumped him in the cell and Cooper had regained consciousness, he was totally motionless. He stood, arms tightly folded across his chest, leaning against the wall at the foot of Becker's cot as he intently watched each breath the wounded man took.

Dake pressed a clenched fist against his aching head. "Let's get it done, counselor," he said finally, picking up a pad of ruled paper and gesturing for Estevan to follow him back inside the cell.

The lawman handed the tablet to Stockwell without looking at the man, knowing the physician would not approve of what he was going to do. His eyes looked on Becker's bloated face as he addressed the man, shrewdly calculating each word as he said it. "You're about to turn into one righteous stiff, Becker," he began. "I'm not going to stand here like the rest and give you some line of bullshit about heaven or hell, or what you should or shouldn't do for the good of your soul, because personally I don't give a damn if you fly or fry. That isn't my job. It comes to this. You know that Folley didn't back-shoot you. That means your friend in the fancy buggy made the shot. Now you can lay there and bleed to death and let that man go scot free, or you can give me his name. I get that name, Becker, and I promise you, that bastard's going to hang. I *don't* get that name, then you can go straight to hell knowing you're the one that let him get away. Your choice, Becker," the lawman finished.

Becker's face congealed and he gasped for breath. He was shaking his head, stubborn in his belief that he was not dying. But already, his fingers were growing numb, and the blood that pooled at his back was cold. A series of coughs racked the man's body, and he lifted a dead fist to his mouth to stifle the pain. Bright red foam colored his fingers, and when he drew his hand away, he gagged at what he saw. It was true, what Dake had told him: He was dying, and the man who had murdered him was getting away. "Kincaid," he rasped vindictively. "Jefferson Kincaid."

Becker saw the smile on Dake's face and realized what he had done. Dake had the name. There was no point now in denying the rest. It was only a matter of time until the lawman found Kincaid, and with him, the damning evidence that would prove what Becker had done.

The man was silent for a long time, his breathing growing shallow as he slipped away, the only sound the noise of Stockwell's pencil against the rough paper as the doctor continued to make notes. And then, suddenly, he convulsed and sat straight up. He pointed a long, shaky finger at Cooper Dundee and laughed. "It would have worked," he croaked. "You're still going to pay, Dundee!" he rejoiced. "Ask your brother," he mocked. "He knows! Kincaid has . . ." Becker's voice failed and he tried again. "Kincaid has the . . ." And then he died.

Angela eased through the front door. She had arrived in time to hear Becker's last words, and finished the sentence for the man. "Michael," she breathed. "He has Michael and Niña."

Cooper turned to face his sister, as puzzled by her declaration as he was by Becker's last words—even more confused when he saw that Regan was not with her. "Angela?"

She held up her hand, silencing Cooper and feeling ashamed for what she had to tell him and for her failure to keep Michael and Niña safe, as she had promised. "Tell him, Jonathan," she ordered.

Jonathan Dundee was outside the cell. He stood apart from them all, painfully aware of his aloneness. *But then, he had always felt alone.* "Jefferson Kincaid is Michael's father, Coop. He came to Phoenix to find the boy and to take him." And then, in a sudden need to vindicate himself for his part in everything that had happened, went on. "Regan knew he was here, Coop. She saw him in my office the same night Dake and Stockwell brought you in from the accident."

Cooper was shaking, his skin white beneath the black patch that covered his right eye. "It's just like before, isn't it, Jonathan?" he accused, his voice a flat monotone, the question purely rhetorical. He neither expected nor wanted an answer, choosing instead to remember the deception, the secrets. "You bastard!" he roared. He lunged across the room, stopped cold when Angela stepped in front of him and blocked his way.

She grabbed him, one hand on either arm as she struggled to hold him back. "I'm sick of it, Coop!" she exploded. "Of you and Jonathan and the way you turn your petty quarrels into unnecessary wars! Kincaid has the children. And Regan . . ." She could not reasonably explain the feeling of dread she had for the woman. "Regan had to make the run to Casa Grande." She paused, still trying to reason with his rage. "I heard Bucky Conners tell someone in the street that Kincaid's coach was headed south, Coop. Don't you understand? Kincaid is going to Casa Grande, too!"

Suddenly, Cooper did comprehend. Kincaid had killed to take the boy. He would undoubtedly kill to keep him. "Estevan," he called. Already, he had begun rummaging among the weapons that lined the wooden gun rack.

Reluctantly, Dake moved to help him. "We'll form a posse," he said, shoving cartridges into the chamber of a Winchester. "I want this kept legal," he declared.

Cooper ignored the lawman and then faced him. "You keep it legal, Dake. I'm going to find my family!" He grabbed a loaded rifle for himself and tossed another across the room to Estevan.

Angela caught the weapon midair. "I'm going with you, Coop," she announced firmly, and it was then that all four men realized she was wearing trousers.

Jonathan came forward, grabbing his wife's arm. "No, Angela." He held on to her arm. "I forbid it!"

Determined, Angela unwound Jonathan's fingers from her arm. "How dare you," she breathed. "I'm going, Jonathan. If you were half a man you'd go with us, and you'd help." When Cooper started to object, she turned on him as well. "And if *you* were half a man, Cooper Dundee, you'd accept that help!" Without a word, she spun away from them both and headed out the door.

Thoroughly chastized, Jonathan followed after her. Cooper caught his arm as he passed. "This isn't over, Jonathan."

Estevan barged in between the two brothers, using the rifle Dake had given him as an effective ram. "I'm sick of it, too," he announced bitterly. "Angela's right. If you two had been old enough to enlist during the war, you'd have signed up on opposite sides just for the pleasure of shooting at each other!"

Dake followed them out the door, cursing when he saw that Angela had had the foresight to arrange for horses. "You're deputized," he roared. "All of you!" He spun around. "Conners!" He summoned the deputy, and began issuing terse orders. "I'll need a half-dozen men," he declared.

"Mounted and armed. Ten minutes," he declared. "You've got ten minutes, Conners!"

Dake dismissed the deputy and turned away, heading for the livery barn. Dr. Stockwell called after the man. "Do you want company, Ethan?" Theirs had been an acrimonious friendship, but a good one.

"No," Dake shouted over his shoulder, the word coming more harshly then he intended. He tried again, his voice changing. "No. If Coop has his way, Kincaid won't be needing any doctor."

Kincaid's brougham carriage skimmed across the desert, the pair of matched grays moving easily ahead of the light coach. The animals were less impervious to the afternoon sun because of their light coloring, and their driver kept them at a constant, mile-eating lope.

Frank Gilman sat on his high perch, watching the smooth up and down workings of the animals' rear ends. The horses were magnificent, working in tandem like two creatures that had been born cojoined, and he enjoyed watching them.

There was another reason for his pleasure. In his seat, he was aloof from the man inside the carriage, and for now, out of his reach and away from his scrutiny.

Gilman did not hate Kincaid, nor did he blame him for the long bondage that had united them over the years. His feelings went beyond hatred, because Kincaid was not worthy of even that emotion. You could not, Gilman realized, hate a *thing* that was no longer human.

He did, however, grieve for the children. And yet, he had done nothing to stop what Kincaid was doing. And for that, Gilman was deeply ashamed. There was still time, he thought. Somehow, in some way, he would help the children.

Gilman's reverie was interrupted by a subtle change in the movement and gait of the horses. Without his restraint, their pace was decreasing, so much so that, inside the carriage, Kincaid was also aware of the change. There was a loud thumping at the small door on top of the coach, a pounding that became more intense as the carriage slowed down even more.

The driver stared ahead out over the heads of the grays. And then he saw what the animals had sensed.

A small, partially open coach was parked beside the roadway, the sweating animals standing patiently at ease. There was no one in the driver's seat, no sign of any passengers, and no indication that there had been any trouble. Everything, from Gilman's first observation, was intact and in order.

Gilman reined in, turning around in his seat just long enough to pull up the small roof hatch. "Trouble, sir," he said curtly. "There's a small coach ahead, off the road."

Kincaid cursed, and his first instinct was to tell the man to go on. Reconsidering, he raked open the wooden louvers at his small window and, as they came abreast of the other carriage, changed his mind completely.

He saw the logo on the closed half door—the bold "D" of Dundee Transport—and felt strangely elated. "Pull up, Gilman!" he shouted. "Now!"

Regan heard the sound of the approaching team. She lay flat on her back on the cramped front seat of the open coach, her long body racked with pain. "Help me," she whispered as a dark shadow appeared before her, the man's image blocking out the sun. "Please help me. . . ."

Kincaid smiled. "Of course, Regan," he crooned, mocking her. "Of course, I'll help you."

"Jefferson?" She raised up slightly, unsure of what she was seeing and hearing, and then recoiled at the insanity that had suddenly fired the man's pale eyes. He climbed up into the coach, and as he did, she looked behind him to where Frank Gilman was standing beside the waiting brougham. Michael was beside the driver and, next to the silent boy, an equally pensive Niña.

Kincaid's arms slid under Regan's shoulders and knees. "The baby, Regan," he whispered, his voice suddenly changing. Confusion marred his face, and his eyes seemed to lose their focus as the anger was washed away and some strange veil swept across the pale orbs. His gaze drifted across Regan's face and long body, settling finally on her mounded belly. Reaching out, Kincaid placed his hand on her stomach and felt life stir beneath his fingers. "A son, Regan," he whispered, lifting her up off the seat as if she were a feather. "I want a son."

Unable to stop herself, Regan began to weep. The sudden change in Kincaid's demeanor, his instant tenderness, frightened her even more than the madness she had seen in his eyes only moments before. She was too weak to fight him, and she hated herself for that weakness.

Cooper Dundee kept his horse at a full run. From the moment he had pointed the animal's nose south, he had pushed the dun mare as hard as he had pushed himself. A grim-faced Estevan Folley rode at his side, and behind him, Jonathan and Angela Dundee.

Cooper eased up, impatient with the others as they fell farther behind, his gaze locking on Estevan's face as he turned his horse. He could see the lines that pain had etched across the man's forehead and mouth and knew that the hard ride had been as torturous for Estevan as it had been for himself. *And Angela*, he thought guiltily, turning to face the woman as she came up beside him. He wondered how long it had been since she had actually straddled a horse or used a traditional stockman's saddle.

"Estevan," he called out. "Pull up!"

Already, Estevan was shaking his head. He kicked his horse into a harder run and gestured, cavalry fashion, for Cooper and the others to follow after him. Three abreast, they rode on, with Jonathan still behind them.

Kincaid had moved Regan into his own carriage. He hovered over her, stroking her forehead tenderly with his hand as he spoke to her. "A boy, Regan," he intoned, as if it were really within his power to command God and nature to do his bidding. "It will be a boy."

Regan listened to the man's words, her eyes exploring his face. It was as if he had somehow slipped back in time to their distant, shared past, and had taken her with him. But this time things had changed, and he was taking a different path: He was speaking to her of love, of their child, and of their life together as husband and wife. She knew, looking at him and hearing his words, that he was insane, utterly insane.

Niña was at Regan's feet. Modestly, she had arranged a heavy carriage robe around Regan's knees. "I can help, Regan," she whispered. She patted Regan's hand, her own fingers looking remarkably small beside the woman's. "Dotty had a baby," she went on, "when I was ten." It seemed strange, now, that she had never wondered what had happened to the child.

Regan struggled to remain calm. She crooked a finger at the child, mindful of Kincaid's presence, and whispered in her ear. "We have to be careful, darling," she cautioned. "Mr. Kincaid. . . ." It was difficult to find the right words.

"He's crazy," Niña breathed, her own mouth now next to Regan's cheek. Like Regan, she had listened for hours to Kincaid's rantings and knew that he was mad.

Relieved that the girl understood, Regan nodded her head. "Someone will come, Niña," she murmured, thinking of Tomás and the wire he had promised to send from Casa Grande.

Another intense spasm tore at Regan, her back arching as she fought the urge to push. The contractions were coming more frequently now, each pain lasting longer, and the time between them growing less and less.

Niña stared up at Kincaid, more afraid of him now than she had been in the beginning. She wished desperately that Michael was with her and not outside the coach with Gilman. She straightened up and began to disrobe. "For the baby," she said, when she felt the man warily watching her. The muslin dress she wore over her white cotton shift was still reasonably clean and very soft, and she slipped it over her head and offered it to Kincaid. "It needs to be cut," she suggested. "Something for a diaper." She pointed to a front bodice panel. "And this"—her fingers drifted to the gathers of the full skirt—"for a blanket."

Suspiciously, Kincaid took the garment. The little voices inside his head were tormenting him, whispering their insidious distrust of the girl's motives. She could hurt the child, they taunted. Worse, she could help the woman escape. Kincaid listened to the incessant whisperings, and then, finally convinced that the girl posed no real threat, he nodded and backed out of the carriage.

Gratefully, Regan patted and then let go of Niña's hand, and as she did, she felt a sudden swelling of pressure deep in her belly. There was a strange, gushing noise, the sound of rushing blood and water, and a hard, intense pain that seemed to build without end.

"The baby is coming!" Niña squealed as Regan surrendered to the uncontrollable urge to push. Regan's moaning intensified and soon was echoed by a tiny, angry voice that wailed in chorus to Niña's elated cry. And then Niña's small hands were filled with a miracle.

Kincaid loomed in the doorway of the coach, the makeshift blanket and diaper in his hands. Niña quickly grabbed the fabric, carefully keeping Regan's newborn daughter concealed as she knotted the cord and attended to the cleaning. When she finished, she held up the infant, stroking its soft cheek. "It's a boy," she lied, knowing that this was what the man wanted to hear.

"My son!" Kincaid rejoiced. He reached across Regan's head, intending to take the baby, angry when Niña refused to let go.

"He's hungry," Regan lied, opening her arms to the infant. And then she smiled up into Kincaid's face. "Help me sit up, Jefferson," she asked, her voice soft, calm. There was a calculated helplessness, a dependence, in her tone as she played out Kincaid's fantasy, and the man responded. He released his hold on the child and surrendered it into Regan's arms, watching as she opened her blouse and offered the infant her breast.

The sound of a scuffle outside the coach drew Kincaid's immediate attention. He kissed Regan's cheek and then the child's. "I'll be back, Regan," he promised, and backed out of the carriage.

"Let me go!" Michael struggled against Gilman's grip, his eyes on the cloud of yellow dust on the northern horizon that had begun to diminish behind the cover of rock and tumbleweed. "Damn you! Let me go!"

Gilman picked the boy up in a tight bear hug, his head pressed against the youth's cheek. "Not now, boy," he whispered, hoping that Michael would understand and trust him. "Later. When we can all get away."

Michael shook his head. He had no reason to trust the man, not after the things that had happened in Phoenix. "No!" he shouted. He made a single, vicious backward kick, connecting with the long muscle in the man's inner thigh, and broke free.

"Coop!" he cried, instinctively knowing that it was Cooper Dundee who was waiting for him just beyond the rocks. *"Coop!"*

He sprinted away from Gilman, running pell-mell past the open coach door. He was just beyond the opening when he felt himself swept up off the ground.

Kincaid grabbed the boy with both hands and spun him around. Michael was nothing to him now. The madness within Kincaid had totally possessed him, and he remembered nothing of this dark-haired boy. What he held in his hands now was a total stranger, a man-child who was fighting him and who posed a threat to his newborn son.

Cruelly, Kincaid drew back his hand. He hit Michael hard, knocking him senseless, and dropped him into the dirt. Even then, he was not finished. "Get rid of him, Frank," he ordered.

Gilman shook his head. He'd heard the same order too many times in the past, and its meaning was always the same: Someone or something had to die. He thought, suddenly, of Cooper Dundee's two-thousand-dollar Morgan stallion. Kincaid had ordered the animal slaughtered, too, and his words had been exactly the same. *Get rid of him, Frank.* No longer caring about his own life, Gilman spoke. "No," he said, and for the first time in many years, he felt a little bit clean.

Kincaid whirled, facing the driver. "I gave you an order, Gilman! I expect it to be carried out."

"No," Gilman repeated. "Not this time." He drew himself erect, his shoulders going back, refusing to let Kincaid's madness infect him anymore. "Not ever again." Beyond Kincaid, he could see Michael slowly crawling away into the thick undergrowth at the side of the road.

Kincaid was unaccustomed to such disobedience. He stood staring at Gilman, even more angry when the driver dared to turn his back on him.

Gilman headed toward the front of the carriage and the team. He could only hope that Michael was not seriously hurt and that the boy would be able to take care of himself until help came. "I'm taking the woman and the little girl back to Phoenix," he announced. Raising his foot, he started up into the box.

Kincaid drew the Buntline pistol that had been stuffed in his belt. He cocked the piece, coldly took aim, and fired. The bullet tore into the back of Gilman's head and opened a gaping hole as it exited just above the bridge of his nose.

Chapter Fifteen

Having caught sight of the two coaches parked in the distance beside the road, Cooper Dundee had pulled up his horse behind an outcropping of sandstone and had signaled the other riders to dismount and hobble the horses while he surveyed the situation. Now he stood with his body pressed tightly against the sandstone as he peered around the edge at the scene beyond. His own coach, the open canopied vehicle the Dundee line used in the hot summers, sat empty, the horses pointed north toward Phoenix. Kincaid's coach was just behind it, but facing south. Cooper tried to make out whether there were any people in the area, but the fading sunlight was already too thin to distinguish more than vague movements in and around the vehicles.

Kincaid's single shot exploded the fragile desert quiet, echoing across the flatlands and bringing terrible visions of death. Unmindful of Estevan's hands clawing at him, Cooper leaped out from his hiding place and screamed his rage into the new silence. *"Kincaid!"*

"My God, Coop!" Estevan pulled at the man again, dragging him down into the dirt. "It wasn't Regan," he declared stubbornly. "You've got to believe that it wasn't Regan."

The grim vision filled Cooper again, and a great surge of fear swept through the entire length of his body. "I can't lose her, Estevan!"

Sprinting from one rock to another, Angela joined them. Jonathan followed, choosing a shelter among the rocks some distance from the others. He watched as his wife reached out to comfort Cooper, and then he quickly looked away.

Angela's hand was on Cooper's shoulder. "Can you see anything?" she panted, still out of breath.

171

Both men shook their heads. They knew from the expression on Angela's face that she had heard the shot and that she, too, was afraid of what might have happened. "What are we going to do now?" she asked.

Cooper rubbed at the soreness in his chest. "We wait," he said finally. As it stood right now, they had no other choice. "We wait until Kincaid makes a move."

Angela could feel the tightness in Cooper's shoulders as he withdrew into himself. His expression changed, his mouth set in a grim line that hardened his features and made him look cold. It was a look she had seen many times before, during the years when they were growing up.

It was the same look Coop had whenever he was angry or when he was brooding about the people who had wronged or deceived him.

"Coop," Angela began, her voice soft. "Regan wanted to tell you about Kincaid. It was just . . ." The words faded when Cooper faced her and she saw the glimmer of green ice in his single eye.

"I know," he breathed. His eye narrowed as he explored Angela's pale face, the softness returning to the lines around his mouth. "You think that I'm mad at her, that I'm mad because of something she's done. Regan's the one thing in my life that I'm sure of, Angela. The *only* thing that I've ever been sure of." He inhaled, and the hardness returned to his face. "Jonathan," he breathed, his voice harsh. "It's Jonathan."

Angela felt a sudden need to defend her husband. "He's never lied to you, Coop," she declared truthfully, no longer rubbing at the man's tense shoulders.

Cooper laughed, and the sound filled with a bitter rancor. "No," he agreed. "He's never lied to me. But he's never told me the truth, Angela. He's never once bothered to tell me even the simplest truth about what he feels or what he wants. I could have stomached the lies, Angela. What I can't take is the deception, and what it's cost me! It's got to stop, Angela. It's *going* to stop!" he promised.

Afraid, Angela backed away. She could understand that, in his distress, Cooper needed someone to blame, but she didn't feel that that someone should be Jonathan. "Coop," she breathed, wanting to reason with him.

He shook his head, pulling away from her touch, the hardness returning as he leaned back against the rocks. "I don't want to talk anymore, Angela," he said, pulling his hat down over his eyes. "And I sure in hell don't want to talk about Jonathan."

Kincaid stood beside Frank Gilman's body, the smoking pistol still in his hand. A feeling of confusion overwhelmed him, and he suddenly realized he couldn't remember why he was in this place or how he had come to be here. Yet someone, from somewhere beyond the rocks, had called him by name.

He stared down at his driver, genuinely surprised and shocked to see that Gilman was dead. Even with the pistol in his hand, Kincaid could not comprehend his own guilt. "After me," he muttered. "Someone is after me, and they've shot Frank." The thought penetrated, and he instantly dropped into a low crouch, the gun ready as his eyes scanned the brush and the rock-strewn landscape.

A small whimper sounded from inside the coach, and Kincaid immediately reacted. He spun around, aiming the pistol at the closed door. And then, stealthily, he approached the vehicle.

Kincaid pulled open the door, cocking the pistol at the same time. His eyes narrowed as they adjusted to the dim light of the coach's interior, and he swung the barrel of the pistol in a wide circle until he settled on the still form on the forward-facing seat.

Regan's hand was clamped tightly over Niña's small mouth as she stifled the child's scream. She wet her lips with her tongue, fighting the dryness that threatened to make her mute, and gently called out to the man, still holding on to the little girl and the baby. "Jefferson?" When he didn't answer, she tried again, all the while watching his eyes. "Is something wrong, Jefferson?" For a time, it appeared that he was going to answer her, and then the baby began to cry.

The look of confusion that had marred Kincaid's face changed again, his features, his entire countenance losing the look of injured innocence as the hardness returned. Coldly, he poked at the baby's blanket with the barrel of his pistol. "Breed get," he murmured, incensed when he saw the baby's long dark hair. "Little Indians grow up to be big Indians," he intoned.

Regan pulled the baby to her chest. "*Your* son, Jefferson," she cajoled. "Don't you remember?"

Kincaid laughed, coldly. "Cooper Dundee's breed buck," he sneered. He was lucid now, but just as mad as he had been when the child was born.

He tore the baby from Regan's arms. "Your *husband* is out there, Regan. He killed my driver, and he wants to kill me!" He held up the screaming infant. "I'm going to offer him a trade. The baby for his . . ." Confused, Kincaid's brow knotted, "for *my* life . . ." He laughed at the thought. He had no intention of sparing Cooper Dundee's life, any more than he had of sparing Regan's or the child's.

Still weak from the delivery of her baby, Regan swung her legs off the seat. With Niña's help, she tried to sit up. "Give me the baby, Jefferson. For God's sake, give me the child!"

He pushed her back into the seat. Holding the infant in one hand, he climbed down out of the coach. Unseen, Niña followed after him.

"Dundee! Cooper Dundee!" Kincaid's voice screamed out above the frail cries of the infant that nested in his hand. "Your child, Dundee! I have the child!" He repeated the words a second time, and then fired wildly into the rocks as he ran out into the clearing.

Not realizing that Kincaid was holding Cooper's child, Jonathan returned the fire, shielding his eyes with his forearm as the sandstone pillar in front of him shattered and covered him with yellow shards. He rose up, firing as he ran, not taking the time to aim or search out his target.

Cooper was on his feet. He stared down into the clearing and saw Kincaid lift the fragile bundle he held high above his head. All around Kincaid, bits of gravel and sand rose under the impact of Jonathan's bullets, and for a terrible, long moment, it appeared that Kincaid was going to drop his burden. He hunkered down on one knee, temporarily ducking out of sight, and still Jonathan kept firing.

Enraged, Cooper turned on his brother. "The baby! Goddamn you, he's got my child!" This was the ultimate betrayal. He unsheathed his gun and aimed directly at his brother's head.

"Coop!" Estevan shouted, Angela's voice lifting in unison to his panicked cry.

"There," she screamed, pointing into the brush.

Cooper Dundee turned away from his brother. Not far from where they stood, he saw a brief flash of white and a tangle of auburn hair. "Niña!" he shouted, holstering his weapon. The child heard his voice and followed the sound, running blindly through the scrub.

He ran to her, sweeping the girl off her feet and propelling her into Angela's waiting arms. "The baby," she panted. Proudly, she displayed the small bundle she carried in her bramble-scratched arms, tenderly folding back the white muslin that had covered the baby's face. "Kincaid almost dropped her! I caught her, and then I ran!" She smiled proudly. Her small chest was still rising and falling from her effort, and Cooper gave her a quick hug.

He stared down at his tiny daughter, a myriad of rich emotions sweeping him as he looked into a countenance that was so much Regan and so much himself. Her face seemed no bigger than the palm of his hand, and when he stroked her cheek with his finger, she instinctively searched out the tip with her mouth, just like a hungry bird. The taste offended her, and her voice lifted in a lusty cry of anger and disappointment.

"Regan," he said, when he regained his voice, realizing the danger his wife faced. He was almost afraid of Niña's answer. "Are Regan and Michael all right?"

Niña had begun to cry. She was trembling, the weight of her ordeal finally more than she could bear. "Regan is in the coach," she sniffed. "And Michael. He hit Michael, Coop!" The tears came faster. When she had run away from Kincaid, there had been no sign of the boy anywhere. "I don't know where he is, Coop! I don't know where Michael is!"

Angela wrapped her arms around the child, holding on to both Niña and the baby. "It's going to be all right, Niña," she whispered, desperately hoping she wasn't telling a lie. Gently, she led the girl away from the others and into a place of quiet among the rocks.

Estevan watched after the child and the woman. "At least we know that Regan is alive," he said.

"For now," Cooper answered. "We've got to get her out of there. Before Kincaid . . ." He couldn't finish.

*   *   *

Regan struggled with the awkward metal handle that secured the door of Kincaid's coach. Every sound seemed magnified: the slow turning of the hasp, the rustle of fabric as she slipped down from the seat.

The silence was her enemy, within the coach and without. When she moved, she violated the quiet inside the carriage, and the austere silence outside mocked her. She had no way of knowing where Kincaid was, but he only had to listen to know her every move.

Regan was tired, and that fatigue left her feeling beaten and defeated. She decided that her own safety didn't matter anymore. It was enough to have seen Niña take the baby from Kincaid and to know that she had gotten away. And Michael . . . Regan refused to believe that Michael had not gotten away as well. *Coop*, she thought silently. *If I die, Coop will take care of the children.*

The melancholy thoughts roused the woman, and she shook off the feeling of self-pity and hopelessness. Anger replaced fear, and she refused to give up. Resolutely, she pried open the door and dropped down into the shallow trench beside the roadway.

Michael's entire head ached. He lay in the dirt, resting, a scant twenty feet from the roadway, the knees of his trousers torn and bloodied. Gingerly, he raised his hand to touch the soreness at the side of his face. There was a tender knot just below his left eye, and already the swelling had forced the eye partially shut.

He was more aware of his anger than of the pain. He was angry at himself for being so foolish as to trust a stranger like Kincaid, and even more angry at Regan.

She had lied to him. And for the past two years, from the time she had taken him from Fort Whipple, she had perpetuated that lie. She was his mother, his *real* mother, and she had never told him. *She didn't care enough to tell him!*

Michael lay his head on his arms. "I hate you, Regan!" he murmured. It was a halfhearted denouncement, totally untrue, and he knew it. Aside from their minor differences over school and chores, their relationship wasn't all that bad. It was certainly no worse than other mother-child relationships he had seen and, considering Niña's mother, Dotty, a hell of a lot better than some.

It was the deception that hurt. That and the fact that Cooper was part of the deception.

A subtle whispering of sand and sagebrush interrupted Michael's confused musings. He turned, facing the sound, instinctively keeping himself low against the ground. Fear gripped him as the noise grew louder, visions of prowling animals making his heart beat faster, until the rush of his own pulse was like thunder in his ears.

And then he saw. It was Regan. Slowly, her movements barely perceptible, the woman crept along the floor of the desert, unknowingly following the shallow path that had been cut by her son.

Kincaid was alone. Without understanding the reason, he felt a terrible sense of loss. There had been a child, he recalled, a baby that he had held in his own hand, and now it was gone. But why? And how? He shook his head, unable to remember anything about the baby or how he had come to lose it.

Confused, Kincaid wandered about the clearing. The little voices inside his head were busy again, speaking to him in the many tongues of madness as they competed with the incessant buzzing of insects that had been drawn by the smell of Frank Gilman's blood.

Insanely, and with a useless tenderness, Kincaid propped up the grim corpse against the front wheel of his coach. Completely oblivious of the gaping hole above the bridge of Gilman's nose, he talked to the driver as if the man were still alive. "They've all turned against me, Frank. Everyone. The boy." His brow knotted as he tried to remember which one, Michael's face merging with the faces of his dead sons. "Regan . . ."

The mere mention of the woman's name triggered a rage within Kincaid, and he turned away from his dead companion. "Regan," he said again, almost whispering the name. And then he realized that he had left the woman alone.

Kincaid grabbed the latch on the near door, his pistol drawn and ready. "Regan," he coaxed. "Open the door."

There was no response. Incensed, Kincaid tore the door

open. A dark emptiness greeted him: emptiness and the same terrible silence that had descended on the clearing. The door on the opposite side of the coach was still ajar and seemed to mock him.

Angry, Kincaid slammed the heavy door shut. "Bitch!" he fumed. "Goddamned bitch!" He shouted the words into the silence. "You're not going to get away, Regan! Not again!" His voice rose. "Never again!"

Warily, he searched the ground for a sign, elated when he found a wide path etched in the loose sand. His pistol raised, he began following the trail, already feeling the warm flush of victory.

Horrified, Michael watched as Regan struggled through the thick undergrowth. Behind her, he could see the approaching long shadow of a man and knew at once that it was Jefferson Kincaid who was pursuing her. The late-afternoon shadow stretched out behind Regan: dark, ominous, one arm stretched forward. The clear outline of a drawn pistol loomed black and elongated across the yellow-white sand, the detail so perfect that the shadowy image of the cocked hammer and Kincaid's thumb seemed alive and as capable of evil as the man.

Michael rose up on his haunches and withdrew into the shadows. He poised at the edge of the small trail. Desperately, he wished for Cooper to be there. But wishing, he knew, didn't make it so. Cooper was somewhere beyond the clearing, unable to help.

Silently, the boy watched as Kincaid followed after the woman. The man was taking a perverse delight in his pursuit, staying well behind Regan, moving when she moved, silently resting when she did not. And then, tiring of the game, Kincaid called out to her. "Regan."

Michael held his breath. Regan's face was so close he could see the sweat that had beaded across her forehead. And still he did not move. He waited, somehow knowing that Kincaid was not through.

There was an intense feeling of pride in the boy when he saw Regan had not surrendered to her feelings of fear. She lay still for a long moment, and then, covertly picking up a handful of dirt, she forced herself upright and faced Kincaid.

"I'm not going to beg, Jefferson. Damn you! You're not going to make me beg!"

Kincaid laughed, coldly. "You'll beg, Regan," he promised, thumbing back the hammer on the long-barreled pistol. "Before I'm through, you'll beg God to let you die!"

Michael raised up from his hiding place. He charged Kincaid, mindful of the man's weapon. "No!" he screamed, clawing the man's face. At the same time, Regan heaved the handful of gravel.

The shock of the boy's sudden attack and the shower of dirt caught Kincaid off guard. Stunned, he felt the crush of ninety pounds of raw, boyish fury. It was just enough to divert and deflect his aim and his attention. The cocked pistol discharged, the soft lead bullet impacting harmlessly in the dense sand beside Regan's head.

Cooper heard the shot, his whole body reacting to the noise. He had been expecting something, but the expectation did not dull the shock, and he felt his skin prickling all over his lean frame. "Now," he ordered, rising up from the cover of the rocks.

Guns drawn, they made the charge, recklessly running into the open, unsure of their direction. Without stopping, they sprinted past the body of Frank Gilman and into the thick brush.

Kincaid was down, and Michael was on top of him, pummeling his face and shoulders with his small fists. The madness that had consumed Kincaid had now become the primal force of self-preservation, and his strength increased. Viciously, with both hands, he swung at the boy's head, and when Michael ducked aside, Kincaid used the momentum of the boy's sudden shift in position to break free. He tossed the youth aside and then rolled back onto his belly, his fingers scraping in the dirt for the pistol. Rising up, he spied Cooper and the others. Panicked, he cocked the pistol and fired.

Cooper made his shot on the run, Kincaid's bullet whistling harmlessly past him. There was no time to aim, no time to allow for the lack of depth perception that had plagued him since the loss of his eye. And then he knew the satisfaction of seeing his bullet hit its mark. Kincaid screamed, and a crimson smear of red bloomed on his chest as he collapsed in the dirt.

"Regan!" Cooper dropped down to his knees beside his wife. He held her for a long time and then opened his arms to gather Michael into the tight circle of arms.

"Kincaid . . ." Regan tried to speak, but was silenced by the gentle pressure of Cooper's finger against her lips.

"It's over, Regan," he breathed. He paused just long enough to kiss her. "The rest doesn't matter," he said. He gathered Regan into his arms and stood up.

Angela had joined them. She inhaled sharply, concerned at Regan's lack of color and the dark circles under her blue eyes and the way the woman, in spite of the continued late-afternoon heat, seemed to be shivering. "We have to get her covered, Coop," she said. She turned to Estevan and Jonathan. "We'll need a blanket," she ordered, watching as Estevan sprinted away. "And water, Jonathan." Her eyes challenged her husband silently when he hesitated.

Cooper removed his vest and, using it as a makeshift pillow, tenderly propped up his wife's head. Regan clung to him, her fingers biting into his arms. "The baby," she whispered. "And Michael . . ."

Cooper moved slightly and pointed to the place where Niña stood holding the child. "She's fine, Regan." His eyes lifted to meet Michael's. There was a silent exchange between the two, and it troubled the man. Still, he said the words. "Michael's fine, too." He watched as the youngster marched stiff-backed away from them. Regan was beyond knowing. She drifted off, the physical strain of the long day taking its toll.

Jonathan stood above Cooper, the canteen dangling from his fingers. He stared down at his brother's wife, unable to deny the feelings of awe and wonder that filled him. She had endured so much, and even now, with the scrapes and abrasions on her legs and arms, and her face almost obscured by the tangle of her long black hair, she was still one of the most desirable women he had ever seen. He cleared his throat. "Coop . . ."

"Don't say anything, Jonathan," the younger Dundee answered. He took the canteen without looking up and, using his handkerchief, began bathing Regan's face. "Don't you say one goddamn thing!" The fact that Angela was present did not temper the hardness in his words.

From the distance, the baby began to cry again. For a

long moment, Angela was torn between the child and her sister-in-law. "We've got to get them home," she said finally. She stood up, brushing off her hands. "I'm going to see what's keeping Estevan. And then I'm going to see what we can do about getting one of these carriages ready to travel."

There was a long silence between the two brothers after Angela left. The wall was between them again, the same seemingly impenetrable barrier that had always existed, even when they were children.

They had never talked, Jonathan realized. In all the years when they were growing up and the many years after, they had never really talked. In a rare moment of honest self-examination, Jonathan faced the truth. He had been much happier in the East, among his friends and associates in Washington. Dundee Transport hadn't mattered to him, any more than the home ranch at Casa Grande had mattered. It was just that the preservation of the stage line and the land was something that Cooper had wanted. And because Cooper wanted it, he had coveted it, too.

Just like the last time, Jonathan realized. Two years before, he had aligned himself with Logan Montgomery against Cooper. And this time, he had been in league with Jefferson Kincaid. And to what end?

He felt a need to make amends—a real need, finally, to end the old competition. "Coop," he began.

There was a subtle shifting in the sand behind and to the right of Cooper Dundee, just beyond the fingers of Jefferson Kincaid's extended right hand. Surreptitiously, Kincaid groped for his pistol, his gaze intent on Cooper's back. Jonathan caught the movement out of the corner of his eye and instantly responded. *"Coop!"*

Kincaid was on Cooper's blind side, and Cooper was totally unaware of the man's movement. He reacted instead to Jonathan, raising his head as his brother called his name. The instinct for self-preservation was as strong in Cooper Dundee as the anger and the memories of Jonathan's past treacheries. He saw and sensed nothing but his brother's quick movement as Jonathan reached for and drew his weapon.

All three fired simultaneously. Cooper watched in horror as his bullet smashed into his brother's broad chest, and he waited for a similar impact against his own. It did not come.

Instead, there was the whine of hot air as a bullet spun past
his ear from behind.

"Kincaid," Jonathan murmured. He collapsed forward,
landing on his knees as if in prayer. A large circle of bright
blood spread raggedly across the front of his white shirt.
Numbly, he placed his left palm against the wound in a futile
effort to stop the flow. The blood gushed between his fingers.

Cooper half turned, rising up as he moved, and saw
Kincaid slump into the sand, the side of his face torn away
by the impact of Jonathan's bullet. Sick, Cooper turned back
to his brother. "Jonathan . . ."

Jonathan was still on his knees, a strange look of content-
ment softening the lines on his face. He stared across at
Cooper, a thousand shared memories passing between them
as their gaze met for a final time. And then the light went out
in Jonathan's eyes.

Angela screamed. She raced across the clearing, calling
out to her husband as he collapsed, face forward, into the dirt
at Cooper's feet. *"Jonathan!"*

Cooper stood for a time, an aching deep inside his guts
and chest that threatened to suffocate him. The horror of
what he had done tore at him, and his pistol felt hot and
heavy in his hand. "No," he begged. "No-o-o-o!"

He threw the pistol, hard, as far as he was able. It
arched high into the darkening sky, the last rays of the sun
glinting off the barrel as it spun end over end to disappear
beyond the thick mesquite and chaparral.

Grim-faced, Estevan came from across the roadway. He
was leading the horses and carrying the wooden strongbox
from Kincaid's coach. Beside him, on a sweat-streaked mount,
rode an equally grim and solitary Ethan Dake. From the
distance, too far away to have helped, the two men had
observed everything that had happened.

Cooper faced the lawman. "It was me, Ethan," he declared weakly. "I shot Jonathan."

Dake was already shaking his head. He dismounted and
walked slowly across the clearing, pausing only long enough
to rest a gentle hand on Angela's shoulder. He knew that
Estevan was behind him, just as he knew Estevan would be
the one best suited to comfort the woman.

"No," he said derisively, looking directly into Cooper's
eye. "You're unarmed." He pointed at Cooper's empty holster.

Regan lay behind Cooper, and Dake could see that she was slowly becoming aware. When Cooper started to object, he placed a hand on the younger man's shoulder, his fingers purposely digging into the soft flesh above his collarbone. "It's over, Coop. Twenty years of war with your own brother. It's finished. And you're going to have to live with the way it ended."

It was the lawman's way of saying that Cooper, in his own way, had been as guilty as Jonathan for the trouble that had always been between them. There was nothing to be gained from telling anyone the truth about what had occurred.

Dake released his hold on Cooper. "Kincaid," he said. "As far as I'm concerned, it was Kincaid's shot that hit Jonathan."

Cooper knew better. And when he saw the look on Angela's face, he knew that she knew better, too. "Angela," he breathed, reaching out to touch her.

She pulled away, shaking her head. Her pale face was streaked with tears, and there were more to come as she buried her head against Jonathan's shoulder.

Cooper felt empty. He had lost Angela, just as surely as he lost his brother. "I didn't hate him," he said to no one in particular. "I didn't want him dead!"

"Coop." Regan called out to her husband. She was still weak and did not fully understand what had happened. She only knew that Cooper needed her. "Coop," she called again, opening her arms.

He went to her, burying his head against her neck, and held her for a long, long time.

Cooper Dundee and Estevan Folley walked shoulder to shoulder on the cement walkway in front of the new Casa Grande office, each of them momentarily lost in their own private thoughts. It had been three months since the hell that had engulfed them in the desert just north of Casa Grande, and they were still hurting. The physical wounds had healed, but deep inside, the ones no one could see still festered in the dark corners of their minds.

The move to Casa Grande from Phoenix had been a mutual decision. It was to be a new beginning away from the strained business relationships that existed even after Cooper had been totally exonerated of all the charges that had been filed against him. It was also an escape from the bitter personal memories that still plagued them all. Cooper would ramrod the line, working out of the ranchería just south of town, and Estevan would run the new office. It was a satisfying work arrangement for both men, and one that allowed them the kind of life each enjoyed.

They paused in their walking, turning to watch as two workmen hoisted the new sign into place above the walkway. "Not bad," Estevan said, lifting his glass. A bold Dundee "D" dominated the center of the sign, an equally bold "F" intersecting the letter on the lower right-hand side. "The 'F' could have been a bit bigger, though," he joshed.

In spite of himself, Cooper laughed, a spark of humor lighting his good eye. He rested his elbows against the porch railing, reaching up to scratch the place where the eye patch rested on his right cheek. "Ha!" he retorted. "You know damned good and well my 'D' has always been bigger than your 'F'!" He lowered his voice, as if he were talking about something obscene.

"Like hell it is!" Estevan exclaimed.

"Like hell *what* is?" a young voice echoed. It was Michael, filled with all the high spirits of a boy who was happy and completely secure.

Both men turned, and Cooper shook a finger at his eavesdropping adopted son. He was grateful that the differences between Michael and Regan had finally been resolved, and it showed on his face. "You don't watch your mouth, son, you're going to find out!" he warned.

Michael could see that Cooper was trying hard not to laugh. "Pictures," he said, pointing to the photographer's wagon parked next door to the Dundee office. He made a face, fingering the velveteen collar on the suit jacket his mother had made him wear for the occasion. "For the christening, Pa," he finished.

Cooper followed the boy's gaze. Regan was on the porch, waiting. She was straightening the big white bow on the back of Niña's dress, the same bow Michael had tugged at and untied at least a dozen times during the afternoon.

There was someone else on the porch with Regan, and Cooper shaded his eye in an effort to see. "Angela," he breathed, watching as the woman came out of the shadows.

It was as if the young woman had heard Cooper whisper her name. As she looked up, her pale face somehow different from what he remembered, Cooper wished that she would smile.

Estevan was grinning, and there was a softness in his face that filled his dark eyes. "Regan asked her to come, Coop. To be Teresa's *madrina*."

Godmother, Cooper thought, remembering. Before all the trouble, *before he had killed his own brother*, they had talked about how it would be when his child was born.

And now, after three months of silence and separation, Angela was finally here. Cooper felt Estevan leaving him and reached out, his fingers grabbing at the man's sleeves. Estevan pulled away, shaking his head as he moved down the walk. He paused just long enough to take Angela's little boy from her arms as she passed him, and then moved on.

Cooper stood tall above his sister, his arms rigid at his sides as if he were afraid to touch her. *Worse, he was afraid that if he did reach out to her, she would turn away*. And then, no longer able to resist the need to hold her, he opened his arms and pulled her close. "Angela," he murmured. "I . . ."

She reached up, pressing her fingers against his lips to stop his words, but did not pull away from his touch. "Time, Coop," she whispered, trying hard not to cry. "Just give me a little time."

He held his sister, cradling his chin on her soft, blond hair. He loved her so much, and yet he had caused her nothing but pain. "Regan told me that you're going to San Francisco. That you and the baby . . ." He couldn't finish.

Angela's head rocked back and forth against his chest. "No," she said softly. She was quiet for a long moment, and when she spoke again, her voice was stronger. "I'm staying here, Coop. With Estevan." With that, she slipped from beneath his arms and simply walked away.

Pleased with himself, Estevan joined Cooper. "Well?" he demanded.

Cooper grabbed the man, drawing him close in a joyous, back-thumping hug. "Well, I'll be damned!" he rejoiced.

Estevan nodded at the photographer. "Something for posterity, *hermano*?" he suggested.

They lined up on the broad porch beneath the new Dundee Transport sign, and Cooper watched as Estevan gathered Angela and her son beneath his arm. They fit well, he thought—just as he had always known they would.

Regan tugged at his sleeve. "Mr. Dundee." She smiled. She was holding Teresa, and the infant seemed to greet him, too, her fat cheeks pursing as she blew a stream of bubbles.

Cooper put his arm around his wife and stared out at the camera. He could see their miniature, translucent images in the big lens and watched, smiling, as Michael whispered something insulting into Niña's ear while tugging hard at her long sash. Unable to help himself, Cooper began to laugh.

There was a blinding flash of light and a puff of acrid blue smoke as the harried photographer pushed the button . . . just as Niña's fist collided with Michael's pug nose.